D0961943

SANTIAGO AND THE DRINKING PARTY

for The Beesley's. This
I hope you enjoy
With warm rega
Clay Mag
McCall,
Dec. 3, 1

SANTIAGO AND THE DRINKING PARTY

CLAY MORGAN

VIKING

VIKING
Published by the Penguin Group
Viking Penguin, a division of Penguin Books USA Inc.,
375 Hudson Street, New York, New York 10014, U.S.A.
Penguin Books Ltd, 27 Wrights Lane,
London W8 5TZ, England
Penguin Books Australia Ltd, Ringwood,
Victoria, Australia
Penguin Books Canada Ltd, 10 Alcorn Avenue, Suite 300,
Toronto, Ontario, Canada M4V 3B2
Penguin Books (N.Z.) Ltd, 182-190 Wairau Road,
Auckland 10, New Zealand

Penguin Books Ltd, Registered Offices:
Harmondsworth, Middlesex, England

First published in 1992 by Viking Penguin,
a division of Penguin Books USA Inc.

3 5 7 9 10 8 6 4 2

PUBLISHER'S NOTE
This is a work of fiction. Names, characters, places, and incidents either are the product of
the author's imagination or are used fictitiously, and any resemblance to actual persons,
living or dead, events, or locales is entirely coincidental.

LIBRARY OF CONGRESS CATALOGING IN PUBLICATION DATA
Morgan, Clay.
Santiago and the drinking party / Clay Morgan.
p.   cm.
ISBN 0-670-84341-5
I. Title.
PS3563.0825S26   1992
813'.54—dc20   91-40567

Printed in the United States of America
Set in Bodoni Book

For the crew of
the space shuttle *Challenger*, 51-L,
with love and remembrance

And for Moritz Thomsen
with enormous wings

The author thanks the people of Idaho
and the Idaho Commission on the Arts
for their generous support.

Do you mind if I ask you a question or two?
—Socrates

SANTIAGO AND THE DRINKING PARTY

1

Years ago, down in the Amazon, Santiago set me up. He said, "Lives are stories told over and over. The good ones keep getting better. Think about that, Daniel. And while you're at it, think about thinking. We learn best by thinking, just as fish breathe by drinking."

He said this very matter-of-factly. Then he asked me, "Don't they?"

He asked me this when he was about to die.

I had first met Santiago Benalcazar long before that, before I learned his language and at a time when everyone I met misunderstood me and I misunderstood almost everyone. Years later, when I had grown older and studied Spanish, I returned to learn that he had gone professional. He had given up shrine tending and taken up philosophy as his principal stock-in-trade.

The first time I heard him say the word, he said it slowly —*filo-sofía*—and he said it with such lip-smacking, tongue-tapping love that I thought he was talking about an Argentine movie actress.

But it was for Truth that he lusted, and for Truth, in a way, that he died. He did not charge for his *conversaciones*. He herded chickens and sold lemons, and the people would buy him beer just to hear him talk. Santiago, the sage of the jungle, offered philosophy, free for the thinking. "Just think of it!" he would say, and I and others tried to do that. Some say he caused the disasters, some say he brought on the plague, but he really only started people thinking, which for most of us just fouled things up.

We were all examples of one big truth: People don't change. Situations change and people get caught. I, for example, will sometimes act without thinking. That is what is best about me. But if you give me time to think about something, about anything, I'll take time—and more time—until it is too late. I wait. I wait. I consider and avoid. I have avoided writing this story the same way I avoided living it, the way I avoided going back to Los Puentes Caidos.

I can say a very few things without hesitation. For example, I can say that Angelina and Consuelo were good. Santiago's daughter, Angelina, was perfectly good. The rest of us only served as contrast. El Brinco's daughter, Consuelo, was completely good. Good of heart and pure of mind. Both these women were beautiful. Both still are. Even in these days of confusion, good women like these can exist. My proof is Consuelo and Angelina.

Good men cannot so easily exist. Perhaps they never could, even in simpler days. And although Santiago might have asked me, "But what is your proof?" I might not have answered him, because my proof would have been Santiago. Santiago was as close to good as a man can get, but only because he asked good questions. Actions did not encumber him, until the end. Santiago lived in his open mind, and he was comfortable there.

Hector Tanbueno, that devil, was bad—bad as only men can be bad. Born a primitive Amazon Indian, adopted and abandoned by Ohio missionaries, and believed by tourists to be an American Express tour guide, Hector Tanbueno was the thoroughly modern man. He would put your life in terrible danger, rescue you at apparently horrible personal risk, and then charge it all to your American Express card or give you a discount if you had the cash. When I think of Hector, I still want to kill him.

I met them all in South America, on my first trip down here. It was that first journey southward that got it all going, when I was twenty years old and lost.

I had gotten lost this way. I had just quit college again and had moved back to the Idaho forests to find a new way to avoid commitment. It was easy enough to do in the logging towns; no job lasted long and no company had any commitment to me. I was laid off twice, but I quit three times. It was important to keep ahead of them. "Commitment" was the big word in those days, or maybe it's just a big word at that age, before you get committed by time. To my friends it meant marriage or a job, but to me it meant something worse, something like the end.

One day in Idaho, I was thinning trees for Boise Cascade and I decided to drop an enormous Doug fir that had not been marked for harvest. That was wrong, of course, but I couldn't help it; I had just learned how to use a chain saw. The fir stood as straight and strong as a Titan missile and had no limbs for its first hundred feet. It was four feet through at its butt, and I had to make big sidecuts to get the bar of my chain saw in for the undercut. I began my backcut, but when I had sawed through a third of the way, a breeze came up and set the tree back on my sawbar. It was stuck. I needed wedges, but the wedges were in the company pickup. Then I realized that the pickup was parked directly behind my backcut, one hundred feet from the tree. My boss was asleep in the pickup cab.

I eyed the pickup and I eyed the treetop, trying to calculate whether I would hit the truck. The breeze blew softly, against my backcut, and the top of the tree waved beneath low, white scraps of clouds. The clouds seemed to catch on the treetop, pulling it over toward the truck. I had time to notice all of this before the tree began to fall.

The taller the tree the longer it takes to fall. It gathers speed and power from gravity's commitment to finish a job. This tree took forever. It was already three hundred years old and a hundred and fifty feet tall, but it stretched itself out and grew before it died. I was twenty years old and I felt like ten. The thrill was electric. I shouted as the bole of the tree tilted toward the truck. I screamed, and my boss sat up in the cab. I could tell by the look on his face that he did not understand, that perhaps I was going to kill him.

He smiled at me, a slow, waking-up smile. I grinned back at him, savagely, and in my panic I attempted the impossible. As the tree fell, I put my shoulder and face into the bark of the trunk and I pushed with all my strength. I can still close my eyes and see that moment. The tree drove me into the ground and the percussion from the earth bounced me back onto my feet. Unhurt but senseless, I danced a knock-kneed stagger and sat down on the trunk of the tree. I looked along the shaft of that fallen giant to its crown, where its limbs were still waving their branches. It had folded the company's truck, like a man's wallet, right behind the cab.

Luckily, I had missed my boss. Now I had to saw through limbs to get him out. He was fine. He swore at me the whole time. And when he got out of the truck, he fired me. He told me that made me a free man now, and then he beat me up. He was six foot five and I was five foot eight. He kept knocking me over the tree trunk. Getting beat up like that is like fireworks; it is all sound and light. The blows explode in your ears and they flash in bright black sparks, up from your teeth, back through your eyeballs, back into your brain. I kept getting up to get hit again, thinking that I had to, that that was the way I was raised, until finally he said, "Don't you get up," and I didn't.

"You're a tough little idiot," he said, and he went off and started felling trees. My boss was an artist with a chain saw. I lay there awhile, watching him work, and then I walked into town. With my black and swollen eyeless face, it took me all the next day to hitchhike to Boise. I spent that evening in the city library, hiding behind the bigger books—atlases mostly—researching a reason to do something dramatic. They had an old globe of the world in there that was four feet in diameter—just like the tree—and it showed places that no longer exist, like Siam, Mozambique, and the Belgian Congo. These places made me think of adventure, and I realized that adventurers need no reason, no reason to do anything. I could adventure anywhere that did not cost much money and did not require sophistication.

At that time, I thought I spoke Spanish. I had attempted college Spanish 101 four times in three years. But Mexico was too close and I had seen Tijuana, so I tilted the globe on its axis. Seen from upside down, the world had much more water. There were fewer places to choose from. I chose something Spanish, and I lit out. I would impress everyone with my adventures in South America. To trick myself into going through with it and to show my friends that I was really going to do it, I spent most of my summer's money on a plane ticket to Buenos Aires and a train ride to Patagonia. When I got to Patagonia, I found I had tricked myself well. Patagonia is at the end of the earth—the world really comes to a point—and once you are there, there you are, as they say. You know you have gotten away. You cannot stay there, of course. Nothing stays there. It gets blown off or it sticks to a spiny black scrub and freezes or rattles to death. There was nothing I could do but come back.

Getting there had taken me all of a week and most of my money, and getting back would take six months of trying to find cheaper ways home. I lost a lot of my innocence behind Argentine bus stations and aboard Paraguayan ferryboats stranded in the wrong river channels. On a beach in Brazil, I lost my clothes to a woman who looked like my grandmother. In Peru, I caught pneumonia. I carried a fever for the rest of the trip.

I met Santiago and Angelina on the day I arrived at a jungle river crossing in the upper Amazon, near a place called Los Puentes Caidos. There, the twisted wrecks of two steel bridges burst through the surface of the blood-brown water and provoked a giant whirlpool. An earthquake had taken out one of the bridges, and a flood or a war with Peru had demolished the other. Just above the whirlpool was apparently the only place in the entire Oriente where one could cross the river, and there the buses from the north and the south stopped on the opposite banks and abandoned their passengers.

Within the space of half a mile, the river escaped through a gorge in the green wall of the Andes and disappeared into the wet sponge of the selva. Everything happened in that hard right angle between vertical and horizontal, where the drumming thunder of the falling water was baffled into silence by the jungle. The earth changed from up and down into broad and flat, the air changed from something you breathed into something that stuck to your face, and the river changed from foam and mist into a bulging flood of mud.

After leaving their buses and seeing the whirlpool twisting around the ruins like an eel, the people had to decide. Their buses were turning around. Either they got on a bus again and went back to where they came from or they ferried across the river in dugout canoes. These dugouts were fire-gouged, creosoted logs about four feet wide and forty feet long. They had been carved from the trunks of mighty *guardarropas*, and their Japanese outboards were driven by motorboys who were no more than twelve years old. These boys and the older pilots in the bows of the canoes would stand, to show off their bravery, as they motored their gondolas across the river in waves like amphibious invasions.

The people who risked the crossing took the journey in two ways: some faced the danger in petrified panic and some faced serenely away. I remember one scene very well. A woman threw flowers over her shoulder at the whirlpool's spinning, twisting mouth. Then she clasped her hands to her bosom and prayed. I remember watching those flowers beat that whirlpool, just dip into it and float on by, and I remember thinking that the difference between coincidences and miracles was that miracles were coincident to prayer. I wrote that one down. I had a fever then, and for me at the time, any coincident thought was a miracle.

The people even ferried small trucks across the river on platforms built on two and three dugouts lashed together. From what I could see, the broken bridges had already caught two Isuzu pickups and an army tank. The two trucks were skewered on spines of iron re-bar. The windshield motto of one of the pickups—"I Am the Protector of Women"—flashed its reassurance to the women in the dugouts. Only the turret of the tank showed above the flood, and its cannon aimed upriver. The day I arrived, the whirlpool had caught the trunk of a great *guardarropa* tree. The trunk was too large to pull under, and so the whirlpool spun it around like a great propeller. It revolved slowly beneath a liquid sun that was beginning to soak into clouds.

I got some crackers out of my duffel bag. In those days, I existed on nouns and verbs, food in packages, beer in bottles, and fruit that I could peel. I stood on the muddy bank above the river and looked across to the jungle and the foothills that began their climb into the Andes. Among the white trunks of the *guardarropa* trees and the boles of the chonta palms, white Brahman cattle stood angular and still.

Down by the bank, a group of young soldiers shot their M-16s at the tree trunk as it bobbed around in circles. They paid off bets to each other in cigarettes as they hit the tree or missed.

One of the soldiers saw me and climbed up the bank to check my passport.

"Are you Peruvian?" I thought he asked me. "Or CIA?"

"I am a North American," I told him.

"Obviously," he said. He pointed to the whirlpool and said something in Spanish I could not understand, but it did not sound good. I nodded anyway in an attempt at agreement.

The soldier looked at me as if he hated me and then he laughed. He shouted something to his comrades—something close to what he had said to me—and the soldiers all laughed and pointed their carbines at me.

The soldier lifted my ponytail and showed it to the others.

"Hee-pee," one of the others shouted.

I had a vision of them shooting off my ponytail.

"I do not understand," I said to the soldier in Spanish.

"Clearly, obviously. Never," he said.

He smiled at me. He was hating me more and more. He was thinking—I could see it in his eyes—and I couldn't let him finish his thought.

"Screw . . . you . . . blue," I said slowly in English but in the same tone as his, and I held my breath.

He stared at me a moment, hating me, but he did not understand me either. He was about sixteen years old so I tried to look as old as I was, his senior. He left me and walked back down to the river, swinging his arms widely. The soldiers soon forgot me and resumed their shooting.

Right then, a cloud of green parrots burst from the trees and swirled out over the water so suddenly a shiver chilled through my body. I remembered my fever. I had been sick forever, it seemed—sick, tired, lonely, and cold. Even in the heat, my chills kept my sweat cold. My teeth ached cold; my bones felt cold. The parrots swirled above me and chattered. I shook my head and I wrapped my wrist tightly in the drawstrings of my duffel bag. I retreated up a muddy path to a small bluff that rose above the river. Below me, the colors were noisy. The scramble of shacks and tents, the brightly painted buses, and the people in gaudy polyesters looked like a sudden, swirling circus against the brown of the river, the brown of the mud, and the green of the sodden jungle.

On the hilltop, it was drier and quiet. There, a shrine to the Virgin Mary had been built out of plaster and stones. The shrine was small and ugly, slapped into shape by hand, but the stones set into it were strange and beautiful: river-polished agates, ruby garnets, and quartzite crystals grown into castles. A magazine image of the Virgin smiled out from a metal cardholder stuck into the top of the shrine. A plastic bucket waited below the Virgin. The bucket held coins and shiny trinkets, in the forms of houses, cars, hearts, feet, eyes, and other parts of the human body.

A man knelt before the shrine, praying and trembling. He wore clean calf-length trousers and a torn white shirt. His short, curly hair ringed his round, veined forehead, and his eyes squeezed down into a fervor above his broken nose. He looked like a boxer. He mouthed a prayer and then he raised his eyebrows and opened his eyes, as if checking to see if anything had changed. He regarded the Virgin suspiciously and spoke to her, threatening. I wondered, Had he been tricked by her before? Had he made a few deals and then tried to carry them through? The man held out a small charm shaped like a bus and dangled it above the plastic bucket.

Below us, the soldiers ran out of ammunition. The people began jeering at them now and I could hear bus horns honking from across the river and the whirlpool catching its breath. People jostled each other for places in the next wave of canoes to cross.

The praying man stopped moving his lips. He closed his

eyes and dropped the charm into the bucket. He kept absolutely still for several seconds, leaning expectantly toward the shrine. I stopped chewing my crackers. Then the flock of parrots suddenly wheeled past our heads in a flutter of wings and wind. The man rocked back and opened his eyes. He looked about him wildly, muttering. He saw me and struggled to his feet. He motioned to the shrine and asked me a question, his voice and lips shaking. I could not understand him, but I nodded, smiling, and I offered him a cracker. This stopped him. He fished one out of my package and then he looked down at the ground and muttered again. He glanced back at me.

"Milagro?" he whispered. *Milagro* means "miracle." He nodded. I nodded. We munched on our crackers. Then he took a deep, shuddering breath and screamed at the top of his voice, *"Milagro! Milagro! Un milagro!"* The man stretched out his arms and threw back his head. *"Un milagro de todos los días!"* he shouted.

I was shocked by his shouting, and amazed by the strength in his voice. He had just announced a miracle for all time. Now people were surrounding us at the shrine. The man began telling them a very loud story and I kept nodding. He kept poking me and laughing, and then wagging his finger at the Virgin. Several old women clustered around and began to pat my shoulders and kiss my hands. Some of the men winked and tapped their temples. Someone grabbed my duffel bag. Then a group of them hoisted me and the man to their shoulders and marched us down off the bluff and around through the tents and shacks. The soldiers pointed their empty carbines at me and shot *tat-a-tat-tat!* sounds with their tongues. A boy ripped the picture of the Virgin from the top of her shrine and ran ahead to lead the parade. I held to the hair of the men who carried me and tried to keep sight of my duffel bag. The celebrations continued, nervous and noisy, until we all heard new buses honking from across the river. Those who carried the man set him down with fine ceremony. Those who carried me dropped me on my shoulder. Everyone rushed down to the river to get seats in the first canoes across.

What was to be the day's last river crossing was about to begin, and the people who had put off the danger now fought for a chance at it, heartened by the miracle. The man and I were left standing alone. He grinned at me, his eyes sparkling, and he said something and shrugged his shoulders. He dug deep into his trouser pockets and brought out a steel coin, which he kissed and tossed toward the shrine.

He turned back to me. "I am Santiago Benalcazar de Orellana," he said, bowing.

"Daniel Cooper," I said.

"*A sus órdenes,* Daniel." I am at your service. He shook my hand.

I followed him down the bank to the dugouts. Most of the canoes were already filled, but there was room in a peculiar crooked canoe next to which an old gray cholo pilot was scolding a black motorboy. Santiago and I waded past them and took seats in the stern of their dugout. The old man then cuffed the boy so hard the boy's head snapped back, and the man waded up along the canoe and took his place in the bow. He yelled some derision back at the boy and the boy yanked the starter cord on the outboard. The motor caught and fired. The boy laughed and pointed at the old man and patted the motor.

The boy saw me watching him and he handed me the starter cord. The wooden grip at the end of it was carved into the likeness of a naked woman. The nylon cord entered the grip between the woman's buttocks and came out in front from between her legs. There, it was tied into a frayed pubic knot. I almost laughed from surprise. Then the boy pointed to the grip and he laughed in a way that made me feel like smacking him too. He took back the grip and pulled the cord back and forth through it.

All the canoes headed out into the current, angling upstream in a crabbing progress. I set my duffel bag onto my knees because of the water that spouted through cracks in the hull. Santiago sat on the bench in front of me and held to both gunwales, except when he waved to people who kept cheering him from the other boats. In front of Santiago crouched a boy of about six, bailing with a tin can, and beyond him sat a brightly clothed family.

The flotilla of shrill dugouts plowed across the stream. The bundles of laundry, the chickens bound by the legs, and the babies in shawl hammocks slung across the beams gave the crossing an air of a picnic. The weaving boats crabbed across the river until we all got above the whirlpool. Then the motor in our canoe died.

All the passengers turned at once and the dugout almost rolled. The pilot shouted at them, but they would not listen. The bailer boy shouted at them too; they were hindering his bailing. The motorboy pulled at the starter cord, and nothing happened. He set the choke and pulled again.

Nothing. We drifted like a log, moving with the river, and the heavy water killed our wake. Other canoes passed us by, the people in them watching us curiously. The boy tried again to start the motor and a thin sheen of oil spread out on the river. He had flooded the motor. We could wait for the gas in the carburetor to evaporate—and drift into the whirlpool—or we could open the choke and pull until it caught.

"The choke!" I said to the boy. "Open the choke."

He turned to me. He did not seem as concerned as he should be.

"The choke!" I said again, and then I forced the language.

"Cho-kay! Cho-kay!" I said. I shook my hand and pointed.

The boy turned away from me and heaved on the cord. This time, he yanked it off the pulley. He looked at the cord dangling from his hand and turned back to me. Now he was worried. He looked to the bridge ruins.

"*Sí. Choque,*" he said.

"Yes, damn it. *Choque!*" I said. I would later learn that *choque* means "collision" in Spanish. "*Choque!*" I yelled. "*Choque!*"

The motorboy widened his eyes and nodded. We were drifting sideways now, one with the current. The other canoes still motored onward. The people in our canoe took up my call.

"*Choque! Choque!*"

We neared the bridges. The brown water was so thick that as it washed through the wreckage it folded over and slapped back with a wooden sound. I pointed at the motor. "The choke!" I said. The boy nodded and handed me the starter cord.

We hit the sunken army tank just above the whirlpool. The cannon struck us broadsides. It punched into the canoe above the waterline, ripped splinters the length of the canoe, and knocked a bundle of Clorox bottles out the other side. The canoe spun around the cannon, struck the tank turret just behind where I sat, and rebounded toward the whirlpool. Now everyone screamed, "*Choque! Choque!*" A man fought his wife to keep her from jumping into the river. The pilot stood up in the bow and cursed us passengers. He pleaded to the other boats in the river for help. Santiago held to his gunwales, his eyes wide open and his eyebrows high. I stuck my duffel bag between my knees and grabbed hold. As the whirlpool drew us toward it, I saw the huge tree trunk that still spun slowly inside it. The log barely floated, nearly all underwater. It covered the mouth of the vortex and flattened out the spiral, but I heard the airy sucking.

We drifted closer to the whirlpool and the people in our boat stopped screaming. I heard people in other canoes screaming now, but they were more thrilled than frightened. The pilot gave us all a look of genuine hate and he sat down.

We entered the whirlpool. The bow dipped below water and

the stern lifted into the air. The point of the bow struck the log right in the middle and stabbed beneath it. The pilot and the first two passengers disappeared. There was a muffled *screeeek*, and the gunwale boards ripped from our hands and shot wobbling out over the water. I hung on to my duffel bag. Our bow jammed beneath the log, the scraping vibrated up through the canoe, and brown water poured over the sides and into the sinking bow. With Santiago and me airborne in the stern, the canoe spun halfway around the whirlpool and popped out the far side.

Just like that, we were free. But the bow was in splinters and we floated only because the river was so thick with mud. It was as if there were no canoe. The pilot and the first two people in the bow were gone. That left seven of us adults sitting in a line, up to our waists in the flat brown water. The little bailer boy sat chin-deep, looking after nothing. I hugged my duffel bag and searched the rapids below us for the three people. The bailer boy stood up now and turned around and looked at the motorboy with a sudden sickly grin. The motorboy laughed. Santiago was searching the sky.

The motorboy took his cord and somehow got the motor going. Its exhaust bubbled underwater. We sputtered toward shore, through the eddy below the bridges, and the people ran down the bank to meet us.

Our canoe ran aground thirty yards from the bank. We all stood up and slogged in through the mud. Below us, downriver, a woman in a yellow dress ran away, screaming, along the riverbank. She ran into a graveyard of small white crosses and screamed at the sky. Suddenly, right below her in the river, the canoe pilot stood up out of the water. He raised both his arms and opened his mouth and gulped a great gasp of air. The woman stopped screaming and peered at him. He looked like a bear, as brown as if he were made out of mud. Then he dropped his arms and she screamed again and ran away downriver.

Some of the people on the bank cheered us survivors. They

made Santiago and me shake their hands. Others waded out into the river and stood looking after the woman in the yellow dress as she tried to fight her way through a bamboo thicket.

I kept watching the river for someone else to come up and gasp for air. But the water stayed flat. The people waded out to where their fingertips trailed in the water, and they began splashing water out over the river. For a while they did this without a word, and then one of them—then all of them—began to wail.

The sound scraped down my backbone. Then the people on the bank began to wail too. Those who before had cheered the most now screamed the loudest. A woman in a red skirt began ripping strips off her skirt, tying the strips into bows and throwing the bows out over the river. When the people saw this, they stopped wailing and began to sing. It was like a dirge, with no words, or with Indian words I could not make out. They sang, and they swayed to their lamentations.

Then the buses started honking and the people seemed to forget the tragedy and they left the riverbank. The women in the river started wading ashore, singing and splashing themselves and each other. Even the two boatboys scrambled up the bank and climbed on a bus. I waited around, wanting to do something because two people had drowned. But there were never any sirens, or ambulances, or doctors, or bodies. No heroics, just hysterics, and disappearance and death. I had done nothing, and there was nothing to do. The cholo boat pilot, still covered in mud, trudged up the hill through the grave markers.

I waited another moment, watching the river. By the time I got to the top of the bank, the last bus was leaving. I stopped and I watched it go. Then I saw Santiago. He was standing across the landing. He waved to me and turned, and disappeared into the jungle.

I looked back across the river. Now I had done it. I thought,

This is where you've got yourself: right here. The great log in the whirlpool was gone and the whirlpool itself had changed into a long wave curling below one of the buttresses. What was left of our canoe looked like a wishbone floating away in the water.

The whole scene now looked small and distant. The tent market across the river was far away. The merchants were packing up their wares as the soldiers harassed them. I was alone on the wrong end of two broken bridges. It was beginning to rain.

I was already wet, my duffel bag was soaked, but I got out my plastic poncho and pulled it over my head. I sat down on the duffel bag and spread the plastic around me to cover it. Wanting to do something, I took out my book, which I had wrapped in my poncho. It was a paperback copy of *A Moveable Feast* that I had been traded for a flashlight and that I had read three times that week. I began to read slowly, moving my lips and hunching over the book so it would not get wet.

Reading at sunset always made me feel as though I was going blind. On the equator at sunset, the sun falls straight down. In a few minutes, the colors roll up through the clouds and sink down with the night. When it is raining and you are in the jungle and the Andes rise to over twenty thousand feet just off to your right, the daylight goes from dim to dark in the time it takes to read a paragraph. I read about Hemingway in Paris and how hungry they were but how good it was, all being together and writing. In Paris, the apples were crisp and delicious and the lights came on, but I was left holding my book in the dark, water running down to my elbows.

I felt my fever again. It flowed over my skin in rushes and waves. Whenever this happened, I often stopped what I was doing and lost myself in it. But now I was soaked, and under my poncho I sat huddled in the rain. The sand fleas had gotten through my socks, and my ankles were beginning to swell. I had just watched two people disappear and drown, and I felt so sorry for myself I almost felt good. Santiago once said that self-pity may be protective at times. It is safer than anger at your own stupidity. Santiago said anger at others was really at ourselves, and that if we could see it, anger would break our hearts with sadness. "Wouldn't it?" he asked. To Santiago all emotions were one, all heartbreakers, and they all made him shake his head and shrug. I now feel that sadness is nearer despair. It keeps you from doing what you ought to do.

It got darker. I heard the rain in the river, but I could no longer see it. I did not know if the merchants' tents were still on the other side. There seemed to be no other side to anything right now. I tried to withdraw into my fever, but I couldn't do it. I couldn't take it. I do not know if I thought I was giving up or starting something, but I stood up. I grabbed my duffel bag and began stumbling up the beach in the darkest rain of my life.

At the top of the rise, the hard sand turned into a gravel road. I stood in the road and had no idea which way it led. I peered through the dark until my eyes hurt and I saw dull patterns swirl in my vision. I felt as if I were underwater. I stuck my mouth and nose down into my rain poncho and breathed the thick, wet air. I turned to my left and stared into the darkness. I saw nothing at first, but as I relaxed and let my eyes wander, I began to pick up a faint glow, illuminating the slick greenery of a jungle clearing. I waded toward the glow.

Before I reached the clearing, I stopped. At first, what I saw looked like a flying saucer. Its eerie light shone out of a row of square windows that sent shafts of sparkles through the rain. The light silhouetted several white crosses growing awkwardly out of the ground. As I looked at the scene, the rain ceased, first from behind me and then in front like a curtain of sound being drawn away. The light was coming from the windows of the carcass of a battered old school bus. Its wheels were gone. Its roof was flattened. And it was settled down into a nest of

glistening brush. Through one of its windows, I saw the face of
Santiago.

I took a step toward the clearing, through a shower of black
brush that pulled my hood off my head. I stopped to free myself. Inside the bus, Santiago turned to the window. I waved,
but my hand caught in something over my head and suddenly
a spider's web dropped wetly over my face. It sucked into my
mouth.

I tore the web from my face and stumbled to the bus's folding
door. The broken-out windows were hung with ripped mosquito
netting, and the inside of the bus had been made into a home.
Two hammocks stretched between the windows. Old bus seats
now faced sideways and served as couches. Santiago sat in one
of the seats, his back straight and his head cocked slightly. He
looked the way blind people do when they are listening. His
hand rested on the shoulder of a girl who sat reading a magazine
at his feet. The girl was beautiful.

I saw his mouth move, and the girl looked up and saw me.
I felt like the ghost of a rat who had drowned, but she was
unafraid. She placed a leaf in her magazine and came to the
door. She grabbed the heavy bar opener by the driver's seat and
pulled the door open. She wore only an oversized white T-shirt,
which reached halfway to her knees, and a narrow American
Western-style belt with fake Indian beadwork. She was darker
than Santiago. Her dark hair fell curling past her ears. Her eyes
were olive green, and her eyebrows rose high and arching. Her
eyes were very large and they rode in a wide face above a slender
neck. They were so large that she looked very young, but her
shoulders were strong and her body was a woman's.

"*Pase no más,*" she whispered, inviting me in.

I looked to Santiago. He nodded and waved me in. "*Sigue,*
Daniel. *Sigue,*" he said. I followed his hand and took a seat by
a gas lantern that sputtered near a small stove.

The girl came in behind me and took her place again at

Santiago's feet. She had been reading a *National Geographic* magazine. She studied me now: my poor Argentine tennis shoes, my stained Chilean corduroys, and my Peruvian pullover made from a flour sack. I pulled some leaves and twigs out of my hair.

"Angelina," Santiago said in Spanish, "this is Daniel, the gringo who speaks Castilian."

"Claro," she said.

To me she said, "I speak English," and nodded. Her smile was wide and white.

I nodded and smiled as I wiped web from my face with my shirt. The wetness began to leave me as steam. I could feel some warmth on my shoulder from the lantern's chimney and I leaned toward it.

"I speak English," Angelina said again. She said it well, but I believed her about as much as people believed me when I told them I did not speak Spanish. Of course, I told them that in Spanish—*"No hablo español"*—and this made me an obvious liar.

"How do you do," I said to Angelina.

"How do you do," Angelina said. Her eyes were green and direct. Where her father's eyes looked to a distance, Angelina's focused on mine.

"Do you like hot dogs?" she asked me.

Santiago laughed. "Hah! Like hot dogs," he said. They both watched me.

"Why, yes," I said. "I like them very much."

"Why, yes?" Angelina said. She rose and went to the stove and fixed an aluminum plate of cold rice and cooked bananas. "Hot dogs," she said, handing me the plate and a spoon. She and her father laughed.

"Hot dogs!" he said.

She took her place by Santiago, and I don't remember tasting anything. They watched me while I ate, and I kept nodding and smiling. Santiago still held the expression he had assumed at the miracle, of awe, humor, and expectation. Angelina sat cross-legged on her pillow, her hands pushing her white T-shirt down between her legs. I kept glancing at her legs; they were smooth and brown. I tried to think of something to say.

"That's a very good magazine," I said finally, nodding toward the *National Geographic*.

Angelina picked it up and flipped through the pages. "Do you think?" she asked. She opened to a story with pictures of naked native women. The women held up their naked children by their hands and offered them to the camera.

"This is our country," Angelina said, flattening out the magazine. "These are the Auruna people."

"I like your country."

"It is primitive."

"It is beautiful."

"We do not have much."

"Angelina." I was glad to say her name.

She looked up at me, her dark eyebrows high.

"You have a lot, Angelina."

Her dark eyebrows lowered. "That does not mean much," she said. Then she shrugged and shook her head. "And you have a lot also, and more. You are a rich and blond and beautiful gringo."

At the moment, I could smell myself.

"What are you saying?" Santiago asked her in Spanish.

"I told him he is beautiful, Papa."

Santiago looked at me as if I had appeared out of nothing.

"You are brave, too," she said to me. In the lantern light, her teeth and the whites of her eyes shone like pearl. "All gringos are brave. And rich. Papa told me that after the wreck, only you did not make a big promotion."

"There was nothing to do."

"What did he just say?" Santiago asked her.

Angelina told him.

"Exactly!" he said. "Daniel, you understand."

I watched Angelina. Her thick, dark hair curled back behind her perfect ears. Her nose was small and straight. She stretched her T-shirt down between her legs, across her breasts.

"Yes, she is beautiful," Santiago said, and at that, Angelina gave me a strange smile.

Angelina was more than beautiful.

"And you please her, Daniel," Santiago said.

The next morning I met Hector Tanbueno.

2
_____

I woke to shouting and a pounding on the bus. I now lay curled up in one of the hammocks. Angelina slept in the other hammock and Santiago sat in his chair. He was awake but deep in thought.

"Santiago!" a man called from outside the bus. "San-tia-go! Hey! You! Benalcazar!"

I sat up and swung my feet to the floor. Angelina opened her eyes and smiled at me. It was getting light outside and, through the bus windows, I saw dozens of people. Some stood in groups and families; some huddled around small fires. They were not talking. They were waiting for something. They crossed their arms and held their elbows in their hands, or they held their palms to their cheeks and chins. They shuffled their feet, or they squatted and held their heads in their hands. They gazed toward the door of the bus.

"Santiago!" the man called again.

"*Entre!*" Santiago answered, and shrugged.

A huge man opened the door and pressed himself around the bars and past the coin box. He had to stand sideways, bent at the waist under the low ceiling, and he turned his head to look at us. He wore black rubber boots, a pair of farmer's bib overalls, a white V-neck T-shirt, and a green baseball cap that advertised John Deere tractors. His face was freckled, his hair red. He was so fat that he huffed when he breathed, but he looked as strong as a bull. He was followed by an Indian boy wearing only shorts and a soup bowl haircut. The boy squeezed past him into the bus.

"*Buenos días,*" the man said to Santiago.

"*Buenos,*" said Santiago.

"*Buenos,*" the man said again. He lowered himself onto a seat before he saw me. "Uh!" he said to Santiago. "Gringo?"

The man turned to me. "I'm Lester McGuinness," he said. "I will help you. Where you from, kid?"

"Idaho."

"Huh. Hmmm. Just bumming around, I bet. Just seeing the world?"

"I'm traveling."

"Hmmm. You look like it. But don't you worry, we'll get you cleaned up. Get you a bath and a hot dog. Really. When did you get here?"

"Last night. In the rain."

"Uh-huh. You must be another of Santiago's miracles."

He asked Santiago, "*Milagro?*"

"*Claro,*" said Santiago.

Lester nodded. "Uh-huh." The Indian boy who had followed him into the bus kept smiling at Angelina.

"Old Santiago probably thinks you're an angel," Lester told me. "Ever since he wrecked his bus, Santiago has been responsible for three heaven-sent sightings and a burning bush.

Now people are burying their stillborns around his door and building a picket fence out of the little white crosses. Oh, damn it, yes. I come here from Ohio to spread manure for Jesus and I end up on miracle weed control. Miracles grow like quack grass down here. And bad. It's the Amazon, I know it. It's God's garden, I know, but it can get to be ridiculous. The story now is that Santiago walked across the river yesterday."

"I was there."

Lester raised his cap with his eyebrows. "Unnh? Yeah? Hunh? You get it in pictures?"

"Two people were drowned, but there was a miracle, all right. We should have all drowned and we popped right out."

"Yeah? Well, let me tell you. In any disaster, always someone survives. Now you tell me. Did you see Mother Mary?"

"No."

"No, you didn't. But everybody else did. She held up her skirts in one hand and Santiago's hand in the other and they just sauntered across. They say she appeared to him beforehand and she told him she was going to do it too. Santiago probably proved his faith by going in the canoe with you."

"I didn't have anything to do with it."

"I know you didn't, kid. I know you didn't." Lester slapped his cap across his knee. "All right. Yeah, you didn't. And if that ain't the case. Welp! It's time for Reality Jesus.

"O.K.," he said to Santiago. "What? Hey. *Qué pasó?*"

Santiago related the event, calmly and clearly it seemed, although I couldn't follow the Spanish. Lester shook his round head as he listened. When Santiago finished with what sounded like a question, holding his palms up and leaning forward, Lester said to me, "This joker claims that the Mother Mary did appear to him, but she didn't say a word about the whirlpool. She sounded more like birds' wings. He thinks she said that he was the smartest man in all the Oriente, and he wants to know why she would say something like that. Now he is wondering if maybe she was talking about you, that you're the smartest man, and he just didn't understand her. Do you see what I have to deal with, kid?"

"What did you tell him?"

"I told him he should have got it from her in writing. That's a joke, of course, and he won't understand that either, but that's O.K. We teach Reality Jesus in our church. You know, 'The Lord helps those . . .'—that kind of stuff. Show, don't tell. Teach, don't preach. Lead, don't plead. I'm down here with AgriCristo Amazonas. We're interdenominational. I'm just a farmer, really. My wife's the Baptist."

Lester patted the bib of his overalls and drew his chin back into his cheeks. "This is not going to be easy," he said to me, through his small red lips.

In an ugly, singsong Spanish, Lester scolded Santiago about sin. He used English as a rock to pound in his meaning. "*El orgullo*," he called it. "That's pride." Santiago listened carefully. Angelina and the Indian boy watched Lester the way kids in our country watch TV, passive and mouths open. The people outside watched through the windows and translated Lester's speech to one another.

When Lester finished, he looked around the bus as if he were looking for something else to say. Then his eyes lighted on the Indian boy and he smiled.

"Well, O.K.," he said to me. "Now you look at this. This here is Hector. Hector is a fine new Christian Indian from the Auruna tribe, who are pitiful primitives. His mama and him just walked out of the jungle one day a couple of years ago and we took them in. She died of the flu right off, but Hector did fine. We call him Hector because that sounds like his Indian name, which means 'fox,' we believe, or maybe 'beetle.' "

Hector was still smiling at Angelina. He was short, square, and brown. His eyes were large and dark. He would dart a glance at me or Santiago and then return his gaze to Angelina.

Lester cuffed Hector on his bare shoulder. "Hector, what's your name?" he said.

"My name is Hector," the boy said.

Hector's voice surprised me. It was low and manly. He suddenly looked older.

Lester smiled. "He's got a good *eee*-fect, don't you know."

"Pardon me, miss," Hector now said to Angelina. "Do you like hot dogs?"

Angelina tossed her head. "How do you do?" she said to me.

Hector turned to me. "I learn the English in church. We talk about God."

"We talk, but he don't listen," Lester said.

"But he don't listen," Hector said. His voice was so low. He smiled at Angelina.

"No, you don't," said Lester.

Now Hector whispered to Angelina, "An-ge-*leee*-na."

She did not look at him.

"An-ge-*leee*-na," he said, low but louder.

Santiago caught Lester's attention and shook his head.

"Simmer down, Hector," Lester said.

Hector widened his eyes and nostrils.

"We got to watch this one," Lester said to me. "He's older than his looks and he's getting real itchy. He's got Indian senses and powers, too. The other day he got our little girl, Dorothy, to take off her clothes and ride the pigs. I thought the wife would die."

Hector watched Angelina. He took a deep breath; his rib cage was huge. " 'Gelina!" he rumbled.

"Put a lid on it," said Lester. He said to me, "We just barely got him to keeping his pants on his butt and now he's trying to get into others. Mae makes me take him around with me now. She won't have him around alone."

Then Lester paused. He looked distressed. "And what's

other, what's more, is that things happen around him too. He's like lucky. Not good lucky or bad lucky, just lucky. Indian lucky. It's those Indian senses, maybe. I can't explain it, but it's spooky. Know what I'm saying? Spooky things happen. Or nothing spooky happens, but everybody thinks it did. Like Santiago here, yesterday. What explains that? Jesus does, I'm sure. Or maybe Satan. But not in the Catholic way. No Mary Mother way, no sir, it's Jesus who explains it, but we won't understand it. More in a Christian Science way, maybe. I don't know." Lester stuck his index finger into his right cheek and twisted it. "I'm no Christian Scientist neither. I feel like old Santiago. I feel like I would be the smartest man in all the world, if only I could figure it out."

Santiago was watching all the people gathered outside the bus. Hector was staring at Angelina, but she ignored him. She had her eyes on me.

Lester stood. "We best be going. I'm going to tell all these good dumb little folks to go on home. Come on, Hector."

Hector did not move. He watched Angelina.

"Hector . . ."

Then Hector got a strange look on his face. He held up an index finger and started blinking.

"Oh, oh," said Lester. "Oh no now."

Hector's face took on a dark cast. The skin around his eyes turned dark. He dropped his hand. His eyes darted and his nostrils flared, as if he were picking up a scent.

"Oh no. Oh, damn. Oh, damn!" Lester said.

Suddenly, Hector raised his hand again. He waved his finger at Angelina, as if counting. Lester looked at Santiago and at Angelina and then he looked at me. "Do you feel it?" he asked me. "Do you?"

I nodded, but I did not feel anything.

"Oh no. You feel it too?" Lester said. He stood and grabbed the bus coin box and hugged it close to him. He squeezed it hard and started puffing. I thought he would rip it out of the floor. His fat cheeks turned splotchy.

Hector was nodding his head with his finger now. Then he stopped and he said something to me in his own language. It chilled me. It was low and came from deep within his chest— a question, or a command. Confused, I looked at Angelina. She was watching me.

Then Hector made a sound with his lungs and throat that boomed like a drum. It drummed into my ears. Outside, dogs began to bark, then howl in a high, quavering keen. I did feel something now. I felt almost sick. I felt as if I needed to swallow, but I could not. My feet felt magnetized to the floor. Then the floor jerked. It snapped. Angelina cried, "Papa!" And the whole bus lifted and a tremor rolled beneath us, as if the bus were back on its wheels, rumbling down a rutted road. I held on to the cords of my hammock and wrenched my feet up off the floor. A saltshaker tipped over and rolled off the stove; then the stove crashed over. Lester held to the clattering coin box and a human moaning rose all around us as the people outside dropped to the ground. The tremor rolled under us like a wave, lifting us. I waited for it to drop us. It had to drop us. The earth could not rise forever.

And it didn't. At the top, it left us, waiting.

Outside, people were screaming in terror, but as the tremor stopped, we all caught our breath.

"Temblor!" cried Angelina.

Our hammocks were swinging in unison. The air smelled of jungle gas and spilled kerosene, and the guarana trees rained leaves upon the roof. Lester hugged the coin box. His lips were gray, his eyes were wet, and he breathed in short grunts.

"Oh, damn," he said.

"It was an earthquake!" I said. I felt we were still up in the air.

"Oh, damn," Lester said.

I tried to swallow and I couldn't. Hector grinned like a conspirator. Santiago smiled crookedly. Angelina's eyes grew wild and happy. A few brave people began to peek through the windows.

Lester cautiously released the coin box. He balanced for a moment and then collapsed onto the bench. "No! No! He knows when those things are going to happen! Before anyone else. Did you see it? Didn't he know it? Just before? He says he can smell them."

Santiago held up his hands. *"Presto!"* he said.

"Oh no," Lester said. "And see? It's another damn miracle."

"I am another damn miracle," Hector said. His voice was low and certain.

"Don't say that," Lester told him, almost whining.

"Don't say that," Hector boomed back.

"Maybe things do just happen around here," I said to Lester. "Maybe this is just one of those kinds of places."

Lester looked at me as if I were stupid. "Yeah? Hunh? You got that right."

"Well, look at those bridges," I said.

"Wait a minute. This man Santiago thinks he's a lightning rod for acts of God. He thinks he's a Job, except he takes every disaster like it was a goddamn birthday present. Ten people died when he wrecked this bus and now he's turned it into a Howard Johnson's. And this shitty little Indian kid can smell earthquakes and make little girls take off their clothes. He masturbates and laughs about it. It's sick, boy. It's morbid and it's un-Christian." Lester rubbed his stomach and chomped his teeth.

Angelina slipped out of her hammock. "Do you like hot dogs?" she asked Lester. I could now read the beadwork on the back of her belt. It said, "Ohio."

"Uh-hunh," said Lester.

Hector reached out and touched Angelina's arm. "I am the

miracle," he said to her. Angelina looked down at her arm where he touched her.

Outside, the people were now packed against the windows. The crowd had grown to a mob. People I had seen at the market the day before were now around Santiago's bus, hawking corn cakes and plastic saints.

The people began to chant. "San-tia-go! San-tia-go! San-tia-go!"

They were calling for a hero. Angelina laughed and ran to her father.

"No!" Hector said. "Santiago, no!"

Hector went to the open door.

"San-tia-go!" the crowd chanted.

Hector waved his arms at them.

"Santiago, no!" Hector boomed at the crowd.

"San-tia-go!" the people chanted.

"No! No! Hec-tor!" he thundered. His lungs were huge, like a bellows.

"San-tia-go!"

"Hec-tor! Hec-tor!" Hector shouted. His eyes were bright and wide.

"Hec-tor!" a few people yelled back.

"Hec-tor!" he led them. "Hector!"

The noise grew deafening. Lester McGuinness looked at me and shook his head. "Maybe the end of the world is coming soon," he said. "Forgive me, Jesus, but maybe that's why these people have all their floods and their earthquakes and landslides and plagues. It's because these people believe in them so hard. They want them."

The crowd was now chanting, "Hector!"

Lester took a deep breath. "Welp," he said, and he stood up. "Welp, it's time for reality, Jesus. It's time to unlighten the folds." He squeezed past Hector and went outside to speak to the crowd.

Angelina crawled up on the seat beside her father to watch the confrontation. I lay back in my hammock, overwhelmed. Hector looked over at me in triumph, his eyes now deep and dark.

That afternoon, after Lester took Hector away, Santiago got ready to go across the river and talk to the Virgin. He asked if I wanted to go with him, but I did not.

"Muy bien," Santiago said. "You are not religious and I respect that. You are a thinker and I respect that. You reason things out for yourself. *Bueno*. We will talk about it later. Now, Angelina will care for you."

When he left, some of the people who had been there since morning followed him down to the river. The others soon drifted away.

Angelina and I were alone and the bus seemed smaller. Angelina was excited and happy; she even clapped her hands. She said to me, "Daniel, there is a place for you to wash yourself, up the road."

I emptied my duffel bag onto the floor of the bus and found my kit with the silver comb, the double-edge razor, and the perfumed soap from Argentina. I left Angelina unfolding the alpaca poncho and I walked up the road to where a fresh stream joined the river. Two women were washing clothes under the bridge, so I waded upstream to a deep, clear pocket with a floor of coarse sand. I soaped and scraped in the cold water until my skin burned. I put on my only clean clothes—a pair of cutoff Levi's—and I brushed my teeth for a five full minutes. Then I shaved carefully by touch and did not cut myself.

I combed my hair straight back and tied it with a strip from a banana leaf. I felt natural and clean and my fever burned clear, like a light. My skin had chilled from the water, and the insects left me alone. The air was warm and thick in my lungs and heavy with perfume from the jungle. I stood on the sandbar, above the sun in the water. A small green viper swam across where I had bathed. It made S's in the water and disappeared beneath the bank.

When I got back to the bus, Angelina was out hanging the alpaca poncho in the sun. She had washed it and it smelled clean, of hard soap and lanolin.

"The women at the bridge came to tell me you were singing," she said. "They said you were singing rock and roll. Rock and roll is very good music. They say it has conquered the world." She now wore a shoulderless, short cotton sundress held up by elastic ribbing. The dress lifted as she reached up with the poncho and it gathered and stayed high as she pulled down. She smoothed it proudly and smiled at me. Her dark hair shone in the sun with a deep sheen and her green eyes were streaked with rays. We stood among the little white crosses in Santiago's yard and watched emerald hummingbirds feed at red hibiscus. Streamers of spiderweb drifted in the air.

"Now you are clean and handsome," she said to me. "Skinny but strong. And so very blond and handsome."

"And you are beautiful," I said.

I followed her into the bus. She had spread the small table with a scrap of clean white sheeting. "There," she said. "Just like that, I have food for you. Coffee with sugar, and bananas with cinnamon. And toast prepared with marmalade."

"Perfect," I said.

"And papaya with lime?"

"Perfect."

"And more coffee, with more sugar."

"More perfect."

"And more?"

We stood very close to each other. The light was bright through the windows. I felt the heat of her skin, and I watched her face, but she did not look at me now; she looked down. Her forehead was clear, her eyelashes were thick, and her shoulders were strong and brown. She was breathing fast and lightly. I felt my own breathing, too. She turned her head toward me. The jungle buzzed outside the windows and I felt her breath in the hair on my chest and I almost reached out to hold her.

Angelina fed me fruit and coffee. As I ate their food, I looked around the bus and saw that it was clean and neat. Their few possessions—mostly plates and cups—were clean and well cared for, arranged on a board. It was like a Robinson Crusoe bus, everything perfect. Outside, the jungle was rich and green and the fruit were large in the tops of the papaya trees.

Santiago came back while I was still eating.

"Well?" he said. "If our guest is content?"

"If he is," said Angelina.

"We hope he never leaves us."

"And how are you, Santiago?" I asked him.

"I?" Santiago shook his head, smiling. "*Confundido*. Confounded. The Virgin is silent today, or occupied. It is as if I am the smartest man in the whole Oriente and my mind is all a question mark." Putting his thumbs into his armpits and shrugging his shoulders, Santiago slumped as if he were hanging by an invisible thread. "I'll try again tomorrow. Perhaps Señor McGuinness is correct. Perhaps *you* are the smartest man."

"I think Daniel is the smartest man," Angelina said. She came over and sat down next to me. She put her hand on my knee. This did not bother Santiago.

"And you the smartest girl," Santiago said. "You, my Angelina."

I stayed with them five days. Angelina had hundreds of English words she had been waiting to learn the meanings to, and we read her *Geographic*s together. That second night I could not sleep, thinking about her—quiet in her hammock, dreaming. I held my breath and listened for her breathing. An animal boomed outside in the jungle. It sounded like the noise made by Hector; *Tttunh! Tttunh! Tttunh!*

The next morning I got up and cut back the vines for Santiago and hauled the cuttings across the road. He tried to get me to go across the river with him and visit the shrine. But I made him go alone again and I stayed back with Angelina.

When he was gone, Angelina clapped her hands and got out her pile of magazines. She wanted to be a writer for *National Geographic* and travel to exotic places.

"To know the world," she said.

She sat on the floor next to me, leaning against my leg. She wore a loose cotton dress held up by strings tied in bows.

"To know everything," she said. "I don't want to be in a magazine, or to read in a magazine. I want to write in a magazine and have people read from me what the world is like because I know it. I know it, I write it, they read it—there it is."

Leaning against me, sweet and warm, Angelina read in the magazine a story about Antarctica. "Imagine," she said, "how cold. You would die in a minute, or less."

The smell of the jungle in bloom was full in the air. I watched her brown shoulders, the lean muscle rising to her neck, the shine of her skin, and her dark, dark shining hair.

She fanned the pages. I touched her shoulder with my hand and she leaned harder against me. I returned the pressure and stroked her smooth shoulder. I kissed her hair and she turned and looked up at me.

"Angelina," I said.

I kissed her lips as softly as I could.

She smiled, she took a breath, and she stood and went outside. She brought the alpaca poncho in from the line, and spread it out on the broken-down bus seat.

"There," she said.

I stood. Now she looked shy and she put her arms around my waist and held me close, her face in my chest.

"Angelina!" I whispered.

She shook her head, her face still against my chest.

"Angelina?"

She held me tighter. I kissed the top of her head and stroked her hair.

"Angelina," I said. "Tell me."

Now she looked up at me again. Her eyes were fierce and happy.

I kissed her lips.

"*Así*," she said. *Así* means "thus."

I kissed her again and she kept her eyes open. I pulled her dress down off her shoulder. She moved back. Her dress fell to her ankles and she took a deep, deep breath and put her arms up around my neck.

"*Eso es*," she said to me: This is it.

I ran my hands from her hips into her waist, up her sides, across her shoulders, and down her back, around her waist, and to her breasts. She arched back.

"It is, Daniel," she said. "This is it."

I stepped out of my cutoffs. She folded her dress, neatly and smiling. She picked up my cutoffs and folded them neatly. She had a small hourglass birthmark on the inside of her left breast. The defect was perfect.

"You are good," I said.

"Of course, Daniel."

"You are beautiful, Angelina."

"Of course."

"But you are."

"Of course, Daniel. You desire me."

She reached out her arms and I went to her. We lay down on the alpaca blanket, soft and rich with its lanolin. I kissed her face and eyes and I stroked the smooth skin near her sex.

"Everything," she told me. "Everything, now. Everything. All. This is it. Do not forget it. This is it."

I did everything I knew when I was twenty years old. I was tender and slow and I made love. I was tender until it hurt me with holding back, and I was slow until she shook and she was

dying to finish. Then she was in front and I could not keep up
and I finished later, hurting and laughing, a boy with this beautiful girl.

We breathed together, our sweat sweet between us like fra-
grant oil, my Argentine perfume sharp in the air. I slid apart
from her and rolled onto my back, happy now, delirious, laughing and crazy. Angelina was laughing; her teeth were so white.
I felt the nerves from my fever coursing with fire, my vision in
fibers, the battered bus diffusing in an Eden light, streaking in
shifting rays. I felt if I could stop breathing, I would. Then time
would stop.

We held each other, waiting. A butterfly flew in through the
window.

"Ah! Look. He wants us," Angelina said.

The butterfly landed on my stomach and its tongue uncurled
and took the salt in my sweat. Its wings had panes, red and
clear, like stained glass.

"Now this. This is good luck," Angelina said.

The afternoon passed.

When Santiago returned, he was upset. He said that Hector
was famous again. Hector had found the bodies of the two who
had drowned at the whirlpool.

"Down at the *Boca de la Boa*," Santiago said.

He said the "Mouth of the Boa" was where the river often
coughed up its victims. Hector had floated the bodies down to
the village of Los Puentes Caidos and he was charging people
to look at them.

"That is not honorable," Santiago said. "Money cheapens
everything, death included."

"But Hector is different," said Angelina. "Hector is born
of *los bravos*, of the brave and wild Indians."

"Hector is different," Santiago said.

I watched Angelina. I could not look at Santiago. And I
could not wait for him to leave again. On the next day, when

he went down to the village, Angelina destroyed me with love-making.

When Santiago got back from the village, he looked at me sadly and said, "Ah now, good God, the whole world is growing up. That Hector has built a sign that says, 'Death! Twenty-five pesos.' And the corpses' families were there too, demanding his profits."

"What for?" asked Angelina.

"To buy candles," said Santiago. "Already the dead have to work for their living."

I cared nothing for the dead. I was drained and hungry and sore. Angelina now seemed older than I was. She was serious and attentive; she conferred with her father. They had long conversations about articles in the *Geographic*s. They invented stories about where I came from. I paid less and less attention. When she got up to make her father's dinner, I went outside so I would not have to talk to him. I felt young and jumpy. I was about to turn twenty-one.

On the fourth day, after making love, Angelina and I lay together in the heat and the closeness of the bus. Angelina gazed out the window to the blue sky through the green of the treetops. She kept curling and uncurling a lock of her hair around her finger.

"What are you thinking?" I asked her.

"How good it must be in the United States."

"It's O.K.," I said. "It's better here."

"I don't think so," she said.

That night I heard the animal sound again. I was sure it was Hector, drumming his lungs.

After the fifth day, after loving Angelina, at night when everything was quiet, I grew restless and worried. My fever was back. I thought I could be dying, and I was too young to die. My sweat felt like alcohol evaporating away my body's heat. My bones and joints began to freeze. My jaws clenched. The sensation built and built, until I felt paralyzed. I felt like the frozen husk of an insect, hard and empty, ready to be blown away.

And then it was over. The fever released me and I sat up in my hammock and saw that the bus was filling with moonlight. My duffel bag lay in front of me on the floor. I stood; I picked it up and walked out the door.

I didn't say goodbye. I was going to write Angelina a letter. That's what I told myself, and I had to get out of there. I stepped out onto the gravel roadway and saw the way shining in the moonlight before me. The gravel shone like silver coins, and on either side of the road, the jungle was a soft velvet black. I turned to the left and I started to walk. Then a figure stepped out and blocked my way.

I did not know it was Hector but I hoped it was. I hoped it was and I was afraid it was. The figure was short and square, with a large round skull. The moonlight made its black hair look blue. The moon shone on the figure's broad, bare shoulders and illuminated its bare belly, which billowed with fast breathing. The rest of the figure, its arms and legs and feet, was a black silhouette.

I stood there, facing it, balancing my duffel bag on my shoulder. I wasn't frightened. I felt as I often had felt when I was facing adults and they were waiting for me to say something, to explain myself, to admit my youth and stupidity.

"Well," I said finally. "What?"

The figure rocked from side to side and lifted its arms, which seemed to materialize into the moonlight. Its belly swelled and then vanished into black.

"Ttunh!" it said. It was Hector.

"*Ttunhh!*" he boomed, and then he raised his arms again and he filled his lungs and roared. The sound was deep, full, and deafening. It was a howler monkey's territorial roar, powerful and mean.

I stepped back. "Hey," I said. "Hector. Cut it out."

Hector stepped toward me.

"I said, cut it out, Hector."

Hector let loose a torrent of sound, a great roar of anger. It rocked me and now I felt a faint shudder of fear. Hector raised his face and the moonlight shone on his brow and cheekbones. His eyes were dark and full of fury.

"Ttunh! Ttunh!" he boomed. *"Ttunh!* An-ge-*leee*-na!"

"Get out of my way!" I shouted.

Hector shut his mouth and looked up at me. He looked twelve years old again. He probably was twelve years old, but he was a man and we both knew it.

"Get out of my way," I said again.

Hector growled.

Now I heard steps behind me and I turned to see Santiago and Angelina coming toward us. Santiago held the gasoline lantern in front of him as he marched. Angelina hurried beside him. They came up to us, and Santiago inspected each of us with the lantern. Hector looked smaller in the light.

"I was going," I said to Santiago as he waved the lantern around me.

Santiago looked perplexed and Angelina touched my arm.

"Go away!" she said to Hector.

"An-ge-*leee*-na!"

"Go away!"

"Go home," Santiago told Hector. "Go back to the mission."

He turned to me. "And you. Daniel? What happens? Are you well? Come back to the bus. There is nowhere to go in the night. Are you sick? This is no way to act. Come back with Angelina and me. Are you well? What can we give you?"

Santiago took me by the shoulders and turned me around. We left Hector standing in the middle of the night and we went back to the bus. Angelina walked beside me, but she did not speak to me again. I told Santiago it was time for me to go, and he agreed.

"I wondered when you would leave," he said. "I tell you, I understand. Sometimes one has to go away for a while and then come back. Perhaps you'll come back sooner this way."

Angelina would not speak. Hector roared once, just outside the bus, and then we all were silent.

I left again in the morning.

I sometimes have to laugh, as sad as it all is. I laugh and I tell myself that this is the story and it never gets any better. It needs another lifetime.

I remember, years later, Santiago telling us to take away the pillow. "My head has gotten softer," he said.

Angelina started laughing, and I wished Hector were there so I could kill him again. Angelina kissed the pillow and set it aside. She took her father's hand and kissed it.

Santiago smiled at her. "But don't pull the shroud over my face until you are sure I have stopped talking," he said. "My lips are growing numb now. I may be dead and still talking and you not know it."

He looked for me. "And what if I am dead?" he asked. "Can you hear me, Daniel? Can you see me?"

3

I remember as little as I can about my time back in the
U.S. What I remember best is everybody jogging. It
seemed like the symptom of a mental running in place.

One day, I read about the *el niño* floods in South America,
when the cholos, the Indians, and all the animals had to run
for higher ground. Then I began to have dreams and memories,
and I realized that Puentes Caidos was a kind of higher ground,
where things did just happen and strange people came together.
I thought, When you are running in place, it should be easy to
start over. Maybe when you are lost, you should remember the
last time you were lost and you should try to get back there to
pick up the thread. I wanted to see Angelina.

On my flight back to South America, fifteen years after my
first trip and a year before Santiago's death, I felt a worry like
a hot breath racing down my neck. I stayed awake the entire
flight on the darkened airliner, watching out a black window
and mumbling Spanish verbs. The stewardesses watched me and

kept offering me coffee and drinks, but what I wanted was to go back in time. Finally I accepted a coffee and was surprised by its thick, sweet strength.

My plane arrived before dawn and I did not even stop in the capital city. I took a taxi directly through the old town to the Atahualpa bus pits and lost myself in their depths. There, in the dark, in a dusty gulch beneath the whitewashed adobe walls of the colonial city, anything and anywhere, legal or illegal, was up for sale, and cheap. I was ready. I wanted to buy something. I wanted to buy back my soul. But the highland Indian women who still dressed in black for the death of their Inca now sold Day-Glo weavings of Snoopy flying his doghouse.

Being careful where I stepped and keeping my pack high on my back, I paced through the bus pits. My heart beat to the rich mix of odors and voices, my lungs fluttered in the ten-thousand-foot air, and my skin chilled tight in spite of my location: ten miles south of the equator. Dizzy and winded, I kept moving. In the cold and in the dark, I could not stop moving. I hurried through the beams of headlights and thick clouds of diesel exhaust.

Then, at six o'clock, the sun popped over the Andes. Within a minute, it was day and I was warm. I stood in the sun and I thought I was happy. I felt warm and hungry. I bought a packet of *bizcocho* biscuits but I could not eat them. I kept thinking, I have gotten away, I have gotten away. I had everything I needed in my famous-name backpack and a line of credit at American Express.

I wandered about the pits and practiced Spanish verbs until I found a converted American school bus, painted blue and red, titled "Princess of the Amazons." Its itinerary scrolled below its windows in golden Gothic letters:

La Capital al Amazonia.
Cajamarca–Ybaeza–Quiroga–Chicona–Puentes C.

I asked the driver when the bus would leave. The driver looked at his coachman. The coachman looked to see how many passengers were on the bus and he nodded back to the driver.

"Right now!" the driver said, and he got on and started the engine. The bus started rolling. The coachman, a small man in a T-shirt and vest, wanted to put my backpack up on top, but I would not let him. I won the short tug-of-war and we both chased after the bus. I threw on my pack, took a seat right behind the driver, and set my pack beneath my feet.

The bus was half full. The passengers seemed to be either salesmen with suits and briefcases or highland Indian women in skirts, shawls, and homburg-style hats. One jungle Indian sat in the very back. He wore an Adidas T-shirt and a baseball cap. His earlobes had been pierced and stretched down to his shoulders. He had the back seat to himself.

The bus dived out of the Atahualpa pits where one of the city's sewers shot over a cliff and down a hundred of feet in a foaming brown waterfall. The coachman screamed at the passengers to close their windows. The sewage and the road joined a river in a valley of green fields, white houses, and eucalyptus fencerows. The road wound through a sprawling hacienda, then changed from gravel to cobblestone, then to mud, and passed an ancient monastery whose walls were crawling with roses and graffiti. The coachman pulled a bugle out from under the dash and blasted the people and donkeys we passed. Once, he looked back at me. "I am John Travolta," he said.

The road switchbacked up a mountain, and after an hour, we rose above tree line and traveled along a sharp ridge. At times, I caught glimpses of the pass above us: a cloudy blue gap between two volcanoes. The volcano on the north glistened as a perfect cone and whipped the clouds into curling shreds. The volcano on the south exploded the sky with its jumble of rock and ice. We crossed fields of sedge and flows of lava.

Black-and-green hummingbirds with foot-long tail feathers hovered above white flowers.

It grew cold. At the top, it was snowing and socked in with clouds. We stopped at a small shrine near the pass. The coachman collected coins from us to bribe the statue of a saint. The highland Indians got off the bus and began walking uphill, into the mist. One man with a fishing pole also got off. He turned up his suit coat collar and disappeared down the mountain. I looked back through the bus. Four businessmen were left. The jungle Indian was quietly vomiting into a plastic sack.

We broke over onto the eastern slope, thick in cloud and carpeted with a scrub that deepened as we descended. After an hour, we careened into a hanging valley of pasturelands and wild jungle and we followed a rushing river. For a while I counted the waterfalls.

The bus cleared the mountains and we headed south, skirting the edge of the flat country. The sun felt powerful and wet. Out over the jungle, a damp purple haze lay like a blanket, stretching toward Brazil. I recited my Spanish, "I am, thou art, he is, we are, you are . . ." and watched the jungle go by. We stopped in small towns and settlements of bamboo walls and metal roofs. The salesmen left the bus, one by one, and the heat and humidity grew. I brought out the *bizcochos* and washed them down with water from a canteen I had filled in the States. The first three biscuits were sweet and dry. The last one gagged me. I closed my eyes to fight the nausea, and I fell asleep long before we arrived at the site of Santiago's miracle.

The coachman yanked my backpack from under my feet and I woke up. My head ached and my clothes were soaked in sweat.

"The end!" the coachman said. He examined the French padlocks that locked my backpack's zipper pulls. "These are very tiny locks for such a fat pack. Where are the keys?"

I tried to look out the dirty windows. "Are we at Los Puentes Caidos?" I asked. All I could see was gravel and jungle.

"We do not really go there anymore. It is not worth it. And you are alone. Los Puentes is farther. What does this pack weigh?"

"Fifteen kilos."

"Uh! Twenty. We should charge you freight." We lugged my pack off the bus.

Outside, everything was gone. There were no people, no tents, no buses except the one I had come in on. The two bridges were still collapsing into the river and, across the river, I saw what looked like the crumbling foundations for a new bridge. Downriver, the water had washed away the bank where the little graveyard had been.

The driver, the coachman, the Indian, and I stood by the door of the bus. The coachman blew his bugle and the driver called out, "All aboard! *La capital! La civilización!*" But no one appeared.

"What a bad place," the coachman said to the driver. "This man's pack weighs too much."

"*Sí,*" said the driver. He turned to the Indian. "Well, Long Ears. Where are your women?"

The Indian smiled, showing teeth that had been sharpened to points. He waved with the back of his hand toward the jungle.

"Where?" the driver asked him. "I don't see them."

The Indian waved again and began walking away downriver.

"Savage!" the driver called after him, and then he laughed at me.

"Hey," I asked the driver, "where is everyone?"

"Who?"

"There was a market here."

"Not here."

The two men climbed back into their bus.

"Want to go back to the capital?" the coachman asked me. "Half price and we'll play cards."

I shook my head.

"How much for that backpack?"

"Shut up, Tito," the driver told him.

The bus drove away, its tires crunching through the river cobble. *"Sea, seas, sea, seamos,"* I said to myself. I walked into the jungle.

I found Santiago's bus in ruins, in a vault of vegetation smelling of rot and back in the dark like a scene from a voodoo movie. What was left of the bus was filled with dolls and surrounded by a thicket of crosses. The dolls looked like carnival Kewpie dolls, but there were so many they seemed alive. They spilled out of the holes that had once been windows and they lay in groups and piles on the ground. Some were nailed like little Jesuses to split bamboo crosses; some were clothed and some were naked. Most of the bus's roof had rusted out, and three papaya trees grew through the top. Enormous papayas rotted in the trees. Over everything, vines and creepers grew, and great banana leaves covered the wreckage of the dolls. The bus looked as if it had been abandoned for years. A glass jar sat on the fender, with what looked like a piece of paper inside. I fought my way through the chaos to reach it. Inside was a note.

I hereby notify the public
that I have no personal responsibilities
for the souls of these little angels
so irresponsibly
buried hereabouts.

—S. Benalcazar de O.

The note had been notarized. I stuffed it into the jar and stumbled back into the sunlight. Santiago Benalcazar de Orellana. I felt I had been cast up on a beach and found by a note in a bottle. I laughed, too loudly. He was somewhere around. But the emptiness of the river beach soon made me silent. The heat and the air were empty of everything but the thick, chewable vapor. The road burrowed into green tunnels on both sides of the beach.

The light made me dizzy. My sweat stung my eyes. I tried to remember the last time I had been here, when I was younger, when the place was packed with pilgrims come to see Santiago, the miracle man. I stood in the silver gravel on the river beach and peered into the dark holes the roadway made into the jungle. The sun reflected hard off the gravel. It stung my eyes and ignited the undersides of leaves. On the road heading downriver, lianas hung curling like nooses.

Behind me, I heard a popping clatter in the gravel. I turned to see a man hopping out of the jungle on one leg. He was a black man with gray hair, and he wore a soccer uniform: shorts, jersey, and one knee-length stocking. With each hop, he swung his arms out in front of him. At first, I thought he was trailing his other leg behind him, but as he came up to me, I saw he was an amputee, his stump tied off above the knee by old leather sutures that hung like drawstrings. His jersey bore the embroidered title *"Los Aurunas."*

"Buenas tardes," I called, and he stopped.

He leaned forward and dangled his arms in front of him. He turned his face to me and looked at me curiously.

"Sí. Tardes," he said. He offered me his hand.

When I took it, he leaned into my grip for balance and almost knocked me over.

"Could you tell me," I asked, "where is the village of Los Puentes Caidos?"

The man looked downriver and nodded.

"Far?"

"Far enough," he said. "And double for me!"

He was not joking. "Do you know Santiago Benalcazar?" I asked him.

That shocked him. "Yes," he said. "The philosopher."

"Of that old bus?"

"*Oooff!*" The man blew out his cheeks and nodded.

"Where can I find him?"

The man looked downriver again. "In the village, perhaps. Thinking, perhaps." He let go of my hand and pointed into the jungle. "That way."

He swung his arms behind his back and launched himself forward. He hopped away down the road. I shouldered my backpack and followed, but he soon left me behind.

The vegetation closed around me. I walked in the center of the road to avoid the leaves reaching in from both sides. I was sweating heavily, but the more I walked the better I felt. I recognized some of the plants: the red-and-yellow wings of birds-of-paradise, the feathers of ferns, and the wide elephant ear leaves of banana. Stands of tall palms and balsa grew on the slopes, and thick prisons of bamboo locked up the sloughs.

4

The village looked abandoned. I passed several bamboo houses on stilts, and came to a cinder-block building with an open ground floor. Its sign read, *"Pensión El Norona."* Several hammocks hung from the ceiling. In two of them lay two young white women, dressed in short cutoffs and T-shirts. The woman nearest me had short black hair cut like a bob of the 1920s. Her cutoffs were frayed and ripped up to her crotch. The other woman's hair was red and frizzed by the humidity. I thought they were French or German.

"Hello," I said to the woman with short hair.

She looked at me and raised her eyebrows.

"Do you speak English?" I asked.

She glanced at her friend and her friend nodded.

"Is this village Los Puentes Caidos?"

The red-haired woman nodded. We looked at each other for a moment, smiling.

"I have just walked in from the river crossing," I said.

I looked down the road. The bamboo building next door was in ruins. The only wall left standing bore a sign that read "House of Telephones" but I could see no telephone lines. Down at the end of the street sat another large open building. A man and a woman sat at a table on its ground floor.

"See you later," I said to the red-haired woman.

"Goodbye," she said.

I walked down toward the other building. Its sign read, *"La Cantina Caída"*—The Fallen-Down Saloon. I sat on a chair at one of the tables on the warped, creosoted floor. Both the man and the woman came over to my table. He sat down across from me, and the woman stood at the end of the table, twisting a towel in her hands. I recognized the man as Hector.

He was older now, of course, but he fit my memory. I didn't think he recognized me. His large eyes drooped a little, sadly, and he wore a mustache of a few long black whiskers. His hair was oiled back on his head. The chola woman wore knee-length, dark blue shorts and a crumpled short-sleeved cotton blouse. Her jogger's headband advertised Lagarto, "Lizard"-brand Colombian clothes. Her face was shiny, and sweat or tears lined the creases at the corners of her dark eyes. Still, she was attractive. She looked healthy, and kind.

"What would you desire?" she asked me in Spanish.

"You," Hector said to her tiredly. "You. You. You."

I looked back at Hector. The woman snapped her towel at him, and then she smiled at me.

"A beer," I said. "Very cold, please."

"Oh, ho!" Hector said to the woman. "Well chilled. Like you!"

The woman snapped her towel at him again and left the table.

"Viva Reagan," Hector said to me. "My name is Hector Tanbueno."

We shook hands and I introduced myself.

"I know," he said.

Hector's expression said he knew everything, but I told him anyway that I had been there fifteen years before, when the whirlpool had drowned the people.

"I know who you are," Hector said with some fatigue. "So I knew who you were. I knew you would come here." He looked at his watch. "And here you are."

I began to dislike him, but I wanted to be happy. I said, "I like it here."

"I know. It is very tranquil."

There was nothing happening in the village. A yellow dog walking across the road stopped and collapsed into hair and bones. Hector and I watched the dog for a moment, Hector nodding as if affirming the action. Another dog slunk out from beneath a house and sniffed at the yellow dog. The yellow dog snarled and then raised a hind leg.

"And there you have it," said Hector. "Life in its glory."

"Can you still smell earthquakes?" I asked him.

He stuck out his lower lip. He looked impatient, or proud.

"When I was here before, you predicted an earthquake."

"I know," he said. "Would you like one now?"

The woman brought back a liter bottle of Pilsner Grande and a blue plastic cup. She set them on the table.

"Join me?" I said, to both of them.

"*Obligado*," he said. "Consuelo, a chalice for me, if you please."

Consuelo looked to me for confirmation and then went and brought Hector a plastic cup. She opened a Coca-Cola for herself but went back to the other table. She sat down and smiled hugely at me. Hector waited as I poured the beer. We touched our cups together, toasted Reagan, and then toasted the new President of the Republic.

"May he get what the others got," said Hector.

We drank soberly to that sentiment. We finished the bottle and I ordered another. Occasionally, I glanced down toward the Norona, to see if the two women were moving.

I asked Hector, "Whatever happened to Lester the missionary?"

Hector shrugged his shoulders and stuck out his lower lip again.

"Phffft!" he said. "Lester went away."

"And the mission?"

"Phffft. I do not die for nostalgia."

"Phffft," I said.

Now Hector spoke in English, with a high voice and an Ohio accent like Lester's. "Yeah, hunh. You got it, kid," he said. "You got it, kid." And he laughed. "Lester and the Baptists took me to Ohio. The bug-eye state. Yeah. Now I speak in any English. As good as you. Far out. I'm sure. That's cool, you know."

"*Qué bueno*," I said.

"Darn tootin'," said Hector. "Multiple choice."

We drank more beer.

A swirling of water in the middle of the river caught my attention. I stood and watched for the tail of some great creature to lash through the surface. But the disturbance disappeared.

I sat back down. "What was that?" I asked Hector.

He smiled slyly. "That was Hector," he told me.

This was ridiculous, but Hector looked at me so confidently I said, "No. You?"

"Yes. I am the river," he said.

He nodded. "I am the river, who flows," he said. He began to recite. "I flow out of the mountains, the rocks in the sky. Past the people who should watch the sky, but who watch their reflections in me. The river. *El río*."

I watched him.

"I am the poet," he said. "I am the mountain, who shoulders the dawn. Who lies down in the night when nobody sees."

"That is good," I said.

"This is better. Listen: I sneeze, like a mountain. And people fall dead because they believe."

"That is good."

"That is creative writing," he said. "I got straight A's in creative writing. I express myself. And I don't worry how to spell the words."

We drank on. Then Hector said, "I am the silence after the words."

"The words," I said.

"Ay!" he kept saying, softly, intensely. "Ay! Ay!"

I decided I did not have to like him.

The first floor of the cantina had no walls. It was set on posts. A railing ran around most of it, and the kitchen area was set off by tables and cartons. A wooden ship's ladder climbed up into the second story. On a perch by the stairs, two large parakeets slept, leaning against each other. Outside, the colors of the river and the jungle deepened as the sun's light began to slant off the vertical. I felt cooler now and my sweat did not run down my back. Now it stuck coolly to my skin.

Hector watched me. "I am on fire," he said.

"Yes," I said. "It is hot."

"No. I mean that differently. I mean I am in love. *Enamorado*."

I looked over at Consuelo. She leaned against the icebox and touched her Coke bottle to her cleavage.

"She is very nice," I said.

"No. Not with her. Nor with a mortal woman. I am in love with a goddess. With an angel. With a butterfly with wings. Ay! I am in love with the air I breathe, for she is the air in her breath on wings."

Hector shuddered, perhaps because he impressed himself, perhaps because of the beer.

"Oh, I see," I said.

Hector nodded. "Indeed."

"More beer, perhaps."

Hector nodded. Consuelo brought us beer. She snapped her towel at Hector and smiled at me.

"A thousand thanks," I said to her.

"Millions," she said.

The cold beer made me feel cooler and comfortable. I moved my chair around the end of the table so I could watch the Norona.

"When we were children, we bathed together in the river," Hector told me. "She had a mark on her chest, an emblem in purple, in the shape of an angel, or a butterfly. Two perfect wings spread open to fly. Now she is a woman and bathes at night, obscured. I watch, but I cannot see her. She is like a hummingbird, bathing in rainwater caught by a leaf."

I knew he was speaking of Angelina.

"She must be beautiful," I said.

"Beautiful! You would die if you saw her. You who think Consuelo is pretty."

Consuelo watched us, smiling.

"Consuelo is lovely," I said, nodding to her.

"Consuelo bathes in the daylight. Wearing underwear made in Colombia."

I shrugged. "And what is the name of this woman you love?"

Hector used both hands to spread apart his wet mustache. "An-ge-*leee*-na," he said, his tongue tapping between his teeth.

"Of course. Angelina."

"Without"—he looked at me—"doubt, gringo."

"The daughter of Santiago."

"The same. And dangerously so. For you, perhaps, too. Beware."

A young man came into the cantina from the back. He wore wet swim shorts and carried a towel around his neck. The man was strangely built. He was proportioned like a dwarf—short limbs, long torso, and large head—yet he was as tall as I was. He sat on the bench next to Consuelo and started combing his black hair. He smiled at me and nodded.

I turned back to Hector. "And where is Santiago?"

"Now? Sucking lemons, I say. Or asking his chickens unanswerable questions."

"How is he? Well?"

"Decidedly not. He feels well, but bugs grow in his brains. He is touched."

"What's wrong with him?"

Hector did not answer.

"Where can one find him?"

"One finds him . . . odd."

"Where, Hector?"

"Here. Too often here."

"In the cantina."

Hector closed his eyes and raised his eyebrows.

Santiago was coming to the cantina. I would meet him my first day in Los Puentes Caidos. And then what? Now I felt ridiculous, a feeling I had been able to avoid since I decided to return. I looked around at the town.

"Very tranquil, is it not?" said Hector. "Nothing happens here. Not for you, at any rate. Besides, it's the end of the road."

Across the brown river, the wall of jungle stood soft and impermeable.

"Are there trails into the selva?" I asked.

"There is anything you want."

"Hectorito," Consuelo called. "Look. Here comes the Thinkery."

We saw several groups of men, two and three to a group, advancing on the cantina. The one-legged man hopped along with them.

"Such luck," said Hector. "I must leave you, Daniel. The Thinkery is coming."

"The Thinkery?"

"The philosophers' circle. *El Club*, they call themselves. The Drinking and Thinking Considering Club. The never ending circle of chatter."

"Who are they?"

"All worthless ones. They do Santiago's thinking for him, around and around." Hector swirled his finger by his temple.

"How do you mean?"

"Listen. I must go."

"Where?"

"To make my living. Don't gringos do that anymore?"

"What do you do?"

"I make jungle experiences. I guide all types of gringos into Amazon fantasies. You know me. I am Hector, the Jungle Guide. I was profiled in *Traveling* magazine. I am in the *South American Guidebook*. I am everywhere. Go and read about me in books."

Hector stood, swaying slightly. He said, "Do you have a machete? I will show you her shrine."

"Her shrine? Angelina? Why a shrine?"

"Phfft," Hector said. "For religious observations." He puffed out his lower lip, then glanced at the men approaching the cantina.

"I hesitate to impress you further," he said.

Hector left me and marched proudly through the men, swinging his arms widely. Consuelo smiled at me and shrugged.

"You look like Jack Kennedy," she said. "Imagine! Were you friends?"

My head felt heavy from all the beer and from trying to listen and think in Spanish. I looked down toward the Norona for some activity as an excuse to leave the cantina. The tourist women seemed to be moving around. The men who had somehow chased away Hector entered the cantina and took seats around the tables. Except for one or two badly scarred faces, they all looked civil. One thin young man was freshly shaven and dressed in a white naval uniform. He led an older man with blind, smoky-gray eyes. Several nodded to me as they took their seats. Consuelo began to bring out liter bottles of beer.

Then up the cantina's steps hopped the one-legged man I

had seen at Santiago's old bus, and right behind him stepped up Santiago. He saw me, he stopped short, and then he nodded to me as the others had.

Santiago carried a sack and from it he produced lemons which he gave to each of the men. The men called for glasses and they squeezed lemon juice into their beers. Santiago did the same, glancing at me again, and he made a sour face at me as he sucked on a lemon.

After studiously drinking their beer, the men called to Consuelo to bring another round. Then they asked Santiago to begin.

Santiago stood.

"Friends, companions, and distinguished ghost," he said. "Welcome. Let us say that the Drinking and Thinking Club, our philosophy circle, is open."

And he sat down.

"Bruto! Bravo!" called out several of the men. "That's it!"

And they drank quietly for several minutes while I grew restless. Santiago watched me, but he would look away when I nodded to him.

Finally someone said, "Good. What have we today? Who brings the question?"

The one-legged man stood up at the head of a table. He balanced himself delicately by placing his fingertips on the tabletop in front of him. He drew himself up tall and dignified.

"What have you today, El Brinco?" a man asked him.

"A confoundation," El Brinco said. "I find myself confused by the meaning of good."

The men in the cantina looked at each other and nodded.

"A weighty subject," one man said. "And worthy. What confuses you about good?"

El Brinco smiled. "I recently realized that in my too long life I never saw anything that I could consider absolutely, ultimately good."

The drinkers murmured.

"So, what is good?" Santiago asked the group.

"Food is good," said one man.

"Spirits," said another.

"Talking?" one asked.

"Thinking," said another. "Thinking good thoughts."

"Seeing," said the blind man. "To see is good."

"And is thinking good?" asked Santiago.

Now everyone hushed. They all raised their eyebrows and looked at the floor.

"Perhaps. Sometimes . . ." one man offered. "At least when it does not get one into trouble."

"The good President John Kennedy was good," said the blind man.

Consuelo winked at me. "See?" she said.

"What makes something good?" asked Santiago.

"Being shot like that. With so much ahead of you. At least Kennedy went after Castro." The blind man looked around the room. No one faced his gaze either.

"Something is good," someone said finally, "good if it helps and does not hurt."

"Hah!" El Brinco said. "In this life? In this bad place? Here, whatever doesn't hurt—what doesn't hurt like hell— helps. If it doesn't hurt, it's good. It is wonderfully good. But that should be wrong, shouldn't it?"

"Like what, for example?" someone asked. But El Brinco did not answer him.

"We may be onto something here," El Brinco said. "There may be no good at all, after all. What is it that does not hurt us, finally? Life kills us in the end. Then we are dead and we cannot protest. Look at me now. See, I am dying in bits and pieces. First, the Peruvians got my good leg. Now the toenails on my bad leg are going. What next? My ass? My balls?"

"Is it life that kills us?" asked Santiago. "I am not so sure."

Again there was silence.

"Then love, gentlemen," someone asked. "What of love? Good? Or bad?"

"Love is good, of course."

"Unless you catch the itch."

"Or enrage the husband."

"Or give the husband the itch."

"Or!" said a man wearing a ball cap. "Or if your woman breaks your heart."

"Then, of course, Jesus, love hurts."

Jesus, the man in the ball cap, wore an expression of unbearable pain.

The misshapen young man in the swim shorts now spoke. "Look at Jesus! This hurts him now! I did not know. How did your woman break your heart?"

Jesus was stricken. He sighed but could not speak.

"Ah!" the blind man said. "Napoleon, my friend. We have struck the vital nerve of Jesus. See? Love kills. It killed the original Jesus, too."

Now everyone looked at the blind man. His eyes became smokier. "I killed a man for love, once," he said quietly. "Don't try it. It wasn't worth it."

All the men looked hurt now.

"And I killed a man for happiness, once," the blind man said, "only to find that happiness was the least of my worries."

"And worries . . ." the young man called Napoleon began, but he shook his head. He couldn't finish.

Santiago watched his friends expectantly.

El Brinco stood up on his one leg.

"We are in a mess here," El Brinco said. "We have lost our track again. Quickly, Consuelo! Bring around more beer."

The young navy lieutenant stood up. "Gentlemen," he said. "We are indeed on the wrong highway. Love is other than good. 'Good' is a word, which merely describes. While love . . ."

The lieutenant waved an open hand in front of his face, looking for his word. "Love . . ."

"Love stinks?" offered El Brinco. His expression showed little patience with the lieutenant.

"Go ahead, Hugo," said Napoleon, encouraging the lieutenant. "Love . . ."

"I said it already. Love hurts," said the blind man.

The young lieutenant struck a noble pose. He crossed his arms in front of his chest and gazed across the river.

"Love," he said. "Love of woman is the highest good. This is why we love our country, no? To protect our women. Mothers, wives, the mother of the son I will someday have. A good and brave son, who cares for me more deeply than I care for myself. These are better than life."

"Balls!" retorted El Brinco. "Balls are the best good. They think for themselves. They don't ask questions. They are always friendly and ready to go. They are blind too, but so what? They have feelings! 'C'mon,' they are saying. 'C'mon! Let's go . . .' "

El Brinco looked around the room for a laugh, but the drinking men took his speech seriously, nodding. El Brinco snorted and sat down. Consuelo offered more beer and Santiago passed out lemons again. He gave me two. The men squeezed the lemon juice into their beers. So did I, this time.

"So what were we discussing?" Santiago asked. He was looking at me.

"Well, women, apparently," said one man finally. "Women, as always."

"And men," said another. "One cannot speak of woman without man being assumed, for comparison purposes at the least. So, let's talk about men, too. For without man, woman would have no reason to suffer."

"Oh, spare me," said El Brinco.

"But that's it!" someone else said. "We are getting close!"

At this moment, the two tourist women from the Norona

Hotel walked by us, outside the cantina. They both wore European string bikinis, which looked wet although they were dry, and Japanese thong sandals that popped against their heels as they walked.

"The subject," said the blind man, "demands discussion."

But everyone else erupted into whistles and catcalls. The blind man jumped up and spun around. "Where?" he said. "What?"

"Jorge," someone said to him. "Jorge! Two naked women are walking by!"

"Oh, damn it!" Jorge said, and put his hands over his eyes.

Santiago was watching me. A silence fell upon the cantina. The men stopped drinking and looked at each other. From across the river came the shrieking of parrots, and I got up and followed the two women.

I followed them down the path through a plantation of flowering hibiscus trees to a larger path, which followed the river. The women turned downstream, stepping carefully over the exposed roots, which were wet and slick. They ducked under an arch of branches and emerged upon a white sand beach where a smaller, clear stream joined the muddy river.

I followed them onto the beach.

On the point of land that separated the two rivers, a dozen dugout canoes were beached and abandoned. Up the smaller river, four local women were bathing. They stood knee-deep in the water. Three of them wore white slips, their brassieres and panties showing white through the wet fabric. Their long wet hair shone in the sunlight and made clear, clean noises as the women squeezed out the soapy water. The fourth woman was the oldest. She wore a black girdle, a red garter belt, nylon stockings, and a great white harness of a brassiere. Her hair was tucked up beneath an orange plastic shower cap. She scolded the younger women and kept them facing out into the river.

The sun lowered behind me as I walked up the beach. The light's declination deepened the jungle colors and reflected off specks of mica in the coarse quartzite sand. This smaller river was about fifty yards across. It was clear, swift in the center, and golden. A wedge of rock rose out of the middle of the stream, and seven small children with wet black hair sat along the crest of the rock, basking like river otters. They waved and called to the two tourist women. Across the river, the jungle grew out over the water. Lianas hung from the canopy and trailed in the stream. Two boys drifted there in a small dugout tied off to a vine. Upriver about three hundred yards, a suspension foot bridge crossed to an abutment of logs. The mountains beyond the bridge were hidden by a tremendous black thundercloud. The jungle was bright against the black.

I stopped and waved to the children on the rock. They all cheered and began showing off by diving into the river from the upstream end of the rock. Their friends snared them as they floated back by.

The two tourist women stopped a short distance upstream. They took soap and shampoo out of their bags and began to bathe, too. Compared to the local women, they looked too thin. They waded out to waist-deep water and stood facing each other as they soaped their bodies.

I settled down onto my haunches in the sand and looked around at the river and jungle. Across the river, the peak of a thatched roof showed through the trees. Down by the river's mouth, several local men were now pulling the dugout canoes farther up on the beach. The jungle in back of the beach looked as if it flooded often. The sand was scoured free of leaves and litter. Broken and bleached branches were caught in the crooks of tree limbs six and eight feet off the ground.

Three men stepped out of the jungle behind me. They all wore T-shirts, tight polyester pants, and black rubber boots. One carried a machete. They walked down toward the river and stopped to smoke cigarettes. They watched the two women in the river.

The dark-haired woman dipped down into the water, neck-deep, to rinse off the soap. When she stood up again, she handed her bikini bottom to the other woman. She began soaping herself below the waterline. One of the three men grabbed the backs of the other two's T-shirts and groaned. They all whistled low.

I sat down on a log and waited. The sun slipped below the tree line and the daylight dimmed. The heaviness of the beer left me and I was hungry again. The two women finished bathing and walked past me back down the beach, and the three men disappeared into the jungle. The children all dived off their rock. Their heads floated like coconuts down to the strand where the two rivers joined.

It was darkening quickly as I walked back toward the cantina. The local women hurried to get dressed before I passed them. As I entered the village, dogs were barking and people were lighting candles and lanterns. The cantina glowed in the light of three sputtering gas lanterns. I went in and sat down by my pack.

Most of the drinkers were still in the cantina, but the conversation had stopped. The men all seemed bemused. Consuelo brought me a beer.

"Do you have Seven-Up?" I asked her.

"Tomorrow."

"Dinner?"

"Tomorrow," she said.

"Any crackers?"

She brought me a package of animal crackers. "A bad night," she said. "There isn't any anything."

Now Santiago looked delighted to see me. He held up both hands and spoke to the other drinkers. "Enough!" he said. "Enough of thought without names. How did the experiment work?"

El Brinco coughed. "Musically. I kept thinking of Sophia Loren."

Young Hugo jumped up. "But that's a name! You weren't following the rules."

"I was not thinking of her name," said El Brinco.

"You were thinking of her corruption, you philanderer."

"Please. I am a widower."

"Miss Loren is married."

Santiago interrupted. "And you, Hugo. How did it go with you?"

Hugo composed himself. "Admirably, Santiago. I thought of peace, tranquillity, harmony."

"Those are names," said El Brinco.

"They are abstractions," Hugo said.

"Names."

"*Caballeros!*" said Santiago.

"I am a veteran and you are a frog." El Brinco slowly stood up on his one leg and hopped around the table toward Hugo.

I looked away and busied myself with my animal crackers and beer. The crackers in the bottom of the package were wet. I sniffed the package.

Consuelo came over and sat down across from me.

"These crackers are bad," I told her.

"I wish we had a telephone," she said. "I'd call the police."

"There are police around here?"

"If we had a telephone, we would have police."

El Brinco balanced himself across the table from Hugo. "Stand up, frog," he said.

Hugo did not look up. "On two legs," he said, but meekly. "On two legs, when I desire." He looked at his hands on the table.

El Brinco picked up Hugo's bottle of beer.

"Of course, Brinco," said Hugo. "Please. Have some beer."

"Thank you." El Brinco poured the beer onto Hugo's hands.

Santiago looked over to Consuelo. "The lights," he said.

"Again!" cried Consuelo. She stood up and went around to the lanterns, turning them off, one by one.

As the cantina fell into darkness, I saw Hugo still sitting on his bench, looking down into his wet hands. El Brinco picked up Hugo's plastic glass and drank from it.

"What a life," El Brinco said. "Oh well. Forgive and forget. Forgive me, Lieutenant, and I forget you."

"If you weren't a veteran . . ." Hugo said quietly.

In the darkness, I heard the benches pushed back and the men stumbling out of the cantina. Santiago was at my shoulder. "Daniel! Welcome! I thought you were a ghost. When you followed the women, I thought you were the devil. When you returned, I knew you were a man. But how? How are you here? Are you hungry? Let's eat."

I followed him out into the open, where lights from other lanterns shed some light. Santiago held on to my shirtsleeve. "We may have learned something tonight. About names. It always comes down to names. Names of places. Names of things. Names of men. Calling names. But a man without a name is an animal, isn't he? Ah! You must be hungry like a wolf. Hah! Come!"

Santiago pushed me in front of him as he walked. I had to pick up my feet to keep from tripping, and I walked in a blind, awkward march, holding my hands out in front of me. We followed a trail, invisible to me, up the slope above the village.

We stopped at a bamboo house like all the others. A light was on inside.

"We are arrived," Santiago said. "Angelina!" He pushed open the door to his house and then got behind me and pushed me in through the doorway.

The first thing I noticed was a heavy fragrance. The air was very still inside the room, but cool. I felt something like a mist. A lantern burned low on a table by an open window. A chair and two boxes had been set around the table. The walls were dimly lit, and shelves climbed up them from the floor to the ceiling. Plants lined the shelves. I stepped closer to look at one of them. At first, the plant looked more like an animal. It was a whitish pink, lobed, and formed like a naked baby bird just opening its wings. As I peered closer, I took a breath, and its sweet odor knocked me back.

"Orchids," Santiago said. "Be careful. They give me dreams. That's why we keep them outside."

I followed his upward glance. The room had no roof. Stars glittered in a black sky.

"It leaks like a waterfall," Santiago said. "But we like to study the stars."

I turned back to the shelves. Above the orchids, objects were pinned to the bamboo wall. One had reflecting eyes that seemed to open and close as I moved my own head back and forth.

"What are these?"

"Those? Butterflies. The business of Angelina. She sells them to scientists and rich collectors. A good business, no?"

I could not really see the butterflies in the dim light, but as I leaned closer, I noticed I could almost see between the bamboo slats and into the next room. A lantern burned brightly in there, and someone moved back and forth through its light. Angelina. A light tapping followed the shadow.

Santiago touched my shoulder. "Around here, people say that butterflies are so beautiful they do not need souls. That would mean that, with my ugliness, my soul would be a marvel!" He laughed merrily. "Not funny? Well, to get that joke, you would have to have my face." He laughed some more. "My son! You are too intent. Ah! That specimen, there? That butterfly is called the blue morpho. Now there is a name for you. It signifies the 'blue sleep of death,' and she shows such life. That butterfly flies like she is dangling by a string held in the hand of God. Up! Up! Up!

"You ought to see how Angelina lures the morphos to her. My daughter! It is almost a scandal. Here is the story. It is scandalous, so listen. Angelina takes off her clothes. My daughter! Then she covers herself in the blackest mud and disappears into the riverbank. If you came upon her unaware, you would not see her. You might see some clothes, neatly folded, and wonder, What? But if you saw her, and knew it, the fright would kill you. She could catch your soul and pin it to her wall. Ho! Ho! No. But no." Santiago poked me in the ribs and laughed. "Well. I mean she hides in the shade by the side of the stream and waits until all is in its noonday stillness. I don't think she breathes. Butterflies breathe with their wings, you know. Open. Close. Open. Close."

Through the wall, I watched the motion around the light.

"There, in her invisibility, Angelina waves in the sunlight a swatch of silk of the holiest blue. Think of it. Silk! Spun by the magic of a worm in China. To catch the magic of a butterfly here in America. That's magic. And that's international commerce. Anyway, the morphos fly to Angelina by the dozens. They mate in the air around her. Up! Up! And when they are spent, they land upon her and drink the salt in the mud. And she becomes a blue shadow, covered by their wise blue wings, opening, slowly, closing, closing, opening. Her eyes must hypnotize them. Now open. Now closed. No?"

I tried to see through the wall.

Santiago cleared his throat. "At least that is how that bastard the poet Hector wrote it in the poetry contest for the big newspaper. And he won! I don't know how. What do you think of poets, Daniel? What are you looking at?" He leaned over next to me.

Santiago laughed. "Son. My son! What are you doing? You will hurt your vision. Angelina!"

From the other side of the bamboo partition, a voice spoke softly. "Yes, Papa."

Santiago chuckled. "I speak English," he said to me.

"How goes the dinner, Angelina?" he asked in Spanish.

"It is almost ready," she said, again in English.

Santiago asked me, "What did she say?"

"She said, 'Ready. Almost.' "

"Of course she did. Please, sit down."

Santiago pulled out the only chair for me. "You must. Angelina would insist." He sat down on one of the crates. "We'll have Angelina sit with us. Are you hungry?"

I nodded.

Angelina entered the room, carrying plates and spoons. She stopped when she saw me.

"You. Daniel," she said.

I started to rise.

"Don't get up, Daniel," Santiago said.

Angelina left the room.

"Bring a plate for yourself," Santiago called after her.

I started to go after her, but Angelina came back through the doorway and looked straight at me. The whites of her eyes reflected the light, and her clear green irises shone like the eyes on the wings of some of the butterflies. She wore sandals, blue shorts, and a white short-sleeved blouse buttoned at the collar.

Santiago leaned forward and turned up the gas. "I want to see what I want to eat," he said. He began to stab at his food with his spoon.

Angelina sat down next to me and set her plate on the table. She was Santiago's daughter, but her features were perfect. Santiago looked as if he had slept on his face all his life. Angelina was as I remembered her, and more beautiful.

She looked at me. "I do not hunt butterflies naked," she told me.

"There is a lot I don't know," Santiago said. "Please, Daniel. Eat."

The meal looked like fried bananas and chicken.

"It's bat meat," Santiago said. "Hey? What's the matter?"

"See?" he said to Angelina. "The power of a name."

"It is a chicken, Daniel," Angelina said.

"Now," said Santiago, "you should be hungry again."

I was almost too tired. Santiago's hands were quick with his food. Angelina's perfect fingers moved smoothly above her plate. My hands shook.

"Tell me, Daniel," Santiago asked. "What does my daughter think of Hector? Go ahead. Ask her."

"Angelina," I said. I liked using her name. "How do you think of Hector?"

"Rarely," Angelina said.

"Rarely," I told Santiago.

Santiago nodded. "Just so. *Ni mariposa ni polilla*. Neither wine nor lemonade. I don't know what he is. Now, Angelina, tell our guest the difference between a butterfly and a moth."

Angelina said, "One difference is that when a butterfly alights, she closes her wings."

Santiago looked at me, his eyes widening. "Just so," he said. "The butterfly would hide her beauty."

I nodded. I could not finish my meal. My stomach cramped around each swallow of food and I had to wait before I could take another bite.

"You eat like the Frenchwomen, Daniel," said Santiago, *"Más gusto! Más gusto!"*

"Gusto," I repeated.

Now Angelina spoke. "It is a wonder to see you, Daniel."

"Yes," I said.

"Tell us. How are you doing?"

"Very well."

"I'm sure you are," she said. "Please. Tell us about your successes."

"Yes, tell us, Daniel," Santiago said. "How rich are you?"

"We would be happy to hear," Angelina said.

"Yes, indeed. We were sad when you went away. Angelina was so sad."

"I am recovered," Angelina said. "But we knew you had

another life, Daniel. You had successes in front of you. Such
successes. The United States is a grand place, don't you think?
We all know that—everyone tells us. Even when they tell us
different, we know better. So tell us. What have you done?"

"Well. I went into business," I said.

"Of course you did," Santiago said. "You went into business.
Business is the business of a successful man. It sounds so
simple, doesn't it? I mean, when one hears it. But I know it is
difficult."

"What did you sell, Daniel?" Angelina asked me.

"It's not easy to say."

"I'm sure it isn't."

Santiago clucked his tongue. "It never is, is it. Does one
say, I sell land? Cattle? Oil? Or better, does he say, I sell
productivity, nutrition, energy? That may be the way to say it.
You could say you sold possibilities. The future! Is that what
you sold? The future in America, is that what the gringos sell?"

He continued. "Angelina sells butterflies. But that isn't exactly right either, is it? What does Angelina sell? Beauty?
Dreams? Rarity? Nature? The smaller the item the more it is
worth. The rarer, the more valuable, right down to the last
example of an entire species. Right down to nothing, almost. I
say almost because nothing is still worth nothing." He laughed.
"Nothing will always be plentiful."

Santiago paused to think. He hummed as he chewed his
food.

"Very well," he said. "Everyone sells something. Now me,
I sell questions. Or rather, I offer ideas for barter, perhaps.
You take my question, you borrow my idea, and then you pay
it back, with interest, improved. We are both richer."

Santiago sputtered happily. "Hmmm. But that brings us to
another question. How many times may an idea be improved?
How many times may a question be asked before it loses its
shine? How many times can I ask, Who am I? before someone
replies in the derogatory? The answer is this. *Very few times*."

Angelina sat quietly beside me. I felt I should say something. "I suppose one could say that I sold ideas too," I said. "I was a public relations specialist."

"Ah! I knew it! A specialist!"

"How much are your ideas worth?" Angelina asked.

"Six thousand dollars a month, plus benefits and bonuses."

Santiago coughed. "Plus! Plus? And how many ideas did you think up a month? Was every idea a new one?"

"In the agency, we said that nothing was new. We said that every idea was derivative. Our job was to make people think it was new. We made people want to buy it."

"Derivative!" exclaimed Santiago. "Imagine!"

"How did you do that?" Angelina asked.

"What?"

"How did you make people want to buy your idea?"

I looked at Angelina. I wanted her to trust me. "We tricked them," I said.

Angelina broke into laughter. Santiago pulled up short and watched her. I watched her for a moment. Then I started laughing too.

"We tricked them," I repeated, and this kept her laughing.

I laughed like a fool. The Spanish was locking up my brain. The back of my neck began to ache and stiffen.

"This is wonderful," Santiago said. "We must talk often, Daniel."

Angelina whispered, "But Daniel is fatigued." Her hands rested on the tabletop. "He has had a long voyage. We are not sure why he is here."

"Why are you here?" Santiago asked.

Angelina's hands were perfect. I raised my head and looked at Santiago. "I am tired," I said.

"Manifestly, my son. Would you sleep here or at the cantina?" I could bring no expression to my face. I looked at Angelina.

"At the cantina," I said.

"Of course. We can share coffee in the morning."

"You have a beautiful daughter," I said to Santiago.

Santiago led me back through the jungle. The cantina was so dark Santiago had to help me up the steps. I felt my way along the outside railing to my backpack, worrying vaguely about biting insects. I had netting somewhere inside the pack, and somewhere I had a flashlight, but my pack was too full and too well locked to open. I set the pack on a table, climbed up with it, and laid my head down on the hard nylon. I realized that I had come back with no plan. My stomach cramped. My bowels began to churn. I lay as still as I could and took short breaths, moving only my diaphragm. An ache began in the back of my skull where it lay on the backpack. I felt my heart beating. The beating grew stronger and stronger until I felt my whole body rocking with each beat. I held on to the edges of the tabletop. The dark lantern above my head creaked as it swung on its bail and a soft tremor passed under the earth of Los Puentes Caidos.

5

In the morning, I sat with Hector on the front step of the cantina. Hector watched me as I drank a cup of bitter instant coffee and ate sandwiches of crackers and bananas.

"What a bad breakfast," he said.

"I am hungry," I told him, "and there isn't much to eat around here."

"I could live on air," Hector said. He held his hand in front of his face and blew into his palm.

The morning air was warm, thick, and rich. It smelled of damp dust, ripe bananas, fish in the river, and the sweepings of Consuelo, who was wearing down her broom on the packed dirt yard which was paved with the caps of beer bottles.

"You could not live on air for very long," I told Hector. "Air lacks the ten essential vitamins."

Hector laughed. "Consuelita! Did you hear that? Daniel must be a scientist."

Consuelo stopped her sweeping. "You must be a Peace Corps," she said to me.

"If that is so, then he should finish the public showers," Hector said.

"The Peace Corps showers stink, Hector. People make their messes in them. Besides, we have the river. So why finish the showers?"

"For the tourists, of course. Hey, gringo. Did you ever notice that the words *turista* and *terrorista* sound much alike? And *triste*, also—sadness. Is that a coincidence?"

Consuelo shook her head and sat down next to me on the step.

"This coffee is bad," I said to her.

She shrugged, and began to stare at the side of my face.

"Handsome one," she said. "The government makes it that way on purpose. They export all the good beans. Go tell it to the President if you want a good coffee."

"I could not live on the coffee," Hector said.

Roosters began crowing around the village, although it was well after sunrise.

"The little roosters are getting up," I said.

Consuelo giggled. I had said something funny in Spanish, but Hector did not react to it. "Stupid birds," he said. "Every day to be surprised by the sun."

"Do you really think they are?" Consuelo asked.

"I spoke poetically, my flower. And so did the gringo."

Consuelo looked at me and giggled again. She reached up and stroked my cheekbone with her finger. *"Gringuito,"* she said. The atmosphere thickened, dense and breezeless. I felt if I moved I would begin to sweat.

The village square was a dirt soccer field with a goal at one end. As we sat on the cantina step, two men carried a small coffin out into the middle of the field. The men wore black suits and black shoes, and their dark hair shone with brilliantine. A young woman carrying flowers and two older women with Bibles followed the men out onto the field. A dozen children crowded around the women. The boys walked stiffly in their long pants and starched shirts.

"*Ay! Dios! Otro. Otro angelito,*" Consuelo said. "Another angel baby."

The women and children lined up in a loose column behind the two men. The children stood in order, from the biggest to the smallest. They all carried small green crosses made from strips of palm fronds. The youngest children carried tiny plastic dolls.

Hector softly recited a poem. "Angel babies need no wings. They are too light to fall. Hold your breath, or you may breathe them in. Bow your head, for they may bless you as they rise."

Consuelo began to cry. "Oh, Hector. Hector." I put my hand on her shoulder and she leaned against me.

When the funeral procession began to march away, Hector put his hand to his mouth and whistled a high piping note. The children turned and saw us. The smaller ones waved their dolls to us. Two older boys changed their bamboo crosses into toy swords and played like they were pirates. Hector lay back on the floor and laughed.

"For the devil!" he said.

"Hector!" Consuelo scolded him.

Santiago did not show up for coffee that morning. Hector said it was because Santiago was unreliable. Consuelo said it was because the sight of children burying children made him sad. Still, I felt content then to watch their procession march into the jungle. The village looked beautiful to me. Women swept the dirt in front of their homes. Pet monkeys chased kittens and caught them by their tails. Across the square, three men worked on an old bicycle. They were laughing at a wheel that was bent nearly in half. They would laugh until they lost their breath. Then they would wait and point at it and start laughing again.

Beyond them, the Pension Norona hid the mysterious tourist women somewhere inside. Next to it, the collapsing House of Telephones looked like a giant paper airplane crashed on the banks of the river. Above us, the second floor of the Cantina Caida hovered like a magician's illusion. Across from us, an open-front store—its sign read "Store"—spread out its wares in the sun. It sold everything from rice and bananas to religious medallions and boa constrictor skins. Down by the river, the small and squalid navy building wore a brass padlock the size of a pie pan on a door next to a broken window. All around us, above the square, the huts and houses of the village climbed the hillside. Laundry hung like kites from trees. Pet macaws screamed from windows. Two houses had lost their foundations and they spilled down the hillside in a bright wash of boards, bedsheets, and dishes. A man was lowering himself on a rope to pick through the debris.

I drank several coffees, as bad as they were. After a while, Hugo came by, dressed in his white uniform and wearing an ensign's cap.

Hector greeted him. "Admiral! Has the good ship *Beer* yet set to sea?"

"She is away," Hugo said. He took off his cap and secured it beneath an epaulet.

"Well done, my Captain," said Hector. "Another week vanquished." He whistled through his fingers as through a bosun's pipe. Across the square, the men working on the bicycle stood up and saluted smartly.

Later that day, I moved into the cantina. I made a room upstairs by stacking empty crates to make a wall with open shelves for my gear. I sawed a hole in the end-gable for a window that looked out on the rivers' confluence. I stretched mosquito netting over my new window and hung more netting over the doorway. I sawed another window in the front end-gable and hung my hammock between the rafters so it would catch the night breeze.

One-legged El Brinco helped me in my undertaking. I learned he owned the cantina and he was Consuelo's father. After a storm blew rain right through my bedroom and out the front window on my second night in residence, Brinco demanded damages. He wanted storm shutters built from old crate lids, which advertised a beer he did not sell.

"Beer is beer," he said. "And I sell beer. Such is my sentiment."

El Brinco thought my staying at the Cantina Caida would attract the business of other gringos, who always stayed at the Norona. The Norona, of course, had real rooms to rent. And the Norona organized tours into the jungle, led by Angelina and Hector, to hunt for butterflies, to fish for piranha, and to visit the primitive Aurunas. Christianized Aurunas brought their handicrafts to the Norona to sell, where a stout, mean woman named Mama Cuchara served the tourists dinners of vegetarian spaghetti.

"Imagine. Spaghetti with rice sauce, in bricks," El Brinco said. "And the conversation is better here. Very elevated. And beer is beer. Mama Cuchara buys her beer from me at patron's prices and then resells it more dearly to the gringos."

His belief in beer served Brinco well. He supplied the beer that Hugo shipped off by dugout canoe, every other Wednesday, to the army garrison, two hundred miles downriver on the frontier with Peru. El Brinco complained that Hugo was too honest and difficult. He said the Navy would never let Hugo near the ocean. He said, "Hugo would find a regulation against tides."

Whenever the beer canoe left Los Puentes Caidos, Hugo screamed at the boatmen that they would be court-martialed if they so much as touched the beer of the Armada of the Amazon, or otherwise jeopardized the vigil against Peru.

"We are civilians, you waterhead," the boatmen called back. "We don't have to listen to you!"

"Return to port!" Hugo commanded, but the beer canoe drifted away with the current.

"And they are war veterans, too," El Brinco told Hugo. "You have to let them go."

El Brinco had lost his leg to infection during one of the wars with Peru. He said, "I have given my part. Let others give their parts, from each according to his parts."

Hugo said he would give his very life, as soon as his life gave him the opportunity. El Brinco wished it would be soon.

El Brinco and his daughter, Consuelo, slept downstairs in the cantina. El Brinco wrapped himself up like a cocoon in his hammock. Consuelo slept on a cot in the kitchen—safe, said Brinco, from the entire village. Consuelo laughed when he said this.

On my third day in the village, Hector came to get me.

"Quick!" he said. "I will now show you the shrine to my sanctified Angelina. Do you have a machete?"

"Is it far?" I asked.

"Yes, of course! Get your machete. I will show you."

Hector was pleased with my American-made machete. He said anything made in the City of Industry, California, was sure to prevail over nature.

"That's a joke," he said.

"Should I wear long pants and boots?" I asked him.

"Americans always ask what they should wear. Europeans never ask. They tell me what to wear. 'Wear the safari shirt, Hector,' they say. 'Do not wear the Ronald Reagan T-shirt.' Then, when we get to someplace, of course, they all want to take off their clothes."

I wore shorts and my canvas shoes. We walked up the road toward the fallen bridges and ducked into the jungle at the top of a rise. Hector did not follow any trail that I could see, and it seemed he used my machete only when he did not need to. He took care where he stepped, and I stepped where he did.

"Are there snakes around here?" I asked.

Hector nodded. *"Culebras,"* he whispered. Vipers.

"What do they look like?"

"Like two small holes in your ankle, gringo."

I checked my ankles. We hiked uphill for half a mile. I felt better every time we broke into an opening. The dense vegetation always seemed to grow in the same patterns, and though I often turned to look back, I found no way of mentally marking our trail. I tried to breathe evenly and walk easily, but I sweated like a horse.

We stopped at a tall, branching tree from which hung long catalpa-like seedpods. Hector picked up a fallen limb and used the crook near its end to hook down several of the pods. He broke them open. Inside were smooth black seeds wrapped in a wet white fiber. He stuffed a handful of the pulp into his mouth and began spitting out the seeds.

"Take," he said.

The pulp melted in my mouth. It tasted like a light, sweet cinnamon.

"What is it?"

"People here call it guava. Isn't that ignorant? Guava is something else."

"It is good." I looked around as I ate. Now I saw the pods hanging everywhere. "This is a paradise," I said.

"You sweat like you are elsewhere," said Hector.

We hiked another quarter mile and veered off the ridgetop to the right. We dropped a couple hundred feet through tall, stiff grass to a solid wall of vegetation. Hector turned and smiled at me and ducked into the thicket. I approached where he had disappeared. There was not a sign of him.

Then Hector spoke from a yard away. "I am the selva," he intoned. "The forest Eternity. Disappearing into myself. *Entre*, Daniel, and disappear."

I reached into the green wall of leaves and vines. Hector grabbed my wrist and pulled me inside. I was now in a tunnel of hot, close green. Hector sat grinning on the end of a large piece of plywood that had once been a sign. It advertised a popular drug. "Finalina," it said. "For the Pain of Your Life. Always at Your Pharmacy." The sign was the only hard shape in the tunnel. I sat down beside Hector.

"Look," he said. He carefully pulled aside some leaves and suddenly we were looking out over a small rocky canyon. The canyon's other wall was barely thirty yards away. At the bottom of the canyon, twenty feet below us, a clear stream dropped from basin to basin of purple water-polished rock.

"This is it," Hector said.

I nodded. "This?"

"Yes. My shrine to Angelina. Below is where she captures my soul with the butterflies. She will be here soon. She left before we did."

"You watch her here."

"Pffft! Elsewhere, I watch her. Here, I worship her. To me worship is a private matter."

"But you hide from her."

"Of course. To keep it private. Besides, I believe she knows I am here."

We sat on the signboard in the steamy heat. A damp white powder covered the board. I touched my finger to it and smelled it. "That is DDT, Daniel. The old, good stuff. One can sit here for hours and not be molested by a single insect or spider. Once, I found the prints of a jaguar who rested here. And perhaps also he watched Angelina."

I saw the powder caking the seat of Hector's pants. I imagined a jaguar licking the DDT from its paws.

"This is a good place to come," Hector said. "Even when Angelina does not come here, someone often does. They do strange things in these pools."

"Hector, you are a voyeur," I said.

He shrugged. "The thing you have to know about Puentes Caidos is that Puentes is where people come to watch others.

And to be watched, too. We have three groups here—the tourists, the villagers, and the Aurunas. The tourists want to see the jungle, but they want to see the Aurunas most of all. They want naked savages dancing to their desires. The Auruna women wear nothing but strings around their waists, and of course, the disks in their ears. The women have no pubic hair, Daniel, and this makes the tourist men very interested."

"Ridiculous," I said.

"See? You are interested too. The Auruna men, too, wear only the strings, but they tie the strings to their foreskins and hold their penises always erect. This interests the tourists very much. Sometimes the excitement of the tourist women excites the Auruna men and the Aurunas have to unleash their penises. Then the tourist men get angry. It has gotten dangerous, sometimes."

"I don't believe it," I said.

Hector nodded. "I don't believe it. I don't believe it, gringo. The villagers, too, are watchers. They watch the tourists. To the villagers the tourists are like kings and queens, or movie stars, walking television commercials. Riches with arms and legs. They imagine the U.S. is a country where everyone wears a TV on his shoulder."

Hector looked back out through the foliage.

"Now," he told me. "We watch."

Within a few minutes, Angelina came into view, stepping from stone to stone. She wore canvas shoes, canvas shorts, and a blue short-sleeved blouse whose tails were tied across her stomach. Her dark hair was tied back by a blue bandanna. She carried a canvas bag, slung over her shoulder like a fisherman's creel, and a butterfly net. She stopped, twenty feet below us. I heard her feet tapping on the stones. I heard her breathing. I felt embarrassed to spy on her. I looked at Hector. He was in rapture. Angelina set down her shoulder bag. She knelt beside it. Her legs were long and brown and as gracefully shaped as the rock had been shaped by the water. The sunlight made its way through the forest canopy and illuminated the dome of her knee. She opened her bag and took out a small square of bright blue fabric. She rose and walked to the edge of the stream, where the water fell off a ledge about two meters high. She looked around at the jungle—and looked at me, I thought— and then she stepped back so her body melted into the purple shadow of the rocks. She held out the blue fabric, into a shaft of sun, and began slowly to waft the blue cloth in the light.

"Now she changes," Hector whispered. "She flies."

The blue flutter of the cloth in the sunlight above the waterfall flashed like a beacon in the darkness of the canyon. It seemed as if the shadow of Angelina were reaching to touch us, and the blue rag at the tip of her fingers were a scrap of blue flame.

"Oh! None can resist," whispered Hector. "I would fly. I would fly! Every time I watch her, I feel stronger."

Suddenly, from out of the jungle, from above us, another patch of bright blue appeared. Again and again, closer and closer, an enormous blue butterfly appeared in the shafts of sunlight, and always nearer to Angelina.

"The blue morpho," whispered Hector. "The bluest shape of the smallest death."

The butterfly's wings beat so slowly that it seemed not to fly but to hang by an invisible string tugged at from above by a rhythmic, hypnotic hand. It circled the scrap of fabric in Angelina's hand and she matched the pulse of its wings. The butterfly made three passes. Then Angelina's hand went still. The butterfly lighted on her smallest finger. It closed its wings, and it disappeared.

The net fell over it.

"Pah!" panted Hector. "Now! I have died!"

I took a deep breath. I felt cold.

Angelina stepped into the sunlight and pressed the butterfly between the pages of a tattered *National Geographic* magazine. Two other blue morphos now appeared in the air around her.

Angelina stood in the sun and watched them for a few moments. Then she put the magazine back into her shoulder bag and walked away down the canyon.

Hector turned to me. His eyes were brimming with tears. "What ceremony," he said, and then in English, "Hey, man. What a trip."

I tried to say something in Spanish.

"I know how you feel," Hector said. "You should give me five dollars."

We returned to the village. I did not want to pay him, but Hector hung around the cantina until I got him the money.

"Next time, you get a discount," he said.

I wanted to go talk to Santiago. I wanted to see Angelina. But I was afraid that Angelina knew I had watched her, and I felt ashamed.

The next day Hector showed up at the cantina with the two tourist women from the Norona. They wore Levi's and T-shirts and had little nylon daypacks. They each carried a handmade butterfly net. Hector wore his khaki safari shirt, black pants, rubber boots, and a pair of Ray-Ban pilot's sunglasses.

"Daniel! Oh, Daniel!" he called musically from the yard in front of the cantina.

I stepped out into the yard and said hello to the women. They did not appear eager to meet me. Hector put his arm around my shoulder and spoke to them. "Daniel is my guide assistant," he said.

Hector winked at me. "Daniel is at your service."

This time the women said hello. "So, you are the jungle apprentice," the red-haired one said in American English. Her smaller companion would not look at me.

"An expedition!" Hector said. "Today we chase the deadly blue morpho."

I nodded. I could not tell if Hector was serious.

"There is danger," he said to the women. "But no bad danger, if we keep close." He nodded. "There is beauty, too.

Promise me, Kate," he said to the larger woman, "you will do as I say."

Kate nodded.

"You promise?"

"I promise."

"Good. Good! And you. Promise me, Cynthia?"

The smaller woman shrugged.

"Your promise," Hector said to her, "is like a sky full of gray that will not rain."

Kate and Cynthia glanced at each other.

"Hector is a poet," I told them.

"Oh, really?" asked Kate.

This pleased Hector. "Yes," he said. "I am the poet."

"Are you published?" Cynthia asked.

Hector looked at me.

"Are you in books," I said.

"I am famous," he told them.

Hector led us back to the canyon, but this time we followed the path Angelina had taken, along the stream rather than up the ridge. This path was easier. Fast water had carved steps into the rock and kept the vegetation away. The rock was so polished that the place looked tended and tame compared to the wildness of the ridge above it.

Early in the hike, Hector stooped to pick up a handful of leaves that had been crushed by the side of the stream. "This is barbasco," he told us. "The women put it in the water and this way they kill the fish."

"Why?" Kate asked.

Hector looked amazed at Kate's ignorance. "For fish," he said. He tossed the leaves onto the still water.

"Will that kill the fish?" Kate asked.

"Here, the fish here are already killed."

Farther up the stream, Hector stripped some spear-shaped leaves away from a fat, greasy vine.

"This is the plant for no babies," he said. He handed the leaves to Kate. "You eat a little leaves, you have no babies for a little time. You eat many leaves, you have no babies for many times."

"Jungle birth control," Kate said.

Hector nodded. "You want to eat some?"

Kate dropped the leaves. "No," she said.

"Then be careful, Kate." Hector smiled at Cynthia.

We clambered up a waterfall and entered a narrow canyon. The walls rose straight up. They were covered by vines and leaves so thick that they hid the rock behind them. The stream flowed through a channel it had carved in the flat rock floor and through a series of deeper basins. At the end of this gallery, the streambed climbed away again like a steep flight of stairs. I stopped as I entered the place. It was where Hector and I had watched Angelina catch the butterfly. I tried to pick out the blind from where we had watched.

"Oh, my God," said Kate. "This is beautiful."

She and Cynthia wandered around the gallery, touching the orchids that hung from the walls and peering into the clear pools. I went to the place Angelina had stood and studied the wall of the canyon. It was a solid matting of vines and creepers. Birds-of-paradise poked their beaked blossoms out of the thicket.

Hector came up to me. "Yes, Daniel. That is the wall of watching. Look. Can you see yourself? Perhaps she watches us?"

He sat down next to the largest pool. "The morpho is coming," he said to Kate and Cynthia. "But not yet. Don't worry. Relax yourselves."

The women roamed around the green gallery.

"What's farther up the stream?" Kate asked him.

"Jungle. Caves. A jaguar. A volcano," said Hector. "Like here."

He walked over to where Cynthia was studying a spiraling

vine with delicate, light green leaves. "You find a good one," he told her. "This vegetation makes you go dreaming."

Cynthia sniffed the vine. "Dreaming?"

"Big dreaming. The Aurunas use it to see tomorrow."

Cynthia picked off a leaf and crushed it between her fingers. She touched it to her nose. "Do they eat it or smoke it?"

"They drink it. It needs cooking. And magic words. It tastes bad. Like shit." He waited for her reaction.

"Do you know how?" she asked him.

Hector smiled. "Did Daniel tell you? I am Auruna too. I can mix up some good shit if you want it." He went back to his place by the pool. I sat down next to him and soaked my feet in the cool water.

"The morpho is coming," Hector said to the women. "But first, swimming?"

Kate and Cynthia looked at the water in the pools.

"It looks lovely," said Kate. "But unfortunately, we didn't bring our suits."

"You wear the water," Hector told her.

Kate looked at me.

I shrugged. "Don't worry about it," I said.

"Don't worry about it, Kate," Hector said. "Daniel protects you."

I shrugged again.

"Latin America is so weird," she said to me.

"Yes, miss lady," Hector said to her. "Very weird."

Then Cynthia crossed her arms, grabbed the tail of her T-shirt, and pulled it over her head. She reached behind her back and undid her bra. Hector clapped his hands quietly. Kate turned around and looked away. Cynthia stepped out of her shoes and slipped off her Levi's. She smiled toward Kate and glanced at Hector. Wearing only a pair of white nylon panties, Cynthia stepped into the pool in front of her.

Kate turned back to her. "Cynthia. You're going to get us into trouble again," she said.

Cynthia waded in up to her knees. She reached down and skimmed the water's surface with her fingertips.

"You are beautiful, Cynthia," Hector said. "As you touch the water."

Cynthia straightened and looked at Hector. Her large eyes were dark and strange to me. Her skin was white against the dark green of the jungle wall behind her. Her shoulders were narrow and her breasts were small, with small pink nipples. Her hips were wide, and she stood with her weight shifted onto them. She was out of a Renaissance painting. She laughed, looking at Hector.

"Cynthia!" Kate said. She turned to me. "We're safe, aren't we?"

"Sure," I said.

"We had better be," Kate said to Cynthia, and she shook her head.

Then Kate turned away from Hector and me and began taking off her clothes. When she had stripped down to her panties, she stepped quickly into a pool and sank to her chin. Her red hair dented the silver surface of the water.

She turned around to face me. The coolness of the water made her catch her breath. Her pale pink body distorted in the water.

"You are beautiful, Kate," Hector told her. "You are alive in the water."

"You are weird, Hector," Kate said to him. She laughed and turned around to face Cynthia.

Cynthia sat down on the side of her pool and took off her panties. She slid off the rock into the water. I wanted to go swimming too, but not with Hector there.

Hector turned to me. "I will live forever, Daniel," he said.

It was cool by the water. The patches of sunlight moved across the leaves and rock. Kate and Cynthia swam in the pools. After a time, Hector stood and went to the rock where Angelina had earlier caught the butterfly. He took a piece of blue aluminum foil from his shirt pocket and held it out into the sunlight. He slowly waved it in the light for a minute or two, until a blue morpho butterfly appeared above us in the air.

"Oh, look!" said Kate. "Look at it! That's it."

Dipping and rising, the big morpho circled Hector's hand. Hector matched his movement to the slow beat of the butterfly's wings, and the butterfly circled closer and closer to his hand. When the morpho was inches away, Hector snatched the cloth out of sight, into his palm. The butterfly faltered, and then flew in widening circles up to the top of the canyon. It hovered there, watching.

"Cynthia," Hector called. "Come! You will seduce the morpho. Come!"

Cynthia climbed out of her pool and walked past me to Hector. She stood looking up at him standing on the rock. She held her hands in front of her, holding one finger in the other hand. Hector gave her the blue foil and stepped down beside her. He examined Cynthia's body. Then he said, "*Arriba*. For the morpho." Cynthia stepped up onto the rock and gracefully positioned her feet. She stretched up onto her toes to reach the band of sunlight with the scrap of blue foil. She had to hold her other arm behind her for balance. She began to flash the foil in the sun.

I looked at Kate, who had risen from the water. Kate held her hands across her breasts.

"Oh, my God, Cynthia," Kate said. "I wish I had a camera. I wish you could see yourself."

Cynthia was an actress, a moving sculpture. She stretched herself more. She waved the foil in the sunlight. The blue morpho butterfly began a descent toward its prize. As it neared her, Cynthia knew to match her hand's flight to the butterfly's. As the butterfly flew past her face, Cynthia stopped moving. She was stretched out to the sun like a statue, her skin white as ivory. The butterfly landed on her wrist and slowly opened and closed its wings. It was larger than her hand.

"Now, Cynthia," Hector said. "The blue morpho chooses you for his lover. Will you love him?"

Slowly, Cynthia drew her hand down to her face. The butterfly opened and closed its wings, and blue light pulsed in reflection on her throat and her face.

"What do I do?" she whispered.

"Close the eyes, Cynthia," Hector said.

Cynthia closed her eyes.

"Now breathe, Cynthia. Breathe."

Cynthia breathed in. She spread her arms as she did and the butterfly left her hand.

"Oh, my God," said Kate. "Are we in a movie?"

With an easy upsweep of Cynthia's net, Hector snatched the morpho. He took it out of the net and pinched its head to kill it. He opened its wings and held it up to Cynthia.

"Perfect," he said. "Like an Englishman. Dead."

Cynthia stood looking down at the butterfly, her hands and arms now covering herself. She was shivering. Kate got out of the pool and quickly pulled on her pants and shirt and stuffed her bra into her daypack. I went up to Hector and looked over his shoulder at the morpho. It was five inches across and its wings were blue and metallic, like mother-of-pearl.

"You get your money's worth," Hector said.

Kate and I led the way down the stream. Cynthia held back with Hector.

When I got back to the cantina, Consuelo told me that Angelina was off with a British Broadcasting Company filming crew.

"She is acting like a movie star and swimming with the sacred dolphins."

She told me the dolphins were sacred because they were the souls of the *angelito* babies who die before they are baptized.

"They are pink-and-gray fish," she said. "And the mother fish have breasts. They are like pink, naked fish with breasts, if that can be so. And worse, and better, the male fish have male parts hidden inside them. I have seen them. And girlfriends of mine have touched the parts. They have played with these parts—I mean it. And the mother fish sometimes have human babies inside them, little love babies that look like the babies that come out in miscarriages. I have seen these babies, too. They come from village men who have been seduced by these dolphins and then go home to their wives. Or else they happen when village women themselves go straight to the men dolphins."

Consuelo lowered her voice. "The men joke about it, but it is serious business. You know the great dwarf we have in the village—Napoleon Elefante, Angelina's assistant? He . . . Well, it is said he is the product of dolphin and human. And I believe it—although Napo cannot swim. I believe it because his arms aren't long and they aren't quite flippers. What do you think? I think the English should stay out of their waters."

"I thought butterflies were the souls of dead babies," I said.

Consuelo snapped her chewing gum and flashed her eyes. "Who knows?" she said. "You should see them. And besides, everything is possible. Go ask Hector."

That evening Kate invited me to dinner at the Pension No-. rona. It was my first big meal since I had come to the village: a cube of spaghetti cake topped with cooked bananas and cinnamon. I had to wash it all down with two warm Cokes.

After dinner, Kate told me Cynthia had left with Hector to see the Auruna Indians.

"Just who are these Indians?" she asked me.

"They belong to a primitive tribe," I said. "They live off the land and they don't wear any clothes."

"Oh, great," Kate said.

"Don't worry. The ones around here live off the tourists. Hector is an Auruna. Or he used to be. He was adopted by missionaries when he was six years old. It didn't work out."

"Where are these Indians?" she asked me.

"I don't know. I haven't gone to see them yet."

"How long have you been here?"

"I don't know. Less than a week."

"Less than a week? I thought you were an old-timer. Well. Whatever turns you on, I guess. We're leaving tomorrow, if I can get Cynthia to go. This jungle stuff is too thick for me. We're going to Cuzco to see the Incas and stay in a hotel. How long are you staying here?"

"I've got enough money for a lifetime. Two, if people keep buying me dinner."

"A lifetime? Here? That could be short. God, watch out, Danny. I think I'd come unglued and do something shameful if I stayed here two weeks."

"Like what?" I said. "Go skinny-dipping?"

Kate lowered her voice. "That was not skinny-dipping. I don't know what I think it was, but it was weird. I know if I stayed here I'd get stuck. I'd get sleepy and lazy. You know, give up. Do something shameful. Marry a local, maybe."

"That's really shameful," I said.

"It is to me. Really. And I would, I know it. I'd drop out, not take care of myself. I'd let myself get dirty. Watch out, Danny," she said.

At that moment, Kate was wearing soiled white jeans and a wrinkled Hawaiian shirt. Her red hair had curled up kinky from the humidity, and wet strands stuck to her forehead. I was wearing an old pair of basketball shorts and a ripped T-shirt.

"People around here are very clean, Kate."

"I know," she said. "But they know how to be. I need showers and deodorant. Here, I'd be like an office plant that escaped and went wild. And married a weed. No thank you. I need control. I am not a libber. What do you need, Danny?" She looked over her shoulder. "When do you think Hector and Cynthia will come back?"

"Soon."

It was starting to get dark. I was watching the cantina, and it looked as though Santiago's drinking and thinking club was gathering for another evening. I stood up.

"Well, thanks for dinner," I said.

"Don't go," Kate said.

I sat back down. "Why don't you join us at the cantina," I said. "The people over there can get pretty interesting."

"That's all I need right now. What do you think Hector and Cynthia are doing?"

"I don't know. Looking at naked Indians. Or they're on their way back."

Kate shoved away her Coke bottle and leaned toward me. "What do you do when you get back to the States?"

"I haven't thought about going back."

Kate smiled. "Are you married or something? No. Wait a minute. I know. You just got divorced. I can see it."

I shook my head. "I just don't have to go back for a while."

"Of course not."

"I'm here because of myself."

"Obviously. I understand. But everybody's in South America for a reason, aren't they? Drugs, fantasy, import, export. They're all writing a book or something. Aren't you? Everybody I meet says, I'm writing a book. I'm working on a Fulbright. It's not like Europe, is it, where people can go for no reason." Kate was relaxing. "Where do you plan to go next? After here?" she asked.

"I think I'm staying here, Kate."

"Then you must have a reason. That girl in the cantina."

"Consuelo?"

"She's sexy."

"I like the climate."

"The climate?"

"It's warm."

She nodded. "It's erotic, isn't it."

"I guess it is."

"Well, I think it is. Except it's oozy, too. And kind of squirmy. You ought to see our room."

"Is it oozy, or squirmy?"

"Definitely squirmy," Kate said. "I mean, what can you do? You can't close the window because it's too hot. And then you worry about bugs. Have you seen some of the bugs? A kid tried to sell me a beetle as big as my fist. So I just squirm around, until the bed gets sweaty. Can't turn on the light because the light brings bugs. I guess you couldn't mind getting all sweaty."

"It's healthy to sweat. And there's always the river."

"There is. I bathe in the morning. Then I spend the day in the hammock, getting ready to bathe, reading a book about unleashing my true potential. Did you know self-help is becoming a religion? Did you?"

I had to laugh.

"I bet you did, Danny," she said. "I can see you're a thinker. And I can see you're upset and you're going to stay here and think—just think—until you figure it all out."

"Maybe I am," I said.

"Maybe you are. I like you, Danny."

"I like you."

"Can I call you Danny?" Kate smiled, but now she looked sad. "It's all too weird. We are all too lonely. Traveling is the loneliest thing you can do. Have you thought about that? You've got to kid yourself all the time. You develop real intense things with other travelers. You tell them everything. And then you never see them again. Things happen that you would never let happen at home. They say that travel makes the world smaller, and it does. But not the way most people think it does. It makes people smaller too. Like children, I guess. I think it gives them excuses. It takes away their shells."

Kate looked to see if she had more Coca-Cola, then unwrapped a piece of hard candy. "Don't you think that was pretty weird back there?" she said. "Four people who don't even know each other go off into the jungle and the women take off their clothes. Of course, the men don't take off their clothes, and I'm glad you didn't. You just watched Cynthia."

"You watched her too."

"I know. That was weird too. God, what a world. That's the world. Don't you see? Men telling women to take off their clothes."

"Now wait a minute. I didn't."

"I know you didn't. It was Hector. But don't you see? That whole scene just showed something. About men."

"And women maybe," I said. "Cynthia enjoyed herself. And I am glad I went."

"I'll bet you are. But let me tell you about Cynthia. When we were up at the capital, Cynthia went off with an army captain to the cavalry's horse pastures and ate magic mushrooms. Now she says she doesn't know if he ate any mushrooms or not."

"So?"

Kate set her jaw and watched me.

"Danny, you're a kind, good person, probably," she said. "I mean, I'm sure you are. I'm just worried about Cynthia. She's the liberated one and she lets men use her all the time, just like she likes. I'm all uptight. *El capitán* Jaime was O.K., she says, because he is a captain in the cavalry and they don't have cavalries anywhere in the world but this little country and it was like going back in time on the mushrooms. I'll bet it was."

"Cynthia is doing what she wants to do."

"That's what she says."

"She'll do fine," I said. "She can get out at any time."

"I'd like to get out now," said Kate.

"So do it," I said. "Get out. I got out of what I was in. That's why I'm down here."

Kate eyed me. "Looks great," she said. "You're doing great. Just look at you." Then her voice shifted. "No, Danny, I'm sorry. I didn't mean that. Please tell me. What's it like?"

"I haven't been out long enough."

"O.K. . . ."

After a moment, Kate said, "I couldn't leave Cynthia. Not down here. It's so weird down here. Have you noticed that all the gringos seem to be traveling around looking for other gringos? Then they either want to fuck each other or avoid each other. They wouldn't even notice each other back in the States, but here they want to get weird as soon as they can."

Kate suddenly looked distressed.

"This traveling is killing you, isn't it?" I said.

"No. It's not that."

Kate was rubbing her fingertips across the tabletop.

"Oh, shit. Oh, shit. I'm sorry I said 'fuck,' " she said.

"It doesn't bother me."

"It bothers me. It all bothers me. I don't say 'fuck' in Eugene. I wish I knew you in Eugene."

"Relax, Kate," I said. "Come on over to the cantina. I'll buy you a beer. We'll listen to a local version of *Prairie Home Companion*, the Amazonian Kiwanis Club discussing current events."

"I can't speak Spanish."

"Just watch their faces."

"No. I'm going to stay here and read. Somebody gave me a Penguin paperback of *Caesar's Conquest of Gaul*. Now, that's a weird book to read down here."

"Well," I said, "beware of the bugs. Maybe I'll come back in a while to see if you've changed your mind."

"Maybe," said Kate.

The group at the cantina was beginning its deliberations when I got there. An old farmer named Presidente Wilson had lost his motorcycle to an army guard at the provincial border and he wanted to know how to get it back. To El Brinco's horror, Santiago led the discussion from one of practicalities—whether to steal back the motorcycle or to pay a bribe—to a discussion on the philosophy of government.

Santiago paced the cantina, his bald head shining in the

lantern light. He handed me half a lemon. He said, "We should ask, What is the best form of government?"

"A dead one, clearly," El Brinco said.

"A kind one, clearly?" Presidente Wilson said.

"No," said Hugo. "A strong one, of course, and honest. And very visible, to inspire us all to faith and to order."

"Spare me, Hugo," El Brinco moaned. "And spare yourself my indignation."

Hugo ignored El Brinco.

"Look at me, Huguito," El Brinco said.

Hugo would not look at him. Hugo sat very straight in his white dress uniform.

"At least take off that silly cap," said Brinco.

Hugo took off his cap. Consuelo brought me a beer and sat down next to me on the bench. Her thigh touched mine and immediately our skins were slick with sweat where they touched.

"Oooh! It's hot!" she said. She wore a sweet perfume. "Don't you think it's hot? Huguito is very cute, I think." She whispered into my ear, "*Muy guapo*. You too!"

Her father, El Brinco, shook his finger at her.

Santiago continued his discourse. "Perhaps we should ask, What is the reason for government?"

"Freedom?" said Presidente Wilson.

"Freedom from what?" asked Santiago.

"From the government," said Brinco.

"No. From ourselves," said Hugo.

"Hugo, you are a moron," said Brinco.

Santiago continued. "But why? And how? To be free from ourselves? How? Do we keep ourselves enchained?"

Hugo stood, avoiding Brinco's glare. "No, Santiago," he said. His sincerity made his lips tremble. "Rather, without government, we would keep ourselves unbound and misdirected. A strong government gives us a freedom, that is, within bounds, and directions, to better direct ourselves, thus." He pointed. "In a forward-facing manner."

"Ha!" laughed Brinco. "Down the river."

Now Presidente Wilson asked, "And what of my motorcycle?"

Hugo looked at Wilson as if he had forgotten the connection.

El Brinco said, "Old man, despair. Your motorcycle cannot help you now."

"So what can we do about it?"

"We can make a statement," said Santiago.

"A fat lot of good that will do," said Brinco.

"Sometimes making the statement helps the man who says it."

"And what will we state?"

"We have to discuss that. Perhaps we will end up saying, 'The government is wrong.' "

"Oh, my God," said El Brinco. "We are soft in the head."

"Wait," said Hugo. "It is against the law to oppose an act of the government."

The men booed him down.

"Santiago," Presidente Wilson asked, "please, how do I get back my motorcycle?"

Santiago shook himself out of meditation. "My friend Wilson," he said, "you steal it back, of course."

Now Jesus jumped up. "No! If you steal it back, you become as bad as they are. If you act like the government, you become like the government."

"Very interesting, Jesus," said Santiago. "That is very interesting. Then what should our distinguished Wilson do, so people won't think that he is the government?"

"And run from him!" someone said.

"Or pay him taxes," said another.

"He should do justice," said Jesus. "And go kill the individual bastard who dared steal his bike!"

El Brinco laughed and toasted Jesus. "I like your logic," he said. "I'll do it!"

The drinkers all let out a roar and began thumping their

glasses on the tables. Hugo stood watching them, ashen-faced.

Consuelo whispered to me, "That is the naval lieutenant Hugo Rios del Rio. He stands on conviction and principle. That other man, Jesus, gets too excited to think."

El Brinco called to his daughter. "Consuelita! The beer! Sell the beer!"

A celebration broke out. Even old Wilson began to have a good time. Hugo avoided Brinco and joined in a toasting competition. Someone brought out a transistor radio and tuned in a station that played Colombian salsa music.

"Consuelo!" the men called. "This music is yours! Dance, *zambatita*. Dance!"

Consuelo danced with her father. El Brinco performed a graceful one-legged shuffle as Consuelo twirled around him.

Santiago came over and sat down by me.

"Where is Angelina?" I asked him.

"Now? At home, studying. Today? She was on British television! With the pink English searching for pink fish with tits." Santiago chuckled. "Have you ever seen television?"

"Of course."

"Of course you have. It is like a radio with movies. They sell it in stores in the capital. Here, we are on television all the time, but we cannot see it. We with our Aurunas and our dolphins and our hummingbirds. Have you seen English television?"

"Yes."

"Have you ever been on English television?"

"No."

"How does it compare? To North American?"

"Oh, better, I guess."

"Why?"

"It's more serious."

"I thought so. North Americans are not so serious?"

I shook my head.

"That is right. And French television," Santiago said. "How does it compare?"

"I don't know. Worse."

"I would have said so. The French and the German. They are very strong in their ideas. The German television wanted the Aurunas to fight a television war! Only Hector would do it, but he would not take off his clothes."

Santiago's face took on a mock horror. "I used to think that television and movies would be a type of universal form, a very good dream, showing the way things should be. But then I saw some movies. Cowboy movies, with John Wayne. They were good movies, but bad dreams. It did not work. They say North Americans watch much television."

"All the time," I said.

Santiago nodded.

"Will Angelina be here tomorrow?" I asked.

The men took turns dancing with Consuelo, who moved grandly and beautifully, and some men danced with each other. El Brinco was happy selling beer. Santiago took on a posture of deep reflection, sitting up straight with his hands on his knees. I nursed my beer and watched the dancing.

An hour later, Hector and Cynthia stepped into the cantina. Hector wore a dirty pink T-shirt that displayed lightning bolts and the English words FUR OUT! He had a sleepy, sly look on his face. He held Cynthia by her elbow and seemed to guide her into the room. Cynthia was naked from the waist up and she was stoned out of her mind. Her breasts and belly were painted yellow. She wore a dark brown sack skirt like the ones I had seen the Auruna women wear my first day. Her feet were bare and caked with mud halfway to her knees. In one hand, she held a necklace of iridescent green beetle shells strung together on a plant fiber. A garland of crushed orchids tangled in her dark hair. She smiled openmouthed, her tongue flat in her mouth. Her teeth were stained brown. Her eyebrows were high and arched, but her eyes were glazed and half closed. She licked her lips and gazed around the room.

The men stopped dancing. The radio music stopped and an announcer came on, languidly rolling his *r*'s. Someone turned off the radio.

"Oh no. What is this, Hector?" Santiago asked.

"My good gentlemen, this is an *india*," said Hector. He watched Cynthia out of the corner of his eye. "The image of primitive life. A noble savage, without inhibition, without civilization. The natural woman, mysterious and animal. Watch, O my contemporary and distinguished public. The grace of the primitive feminine form, set free!"

Hector guided Cynthia to the center of the cantina. He left her there under a gas lantern and motioned the others to move back. Cynthia stood alone below the hissing lantern. She looked around the room, smiling stupidly. I waved at her to get her attention. She did not recognize me. She breathed short breaths through both her mouth and nose, her nostrils quivering.

Hector spoke to her in the high, birdlike Auruna language.

"Dance, woman," he said in English.

Cynthia began to shuffle from side to side, dipping as she slid her bare feet across the rough plank floor.

"Dis-civilization," Hector the Indian, said to the cholo men.

The men were amazed.

"Oh! Woman!" Consuelo shouted to Cynthia, to no effect. Consuelo turned to me.

I stood up. "Cynthia!" I said.

Just then, Kate ran into the cantina. She grabbed Cynthia by the arm and spun her around.

"Cynthia! Cynthia!" she cried.

Cynthia smiled and dipped and shuffled.

Kate turned to Hector. "Where are her clothes!" she demanded.

Hector shrugged and stuck out his lower lip. "Phffft!" he said. He waved toward the night.

Kate turned to me. She narrowed her eyes.

I could not speak. Over Kate's shoulder, I saw Angelina step into the cantina. I pointed to her. Everyone in the cantina turned and looked at Angelina.

"Come," Angelina said to Kate.

Kate helped Cynthia out of the building.

Lieutenant Hugo Rios got up sputtering and left. Everyone else appeared stunned, including Hector.

El Brinco spoke. "Hector, you are a buzzard."

Hector frowned. "Civilization," he said. "Phffft. There it goes!"

Some of the men laughed. Hector pulled a wad of U.S. dollar bills from his pants pocket. "Look. The client pays," he said, and he put the money on the table in front of El Brinco.

Some of the men applauded. El Brinco nodded to Consuelo and she rose and quietly began to serve the beer. People got drunk. I felt terrible. Once, Santiago sat down next to me and asked, "What did the redheaded gringa say to you?"

I hadn't heard her say anything.

Santiago shook his head. "Names," he said.

Hector took over the direction of the drinking party. He conducted a kangaroo court trial of the government on the charge of stealing the motorcycle from Presidente Wilson the farmer. He played the judge, speaking in his booming bass. He played the government, piping a high falsetto. Santiago stayed out of it. The government was found guilty and sentenced to death. Although many were laughing, the men appeared to take the trial seriously. After the verdict, they became morose.

"Don't we feel like shit," Jesus said.

6

----

ate and Cynthia left the village before I could speak to them. I finally found Angelina with Napoleon down at the beach, seeing to a canoeload of supplies for a scientific expedition downriver. She was barefoot and wore her dark hair in two braids. Her short-sleeved shirt had epaulets, and she had rolled up the sleeves as far as they would go. On her arm, she had a smallpox vaccination scar, white against her dark skin.

I stood in front of her and tried to talk to her, but I couldn't think of what to say. Finally I helped Napoleon put boxes into the canoe as I tried to explain what had happened.

"That was all very interesting," she said.

After she had sent off the canoe and left me there, Hugo came up to me. "What did Angelina say to you?" he asked.

"Nothing much."

"What, for example?"

"Nothing."

Hugo was suspicious. "I want to see your visa again," he said.

A few of the men did not sober up for several days. They lay around the cantina sleeping and drinking. When they had no more money, Brinco put them into canoes going downriver and paid their passages back to their homesteads. Somehow, Presidente Wilson got back his motorcycle. I saw him riding it very soon after the drinking party. It was a battered old Vespa missing its leg guards, and it sounded like a tin billy goat. Old Wilson dragged his rubber boots along the ground and bleated to all his friends.

One morning, I climbed downstairs and saw Hector sitting on the front step. Consuelo was leaning against a post, watching him.

"That was a bad thing you did," I said to Hector.

"Which bad thing, O good gringo of North America?"

"With Cynthia."

"Ah. With Cynthia," Hector said. "Sit down." He moved over on the step for me.

I stepped past him into the humid sunlight. It felt like stepping into a hot shower.

Hector looked me straight in the eye. "The most negative girls most often say yes," he said. "Remember that. This is a negative place. Remember that. Here, bad things happen."

"You took advantage of her."

"Who doesn't," he said, and shook his head.

"It doesn't bother you."

"What? If you feel bad about it afterwards, it makes you a good person? That's the difference between us. Please excuse me. I don't preoccupy myself like other people."

Consuelo called to me. "Daniel. Do you want breakfast? I have fish and plantains."

"Thank you," I said. "And some coffee."

"And that is bad for you too, my friend," Hector said. He raised his shoulders and laughed. "Coffee. The instant bellyache. The worst in the world. But so what? It does not bother you to kill your stomach. So, either leave or sit down."

"Daniel," Consuelo said, "did you hear? Hector got back Wilson's motorcycle for him."

Hector smiled. "Look. I do good things, too," he said. "But I don't dwell. I keep it all equal. One bad, one good. One good, one bad. Pfft. I don't think it matters."

"How did you get it back?" I asked him.

"I murdered a captain."

"You did not."

"It is not clear he did not," said Consuelo.

"So, what is clear and who knows?" Hector said. "And who is to say which captain one speaks of? And when? Perhaps I killed a captain years ago just to set this whole thing up. I think ahead. I am a poet, remember. I am Time, I am Life, I am Death. I murder with word and thought. I killed Captain Jaime for Cynthia in her mind, and it works. She is dumb. She is numb. She is happy. It suffices. Sit down."

I shook my head, but I sat down.

"That's better," he said. "Sitting down is the custom in Los Puentes Caidos. Sitting down and waiting for nothing."

Six vultures were spiraling above Santiago's house. As I watched, the spiral tightened and moved slowly away and up the hill.

Consuelo brought me my coffee and a hard roll. "That fish was rotten," she said. "It would have been bad for you." She sat down on the step and she and Hector shared a cigarette.

"Cigarettes are bad for us," Hector said somberly, and they both laughed.

"Daniel, my dearest," Consuelo said. "My precious Daniel. Don't preoccupy yourself so much."

"Yes. Why are you here, Daniel?" Hector asked. "If you don't like it, why do you stay?"

Consuelo said, "Yes, why do you stay? Nobody stays here. If you are not Peace Corps, you do not have to stay. Those Peace Corps *pobrecitos*, it is they who have to stay. And then they don't stay too long. You must be in hiding. You must have done something very bad in the United States and you had to run away."

"I like that impression!" said Hector. "Daniel the desperado. He won't get caught here. What did you do?"

"He killed a man," said Consuelo.

"Not Daniel," said Hector.

"Of course he did," she said. "That is what I believe. He killed a very bad man and saved an entire town."

"I did not kill a man."

"Of course you did not," said Hector. "I can see that."

"*Gracias*, Hector," I said.

"You say *gracias*, but I know what you did. You cheated on your taxes. That is what gringos do."

"I came here to learn," I said.

That quieted Hector and Consuelo for a while.

"*Bueno*," Hector said. "To learn!" He leaned back on his elbows. His T-shirt had a picture of Donald Duck in a tuxedo. The motto read "Tall Duck and Handsome."

"You should go talk to Santiago to learn," Consuelo told me.

"For what?" Hector said. "I can teach him more. Look, Daniel, at the condors. See them? Do you know what they are looking for?"

"Dead things," I said.

"Do not evade information," said Hector. "The condors are searching for Inca gold."

"Yes, Hector!" said Consuelo. "Show Daniel the Inca gold!"

Hector shook his head at Consuelo, but he said to me, "When the Spaniards conquered the sierra in this country, they found no gold because the Incas hid all of it in the jungle. When the Spanish missionaries came down into the jungle, they kept tor-

turing the Indians to tell them where the gold was. The Indians
became Catholics—that was no big deal—but they would never
tell where the gold was. Finally the Indians rebelled. In Ybaeza,
which was right up there in the hills, the Indians poured molten
gold down into the throats of the priests. All that they could
swallow.

"Only the condors saw the crimes. And some condors live
forever. So only the condors still know where the bones of the
priests are buried. Besides, condors can smell the rot. And
inside the priests' bones, like birds in a cage, there are still the
ingots of gold in the shapes of priests' bellies. Consider it."
Hector patted his stomach. "Big missionary bellies, like Lester
McGuinness."

"So," I said, "you can follow the condors and find the gold."

"It is not that easy," Hector said, "but I have ways."

"Show him!" said Consuelo.

Hector raised his eyebrows and squinted at me. "Do you
want to see?" he asked.

I didn't believe him, but I said, "Sure."

"Sure he does," Consuelo said.

"Good. How much money do you have?" he asked me.

"I won't pay you anything," I told him.

"You'll pay when we get there," Hector said.

"Where is it?" I asked.

Hector nodded toward the spiraling condors and stuck out
his lower lip in their direction. "That way. Follow the condors."

"O.K.," I said.

"O.K. O.K. But first, we drink beer."

So I went with Hector to look for Inca gold. I did not think
we would find any, but I thought I would see something interesting. After I bought a liter of beer, we got my machete and
followed the ridge trail past Hector's hidden observation post
and on up the mountain into the first layer of clouds. The air
became dense. As we left the tall trees, the ground vegetation

grew thick. Hector took my machete, but he did a poor job of clearing the trail. He was a head shorter than I, and several times I pushed through branches into showers of biting ants.

A mile up the ridge, we came to a narrow flow of lava, which had cooled into a river of blocks the size of human heads.

Hector pointed to a place where the lava blocks formed a sort of natural stairway. "Inca stairs," he told me.

"Clearly," I said.

"Did you bring your money?" he asked.

"No."

He nodded, and slid my machete into its scabbard. "This way," he said, and we climbed the lava flow.

When we reached a level bench another quarter mile up the flow, Hector stopped. "This feels like the right place," he told me. "Wait here."

He went into the jungle and I sat down to wait. I began to think about leaving. I could see out over a pattern of small white clouds that floated above the jungle. Each cloud had its shadow directly below it. The balsa trees were all in flower. Several *lisan* trees had lost their leaves and they were now in flames of red blossoms. At the junction of the Norona and the little river, I could see no houses, only a few canoes beached on the sandbar at the confluence. The Norona was low. Below the confluence, it braided out across a wide muddy wash and flowed toward the faded horizon.

Hector spent several minutes in the jungle. From time to time, I saw him come back to where he had first left the lava flow and begin again, pacing off into the vegetation.

Finally he returned to me, carrying a strange contraption made of two tree limbs crossed and bound tightly together. At their junction was tied a tiny humanlike skull.

"Look," he said. "I found it."

"What is that?" I asked.

"This is a locator," Hector said.

"No. I mean that." I pointed to the skull.

Hector laughed. "You don't know?"

"Of course I know. It's a head."

"Very good. But precisely, it's a skull," he said. "A cranium. Of a priest, I believe. Or maybe an Inca."

"It's too small."

Hector pushed out his lower lip. "Too small for a priest?"

"It's a baby's skull. Or a monkey. Where did you get it?"

He waved vaguely toward the jungle. "In a special place, very difficult to locate."

"Where?"

"Over there. Why? What do you think? I killed a baby?"

I did not answer.

"I found it by Santiago's old bus. Bones pop up all over around his bus."

"So, what do you do with it?"

"I use it to find other bones. You will see. Bones attract bones. Like money, you know. Did you bring the money?" He pointed the device at my pants pockets. "*Plata!* Silver! Silver! Silver!"

"I did not bring money. Why should I?"

"To pay me for finding the Inca gold. A little before. A little after."

"I'll pay you in gold," I told him. "When we find it."

Hector looked away from me. He put his hand on my machete. "It does not work that way," he said. "You pay me now and I will show you something that will make you pee in your pants."

"No, Hector."

He looked back at me, blinking. "Look. I did not bring you all the way up here for a stupid nothing. You have the money, right?" He looked at my pockets. "You owe me money."

"Let's find the gold," I said.

He squinted at me. "O.K.," he said. "But it will be harder and you will pay more."

We left the lava and followed the bench around into the jungle. The bench became a hanging basin out of which the stream of Angelina's butterflies flowed down into the canyon.

Hector stopped in a small clearing near the basin's outlet. He extended two ends of his crossed sticks contraption toward me and told me to hold on: the skull would lead us to the Inca bones. The jawless, toothless miniature skull stared straight at me. Its eye sockets were huge and empty.

"And do not speak," Hector told me.

We stood facing each other across Hector's gruesome divining device. Hector kept his eyes on the skull. Soon he began nodding, and I felt a sideways pressure on the device. Hector kept nodding and took a step to his left.

"Do you feel it?" he whispered. "We must follow."

I let Hector lead me. At first, we slowly moved around the clearing, back and forth, sideways like a crab. It was like a Ouija. At times, it did feel as if it were the contraption itself, not Hector, that guided us back and forth, but I wondered how long Hector could keep up the act.

Then I felt a stronger pressure come through the device and we stumbled out of the clearing into a grove of trees so dark there was little undergrowth. Hector was smiling now, nodding and nodding. "This way," he whispered, and we moved slowly away from the clearing.

Hector was breathing harder. He was very excited. He kept glancing up at me and then quickly back down at the skull. "Do you feel it? This way. This way! Do you feel it? No! Do not speak! You are going to scream when you see it."

We were going deeper into the jungle. It got darker. The dead rot of the jungle floor got wetter and I began to smell a deep, foul odor. Hector was shaking and grinning.

"You'll see," he said. "You'll see."

Then I remembered that Hector still had my machete and suddenly I chilled. I resisted the sideways pull of Hector's cross. We staggered to a stop.

"What's this?" said Hector. He looked up at me, but I looked down at the skull between us.

Hector tried to get us moving again in the direction we had been going, but I held firm. The crossed tree limbs between us bowed up and down and wobbled.

"No. This is strange!" Hector said. "What is happening?"

I did not answer. Hector tried to get us moving again, but I would not let him. His divining cross danced between us now and both Hector and I were shaking. Sweat poured into my eyebrows.

"It pulls this way," I said.

"It can't!" Hector mumbled. "What is happening?"

He tried to jerk the device to the side again, but I was stronger. I began to force him back toward the clearing. We took a few tottering steps.

Then the device broke apart and we both fell to our knees.

"Oh, my mother," he muttered.

"What is it, Hector?" I asked.

He stared at the ground between us. "My God. It must be right here," he said. "The Inca gold!"

"No, it isn't, Hector."

"Yes! It has to be. Oh, my suffering Mother of God."

I watched him. He was mystified. He reached down and patted the wet earth around the skull. "Good Jesus!" he said.

"O.K., Hector," I said. "So, what do we do? Dig it up?"

"No," he said. "We can't do that. There is certainly a curse. We would die. Yes. We would surely die."

"Then why did we come here?"

Hector looked up at me, shivering with wonder. "I wanted to show you something that would stop your heart. But here we are! What a place this is. We will be luckier now because we know. And if we ever really need it, we can come back here and get it, the gold, you know. You and I will know."

"So, what do we do now, Hector?"

"Clearly, we celebrate," he said.

"First, you give me back my machete."

All the way down the mountain, Hector was wonderstruck and silent. And we did not celebrate our discovery of the Inca gold. Hector was so shook up that when we reached the village, he just walked away from me.

That night there was no electricity again. Each house burned its one candle and the people went to bed. In the quiet, I took a walk by the riverbank down behind the navy shack, where the cutbank was about ten feet high. I stood on the edge and watched across the big river, darker now than the night. That time of the year was mating season for a species of fireflies that would all flash their lights at once. No stars were shining, but across the black river, a long string of lights blinked on and off.

Then I heard Consuelo's voice below me.

"Oh! What a story, Hector," she was saying.

"That little skull turned around in the air and looked straight at me," I heard Hector tell her. "It hit the ground and rolled over. But it rolled upright. Looking straight at me!"

"What a story, Hector."

"If you ask me, it is up there now, looking down here."

"Ah! And what did Danielito do when the skull jumped off?"

"Nothing! He is ignorance. He did not know what was happening, I am sure. That little head bone up there knew where the Inca gold was. It knew. And now I know too."

"And Daniel too."

"He couldn't find his way back if he had a Yankee radar ticket."

"No, of course not. He was too frightened."

Hector laughed. "No. He is just ignorant. He wanted to dig up the Inca gold."

"But what danger!"

"Hah! I should have let Daniel dig it up. Let him take off the curse."

"No. Not Danito. He is too handsome. Besides, Inca gold will always be cursed."

"It does not seem to hurt the museum of the Central Bank."

"The bank is not a person, Hector."

"No. Nor Daniel either, really. He is a gringo. Perhaps gringos cannot be cursed."

"They are too handsome," said Consuelo.

"They are just devils."

"You are the devil, Hectorito," said Consuelo.

"Yes, I am," said Hector. "And I'm good at it."

They did not speak for a while, although they made some noise, moving around. I sat on my heels and waited.

"There," Consuelo said finally. "I hope you feel better."

"A little."

"Now you can tell me, Hector, about the other baby."

"You will wish I had not."

"Perhaps. But tell me."

"I will give you nightmares."

"Give them to me."

"Very well, Consuelo, I will tell you. Last month, the Indians called me to their village to cure a sick baby. An old *curandero*, a healer, was there, but these Indians would not let him treat her. The missionaries have taught them they need white man's medicine, so they send for me, their white man Indian, to come do the magic. When I got there, they wanted pills. *Aspirinas*, they kept saying. They wanted aspirin, Consuelo, headache pills.

"This baby was a newborn. Ten days old. She was a pitiful vision. She lay in her little hammock, but she was not at rest. She was dying from the stiffness. Her back bent back like a bridge, over. Over! It arched over double, her little heels hard against the back of her head. She arched back in a circle, as stiff as a ring. Her little belly button had popped open, Consuelo. It was bloody and wet. Her little face grinned open like death. She grinned like a little opossum baby."

"No, Hector. Don't tell me."

"Do not stuff up your ears. I will tell you, Consuelo."

"What did you do, Hector? To save her?"

"I told them they were ignorance. Ignorance. We are ignorance, Consuelo. We don't know shit."

"Yes, Hector. We don't know shit. But what did we do to save her?"

"I told them they did not know shit. I told them to let the healer do his work."

Consuelo was pleading now. "What did he do, Hector? Oh, please, stop this little one's suffering!"

"The *curandero* took a blowgun dart and dipped it into curare. He dipped the dart into the monkey poison and he stuck it into the baby's belly."

"And what happened, Hector? Oh no! I know. She became a monkey baby?"

"No, my dear Consuelo. The curare made her go limp. She relaxed."

"Ah! At last."

"At last. The old *curandero* and I breathed into her all night and we pumped her little chest to beat her heart."

"Oh, thank you, Hector. A thousand times, thank you."

"But the little one was dead."

"Oh! Oh, but of course. Of course. How could she live?"

"The curare had killed her."

"Of course it had. I know it. But softly, Hector."

"But softly," Hector said. "She was a very wise little dead angel then, and beautiful."

"So beautiful," said Consuelo.

"But her parents were afraid of her. They would not touch her. I had to bury her by Santiago's bus."

"Don't worry," Consuelo said. "I will pray for you."

"I never worry," Hector said.

"I know, Hector. You are so brave."

I stood up to leave. Hector had impressed me again. Then, as I turned to go, I heard Consuelo say, "Please, I want to put my clothes back on now. The sand fleas are eating me up."

"Put on your clothes," Hector said.

On my way back to the cantina, I almost fell into a hole. El Brinco was standing in it, up to his waist in the dark.

"Ah! Hello," El Brinco said. He was drunk. "Hello, as they say on the telephones."

I thought he might be waiting for his daughter.

"Just out for a walk?" El Brinco asked me.

"I am," I said. "What brings you out tonight?"

"I am burying beer." He shuffled his one foot and I heard bottles clanking. "You can never bury enough beer."

7

———

When anything happened in Los Puentes Caidos, it usually happened at morning or evening. At dawn, the whole village hurried through its few chores. It dressed and spanked its children off to school. It spread out its coffee and cocoa beans to dry in the sun, and then it spent the whole day inside its houses, watching out its windows, or in the shade of the trees near the little river, drinking Inca cola.

At dusk, it gathered at the cooling beach to bathe and flirt and to do its laundry. The women swung the wet clothing through the air, flailing silver arcs of water. I loved to watch them. They slapped the smooth and round boulders. They folded the washed clothes underwater before wrapping them up in their shawls to take them home. Out in the river, teenaged lovers kicked the children off the big rock and nuzzled each other as we watched from the beach. They looked like marine mammals, like seals or sea lions, the boys diving and throwing each other from the rock, the girls sitting together, waiting for their males to rise from the river and shake the clean water from their hair.

During the day in Los Puentes Caidos, gringo tourists provided the action. Because most of them slept late, they missed the big hours of the day, between five-thirty and eight in the morning. They emerged from their rooms at the Pension Norona and found that the village had gone back to sleep. They ate their breakfasts of coffee, fruit juice, soft-boiled eggs, and bread with lard margarine and jam. Then they went down to the beach and photographed the canoes, the monkeys, the parrots, each other, and they swam in the little river.

The tourists came from all walks of life. The wealthy ones came in on American Express Mercedes tour buses and were taken by Hector to see naked Indians. The other tourists included Danish social workers, French engineers, and a Dutch rock and roll band that specialized in imitating Jim Morrison and The Doors.

After dark, everything depended upon whether there was electricity. Santiago told me that for a time candles had been subsidized by the government. He said that had led to long guitar evenings of cigarettes around tabletops and to a renaissance of discussion and democracy. And that had led to the rash of rebellions and rural movements and to the rumor of an army tank rumbling over the divide. Candles now cost what the market would bear. Everyone sold them, but few could afford more than one candle a night.

Electricity was different. It was new and for a year it would be free. Its light was harsh and bright. It made one squint, Santiago told me, and made one think squinty thoughts, about money or women. It made one spend or want more money, and it made women seem hard and real.

That thought suddenly opened up a whole new line of inquiry for Santiago. What was the idea of women? What did women have in common with electricity? Or were they more like a flame?

Was it the magnetism or the heat that attracted men to women?

He went on, asking questions that I was supposed to try to answer. I finally told him I had read that sexual reproduction was a genetic illness caused by an insidious venereal virus, and that we males were merely the infectious agents of the disease.

"Does that make us contagious?" Santiago asked.

Another time, it was Hector who told me that electric light was no aphrodisiac, and that it did not help his poetry. He said electricity's music came out of a radio, usually from Colombia, and caused drunk people to dance the salsa. El Brinco's gas lanterns were not much better.

I pointed out that Santiago's thinking club seemed to persevere under electric lights, but Hector said that just proved his point.

"Just listen to them," he said. "Imagine it's a radio. You are listening to all the stations at once."

Hector once told me, "My mother was fooled by a radio. That was when the evangelist missionaries were parachuting little plastic radios shaped like crosses into the jungle. There were no switches or dials, just the cross and a speaker, tuned to the missionaries' radio station. The little crosses spoke in our Auruna language and told the people to come out of the jungle to get their reward. Imagine, Daniel, what you would do if you picked up a talking cross. You would argue with it. You would correct its pronunciation. But finally you would listen. So of course, my mother took me to get our rewards. She got killed by the white people's common cold and I got Lester McGuinness."

After three or four weeks in the village, most of the villagers still saw me as a tourist. One of the small boys tried to sell me a beetle necklace every day for the first three weeks. Angelina asked me again when I was leaving, but mainly she neglected me, unless I went straight up to her and said, "Excuse me, Angelina." Then she would stop and listen intently. And then

she would look disappointed and answer the question. I wanted
to hire her to take me on a tour, but I feared that money would
ruin me in her eyes forever.

One morning after a nightlong thunderstorm, I woke and
looked out my window. I had a view across the hibiscus trees
to the sand spit between the Norona and the little river. That
morning I saw the entire village down on the strand. The people
were standing in groups, motionless, all facing up the little river.
Couples were embracing, and several fathers had their children
on their shoulders. I pulled on my shorts and hurried down to
the shore to see what they were looking at.

To my amazement, I saw a volcano rise above us, above the
black jungle around us. The volcano was gigantic and it was in
full eruption. I had never known it was there. I stood with the
villagers, gazing up at its gleaming white, spewing cone. The
volcano was perfect. Its slopes rose at perfect forty-five-degree
angles. Its caldera opened toward us—we could see over the
rim—and the plume of white smoke rose from the caldera. The
skies around it, hard against the snow, were violet, like outer
space.

Santiago came up to me. He was almost overcome, his eyes
wide and blinking. "I've only seen Guaguaruca erupt once in
the last twenty years," he said, "and then it was at night, like
an exploding star. It is like seeing God, or the truth, perhaps.
And in broad daylight now, and not knowing what to think."

Angelina joined us. She wore a nightshirt and thongs. She
had waded out into the little river to get a better view of the
volcano, and her legs were wet and she held up the hem of her
shirt in one hand. Her shirt was unbuttoned at the top. I wanted
to see the mark on her chest, but I could not look directly
at her.

"Beautiful," I said to Santiago.

"My father lives up there somewhere," he said. "God grant
that he is all right."

"Angelina," I said.

She flashed her eyes, but she did not smile.

"Yes?"

"That was extraordinary," I said.

Her wide eyes were as green as the gold in the river.

"Yes?" she said.

"Perfect," I said.

Then she looked disappointed.

Santiago and Angelina left me and walked up toward the village. I looked back upriver for the volcano. It was gone, but on the first ridge, near Hector's Inca gold, a patch of palms showed through an opening in the mist. It looked like an island floating in the sky.

For two whole weeks after that, I was the only gringo in Los Puentes Caidos. When I asked Santiago where all the other tourists were, he said, "Who knows? These things happen. Perhaps there is a festival in the capital, or a revolution, or a new movie. Or the *transportes* company went broke. Let me tell you something. Once, after the evangelists all went away, no tourists nor anyone else came to Los Puentes Caidos for almost three months. No one came, and we got hungry. Finally we sent out a search party to find the rest of the world! It turned out that the National Commission on Progress through Highways had closed off our road by mistake. We were erased—pffft!—by bureaucratic error because the Military Mapping Institute was twenty years behind in their maps."

Santiago took out a piece of newspaper and blew his broken nose. The newsprint left smudges on his upper lip. "Now you are making me remember all sorts of things. For example, once, the whole village decided to go on a vacation at the same time. The more people who said they were leaving the fewer people who said they would stay. We had to hire someone from downriver to watch over the village. So you see, a few invisible tourists do not make a winter. Do not worry. If the beer for the army garrison does not show up, Lieutenant Hugo will make his inquiries."

I had come to rely on the tourists for reminders that the world I had come from was as strange as the one I was in. Now I took long walks in the jungle and got to know the natural place. I watched water ouzels pop out of the river and fly away. I watched thin green vipers swim across pools. Once, I thought I saw a creature the size of a sea serpent coiling across the river. It turned out to be two giant otters, each over six feet long; they were chasing each other, swimming and diving. Another time, I watched the little river rise four feet in fifteen minutes. The big rock in the middle disappeared. When it reappeared the next day, someone's house was wrapped around it.

One day, the tinny bray of a loudspeaker broke the noon silence. I stepped out of the cantina to see a little Isuzu pickup charge into town and stop in the center of the soccer field. This pickup was a beauty. Its cab, fenders, and hood were painted up red and gold, with flames, flowers, and a three-eyed lion smoking a cigar. Its metal bed had been replaced by a massive box made from varnished jungle hardwood. And the legend, "*Compro café, cacao, y maíz*"—I buy coffee, cocoa, and corn —was painted on its side.

A tricorn loudspeaker blared from the top of the cab. "Distinguished public! Remote people! Attention! Attention! The first event ever in this part of the world! A movie! From Hollywood! With stars of the cinema! A colossal film brought to you by BetaCine and on our television set! Tonight! Tonight!"

The driver's door opened and two Valalto Indians slid out of the truck. They wore dapper homburgs, reversible wool ponchos of blue and gray, white pajamas, and blue slippers. Their shining black hair hung down their backs in long braids. Both wore Ray-Ban sunglasses and several black digital wristwatches.

The men crossed their arms as their loudspeaker shouted out to the village. Their tape-recorded message filled the village all afternoon. "Citizens of the ends of the earth! Your civilization arrives!"

The Valaltenos struck a deal with El Brinco. They would use the cantina and he would sell beer. The show would begin right after dark. They rearranged the cantina into a theater with seating on the floor, benches, and tables. They set up their VCR and TV near the kitchen door.

The villagers hurried through the afternoon bathing and appeared at the cantina dressed in their best. Santiago and a few others wore suits without ties. Napoleon Elefante wore an apricot leisure suit he had been given by a tourist. But most men wore new sleeveless white undershirts. They rolled up the undershirts to just below their armpits, and they stood patting their bare stomachs and smoking. The women wore black skirts with white blouses or colorful T-shirts that advertised shoes, whiskeys, or American football teams. Hector showed up early, in a double-breasted, wide-lapeled black suit, a yellow shirt, and a green handkerchief ascot. He had greased his hair back with Brillantina. He bummed cigarettes off the men in the undershirts.

Consuelo borrowed my upstairs room to get herself ready. When almost everyone had arrived, she started down the ladder and she stunned us all. All of us men stood up when we saw her, and the sight of her made two teenaged boys start fighting. The parakeets screamed. A baby began to cry. Consuelo descended the ladder in a bridesmaid's dress with full petticoats and a banner that read, *"Señorita Deportiva del Amazonas"*; Miss Sport of the Amazon. Her full lips glowed a bright tropical red. Her eyes slanted Oriental under all their makeup and they flashed, dark and bright. Her eyelashes had grown out half an inch and floated lazily as her eyes opened and closed, one slightly slower than the other. Her petticoats were a dazzling white and her red stocking feet arched as they searched for each rung on the ladder. Before she reached the floor, two little boys dived under her skirts. Unflustered, she beat them on the head with her high-heeled shoes. We all applauded.

Four girls came up to Consuelo and took her hands and kissed them. The girls were dressed as nurses, in white skirts and caps with red crosses. Her father, El Brinco, blew her a kiss across the room. I did too. I hoped she would sit with us.

Apparently, everyone else knew better. The crowd parted, opening an aisle for Consuelo, and at the end of that aisle stood Hector Tanbueno, short and solid in his double-breasted suit.

Hector slapped a schoolboy on the back of the head, and Hector and Consuelo sat down together in the center of the front bench, three feet from the television set.

Now everything was set. The people were ready. The Valaltenos were ready, but it wasn't dark enough yet "for the full effect," as the older one said. "Remember, this is television."

The four girls dressed as nurses began selling beer. They took the people's money in tin cans with paper labels that read, "Help us! Emergency. Earthquake." They did not give change.

"This is all for charity," El Brinco told me.

As we waited for it to get dark, the older Valalteno spoke to us in a smooth Castilian Spanish. *Damas y caballeros*. Distinguished public. Welcome to Los Puentes Caidos, the Garden of Eden in the jungle of hell, the daggerpoint of civilization in the heart of this, this most American wilderness. I bid you health and good welcome."

He flashed a certificate from his wallet. He took a cigarette out of a silver case and lit it. He presented his video equipment. "This," he said, "is a Panasonic television set, the best television set in the world. It is made by the Japanese of Japan. And this is a Sony Betamax, the best Betamax in the world. It is made in Japan by the Japanese." He held up a videocassette. "This is a Hollywood movie. The best movie in the world. It is made in Hollywood by the North Americans, the best—"

Hector interrupted him. "Have you seen *E.T. the Extra-Terrestrial?*"

The Valalteno looked at Hector for a moment.

"*E.T.* was the best movie in the world," Hector said.

"Sir, I was speaking categorically."

"*E.T.* was the best. Categorically," said Hector.

"Very well," said the Valalteno. "I am certain you are correct. But then, as now, I was speaking in generalities."

Now Santiago spoke up. "Very good! Please do, good sir. Please speak in generalities."

The Valalteno wrapped himself in his poncho and glanced at his companion. El Brinco leaned over to me and whispered, "This! This is going to ruin business."

The Valalteno looked as if he thought Santiago was an idiot. He said, "If it pleases you, sir, I will speak more generally. Generally speaking, those movies that are made in Hollywood are on the whole better than those not made in Hollywood."

"Accepted," said Santiago. "Now, what does that say about the movies, as an art, or as an idea, in general?"

The Valalteno hedged. "The brightest stars are found not in heaven but in Hollywood."

At this, the audience aahed.

Now Hector spoke. "Movies are the poetry of the people," he said.

"Oh, my God," whispered El Brinco.

"Let us examine," said Santiago.

"Show the movie!" cried a small boy, but his mother hit him.

"With God's help, my son," the Valalteno said.

Hector left his seat and joined the Valalteno in front of the television set.

"Movies are the picture poetry of the people," he said to the rest of us. He made his eyebrows go together over the bridge of his nose and he raised both hands to continue.

Then Hector's mouth fell open.

From right next to El Brinco and me, out of the gathering darkness, Hugo and Angelina stepped into the cantina together.

Hugo wore his dress white uniform and carried his sword. This was not unusual for him. But Angelina dazzled. She wore a tight, sleeveless, shimmering dress. It was blue green and shimmering, something you would see at a cocktail party in San Francisco or New York. Her hair was pulled back and tied by a bow, she wore high-heeled shoes, and her face was made up perfectly, right out of an ad in a *Vogue* magazine. Her eyelids were shadowed with a faint shining green that made her green eyes luminous. She wore a necklace of iridescent green beetle shells. On one arm, she wore a long white glove. She rested it in the crook of Hugo's arm.

Again, we all stood.

Hugo guided Angelina into the middle of the cantina. A slit on the right side of Angelina's dress revealed her smooth brown leg. They seated themselves on the bench next to Consuelo, where Hector had been sitting before. Consuelo moved over as they sat down. Then she got up and moved around Angelina so she could sit at the other arm of Hugo. Hugo rested his sword across his knees. He looked like a prince in uniform.

He was suddenly a hero. Some boys started chanting, "Hugo! Hugo!" Even El Brinco said, "Ah! God! *Qué lindo!*" But Hector and I watched Angelina. And we were staggered. It was Angelina who made the sun go down, right then, and the world get dark.

Hector forgot all about Consuelo. He came over and stood next to me, and together we stared at Angelina. "Shit!" Hector said in English. "Shit!"

Someone ran across to the generator near the navy shack and fired it up. The Valalteno turned on his VCR and TV. First, we saw a scene with the Mexican actor Cantinflas dressed up like a nun. He was in a compromising position with a pretty young actress who was supposed to be a real nun. Then there was static and a quick flash of cowboys riding horses.

"John Wayne!" Santiago called out.

"Not yet!" said the Valalteno.

Then another scene came up. This one was of palm trees and jungle.

"My God! Look. It's here! It's Los Puentes Caidos!"

But the camera moved in on a bamboo and barbed-wire compound and we saw evil-looking Vietnamese soldiers standing guard. Then we saw an American prisoner of war languishing in a Vietnamese camp.

I had seen the movie. It was one of the *Rambo*s.

"It's Peru!" someone said.

"No," I said. "It's Vietnam."

People turned around in their seats.

"These are North American soldiers," I said, "who are prisoners left there after the war."

"Then tell us the story!" they said.

I translated for them. There wasn't much dialogue.

"Rambo is in prison," I told the villagers, "but the North American military needs him for a secret mission. To go back to Vietnam and get proof that U.S. soldiers are still held prisoner."

I told them that Rambo had only one question for the military: "Are we allowed to win this time?"

The villagers liked that. They were soon spellbound and I stopped translating. They watched Rambo get outfitted for his mission: the knives, the arrows, the camouflage clothing and face paint. They watched Rambo bail out over the Vietnamese jungle but get hung up somehow and be towed behind the plane.

"Why is he doing that?" Napoleon asked.

"Because he is macho," someone else said.

We watched Rambo find the beautiful woman partisan, find the POW camp, free an American GI, fight his way to the pickup point, and then get betrayed by his own people.

"*Qué barbaridad!*" said El Brinco. "The damned officers! Always the officers."

"Brinco's right!" Hector hissed to me, and he left the cantina.

Rambo got caught by the Russians. He was tortured. He was strong. He escaped. Then the beautiful partisan girl got killed. "That's not the way it was supposed to be," Rambo told her, but she was dead. Now Rambo was angry and the villagers around me were in a frenzy. Rambo started killing Russians by the dozens. Once, he lay in ambush by disguising himself as a muddy riverbank. He burst out of the mud and killed another Russian. The villagers screamed.

Rambo was on a rampage. The village that looked a lot like Los Puentes was destroyed, burned to the ground. The people around me cheered.

Suddenly, the electricity went out and the cantina was plunged into darkness. We were all left leaning forward. It was raining outside.

"What is it?" someone asked.

"The end!" Santiago said.

"No. It's the generator," said El Brinco.

"I'll go to inspect," said Hugo. We heard Hugo's bootheels march out of the cantina.

We sat in pitch-blackness for a good ten minutes.

"Well!" said Santiago. "Here. Take away the speaking pictures and we are left dumb."

No one spoke to disagree. They all stared at the blank TV and waited.

"It has made us apparitions," Santiago said, and no one challenged him.

Nothing seemed to be happening with the generator, so El Brinco got the gas lanterns going. He began to sell beer, and everyone stayed quiet and waited. I watched Angelina. She was staring down at something in her hands.

Then Hugo stumbled back into the cantina. His face and the front of his white naval uniform were covered with mud.

"Huguito!" Consuelo cried. "Oh! What happened? Did you fall down the riverbank?"

Hugo's eyes bulged white through the mud. He staggered stiffly past me into the cantina, his legs moving only at the knees. He held his arms close to his sides with his palms turned forward. The front of his uniform was almost black. A set of bare human footprints ran up his back.

"Ambush!" he whispered, staggering in a circle in front of the TV. "Ambush!"

"Dios!" a woman cried. She pulled her children about her. *"Los aurunas!"*

"No-o-o-o," Hugo whispered to her. He made his mouth round and open. His tongue lay red and flat in his mouth. "No-o-o," he whispered. "Peruvians!"

"Ay! Peruvians!"

People began to scream, but the electric lights snapped back on and everybody shut up.

"How do you know?" Napoleon asked Hugo in a whisper. "How, Peruvians?"

"They told me!"

Lieutenant Hugo Rios del Rio slumped to the floor. Consuelo ran to him. She cradled his head in her lap and wiped his face with her petticoats. "Brave, brave Hugo," Consuelo said.

Hugo rolled back his eyes and looked past Consuelo's arm to Angelina. "For you!" he said. "For you."

"Poor, poor Hugo," Consuelo said, and she hugged Hugo's head away from Angelina and pushed his face into her breast.

El Brinco tried to sell more beer. "Before the Peruvians get here."

Everyone looked at everyone else, and then we all looked at Angelina.

We could see in Angelina's face that she was in touch with something strange. She sat in her cocktail dress on the edge of her bench with her hands cupped and folded in front of her.

Her skirt was so tight around her legs she had to keep her knees together and her legs twisted to the side. It was like she was waiting for a cup of tea, but she looked at her hands as if they were alive. Her mouth was open. Her eyebrows arched high and her beautiful green eyes looked down at her cupped hands. Then she unfolded her fingers. There in the palm of her white-gloved hand was a shining blue butterfly.

"Oh! Ahhhhh!" everyone said. "Oh! Angelina!"

"What a miracle!" someone said. I noticed muddy footprints leading up to Angelina.

Then Hector stepped past me into the cantina. He was barefoot and nearly naked, stripped down to his wet underwear and plastered from head to foot in mud. He looked like an Indian Rambo. He held Hugo's sword in his hand. Its blade dripped black-red blood.

"Have no fear, anyone," he told the people. "Those Peruvians shall not return."

Everyone's eyes widened. Hector looked around the room. He then looked at Angelina and wiped the blood from the sword with his fingers.

"Have no fear," he said to Angelina. "Some butterflies live forever."

Santiago stood up and crossed his arms. "Hector," he said. "Have you just killed Hugo?"

Hector cocked his head back. "No, old man."

"Then what?" Santiago said. "Why is Hugo bloodied?"

Hector's eyes narrowed. He shook his head. "Lieutenant Hugo Rios del Rio has saved us."

Hector gazed at Santiago evilly, and he looked down at Hugo. "My congratulations, Lieutenant, you have mortally wounded the Peruvian pig."

Hugo sat up. He was unhurt.

"Oh, Hugo!" Consuelo said.

Now Angelina spoke. "Hector," she said. "Did you steal this from our house?" She held up the blue butterfly.

This time Hector nodded gravely and bowed to Angelina. "I will steal your heart!" he said.

Hector then pointed Hugo's sword at Santiago. "But beware," he said.

"Beware!" Hector said to me.

Hector walked over and handed down the sword to Hugo. He left a trail of muddy footprints on the floor.

Now the Valalteno held up his hands. He was as polite as an Englishman. "Gentlemen," he said softly. "If the war is over, should we show the movie?"

We all watched the rest of *Rambo* and the villagers loved it. The Valalteno backed up the tape and we watched the village burn again. Hugo lay on the floor, his head cradled in Consuelo's lap. Hector, stinking of mud and breathing hard, stood next to Angelina.

After the movie, Hector said to me, "Be careful, Rambo." Then he disappeared into the night.

Most of the villagers went home happy. Santiago was so disgusted that Angelina had to escort him home. El Brinco got drunk and passed out. Consuelo took Hugo down to the river with a big blue bar of laundry soap. She came back into the cantina and asked me for some of my clothes to dress him in.

"Go get his own clothes," I said.

"He needs a change," said Consuelo. "A real change."

I gave her a pair of Hawaiian-print shorts I was embarrassed to wear and the black Grateful Dead T-shirt with its picture of a grinning skull wearing a crown of roses. I went up to bed. From my room, I could hear Consuelo cooing and talking to Hugo for a long time. Later, I think she and Hugo made love.

I couldn't sleep, thinking that was what they were doing. The trees outside were sighing. The river breathed as if it were rising. I tried to think about other things. I had not heard Angelina laugh since the day I returned to Los Puentes Caidos. When she smiled, it thrilled me, but her smile always faded, even when she smiled for her father.

The next day the Valaltenos showed *Rambo* over and over until they got all the money they could from the village. I stayed down by the river, but I could hear the people chant, "Rambo! Hector! Hugo!" The whole village seemed different after that.

Hector and Hugo, strangely, spent more time together, although I'm sure it was Hector who ran barefoot up Hugo's back. And while we all suspected that it was Hector who had killed the pig with Hugo's sword, Hugo did not take the incident as an insult. Now they seemed to be working together: Hugo checking a tourist's passport, Hector checking the size of his wallet. Other times, Hector and Hugo seemed to circle each other like buzzards.

One evening, the navy shack burned. Someone screamed, "Fire!" and everyone ran to get buckets of water, only to go and stand guard in front of their own houses. I tried to help Hugo, but all we had to use were two plastic Clorox jugs with their tops cut off. The situation was hopeless, but with Hugo I knew I had to keep bringing water even when it began to rain.

The rain put out the fire, sparing the half of the shack that held Hugo's bed. His desk and the cage for detained suspects were destroyed. Hugo was beside himself with rage and confusion. He found his scorched sword and pistol in the ashes of his desk and he stormed around the village square shaking the weapons at the sky. Consuelo followed him, carrying a cup of water and a bottle of aspirin. She finally settled him down, and she took him up into my room. I slept on benches downstairs.

The next day Hugo arrested me on suspicion of arson.

"This is stupidity," I said.

"This is formality," said Hugo. "It is unfortunate you were there when a government facility was sabotaged."

"But it doesn't make sense."

"I have to do something. An officer reacts to every situation or he risks losing all respect."

Hugo's lockup was burned, so he handcuffed me to a table

in the cantina. "You are under an arrest of convenience," he said.

I slipped the handcuffs off the bottom of the table leg and went upstairs to sleep.

"You will wear the manacles symbolically," Hugo yelled up to me. "The investigation continues."

After *Rambo*, the young men in the village started wearing camouflage T-shirts sold to them by the Valaltenos. It upset Santiago that the village had been so easily seduced during its one-night stand with TV. I told him that I didn't think the Rambo influence would persist.

"It's not Rambo that worries me," he said. "It is the village's gullibility."

8

In a few days' time, my handcuffs won me an acceptance by the villagers I never would have earned had I simply stayed in the village, even for the rest of my life. The handcuffs gave me a logical occupation, that of prisoner, and a reason for not simply spending my money and leaving. The children who kept trying to sell me Chiclets now desisted. Now, as I stood on the riverbank, they would come up to stand beside me and slip their slim wrists through my free handcuff. Some would solemnly march around the village with me as if they were doing penance. Others thought it was funny to slip a hand into the cuff and hang from it as if unconscious. They loved being dragged by me across the village square.

I almost came to like the handcuffs. I found I could use them to open bottles of beer. The drinking club found this amusing; they made up sayings about the uses of bondage, and their discussions of freedom became humorous and speculative.

Some of them could not look at me while they discussed my situation. They spoke to me in the third person. "How is the prisoner today?" they asked. For a while they called me *el simbolito*, the symbol, and I got a good feeling of how totally abstract their notion of freedom was. One night, Santiago gave the Thinkery a beautiful twist on an old Greek myth. He asked whether the reason the man kept wrestling with the boulder, and never quit trying to roll it to the top of the mountain, was that the boulder was too beautiful for him to leave it alone.

"I have felt such stones," Blind Jorge said, "and I know what you are talking about. They are weighted inside with something significant. They have a heavy coolness about them that becomes an obsession. We must be careful to choose our obsessions wisely."

"Our obsessions should be women," said Jesus. "Women or nothing at all."

This discussion reduced the drinking club to drunkenness and tears. "Pure obsessions purify," Lieutenant Hugo sobbed. "I know this because I am pure." Hugo was wearing a T-shirt that said "Don't ask me. I just work here."

After the eruption of the volcano and the first-ever showing of a movie in the village, the mood of the villagers had been high. They expected good things: some sort of divine good luck from the volcano's blessing and economic progress now that civilization in the form of a Rambo movie had reached the little river's shores. But when nothing obvious happened, they began to suspect a trick. Three rumors came to town that week.

Old man Wilson picked up on Blind Jorge's radio a report that a massive earthquake was predicted for the capital at three that same afternoon.

"Who predicted the earthquake?" I asked.

"The Star Wars people at NASA, in the United States."

"Impossible," I said.

"That's what Hector says. That's what Lieutenant Hugo says.

But tell us, why then are all the schools closed in the capital, and why is everyone sitting outside in the capital city's parks?"

"Because they are ignorant."

"That's what Hector says. But tonight in the capital, the people will all camp outdoors. And so shall we."

And they did. They brought out their babies and blankets to the center of the soccer field and they set up a camp. They had a wonderful time. They danced and played volleyball, and the young lovers were able to promenade for a while and then sneak back up to their parents' empty houses. That evening the villagers lit cooking fires. Somebody butchered a pig and soon an aroma of roast pork filled the air. Some young American tourists joined the fiesta and sang folk songs, which pleased the villagers immensely.

Hector, Santiago, Hugo, and I stayed in the cantina, drinking beer and watching the festivities in the field.

"They are fools," Hector said. "I'll tell them when they can have an earthquake."

"They are having more fun than you are," I said.

Hector turned his big, slow eyes to me and shook his head. "I'll show them fun. I've got plans for these monkeys."

Santiago said, "I hope we don't have an earthquake tonight. It would mean years of enlightenment down the drain. Such setbacks to civilization have happened before."

"Don't worry," said Hugo. "I'll be in charge."

Hector belched and walked to the steps. He inhaled, filling his huge rib cage with the savory air. Then he laughed an enormous, evil, low-throated laugh and aimed it at the people in the square.

There was no earthquake that night. About midnight, it began to rain.

The second rumor came the next day, when some Swedish tourists brought in the news that President Reagan was dying. He had a cancer on his nose and it had spread to his brain.

"My God," said Consuelo, "he must look like those poor miscreants in the penny newspapers."

The Swedes had read the story in a capital city tabloid.

"You're sure of this?" I asked them.

They shrugged their shoulders and nodded. They had read it. Reagan had resigned and George Bush was now President.

That evening I ate dinner at Mama Cuchara's and pumped the tourists for information. They asked me what kind of president George Bush would be.

"Better," I said, but I had no idea.

Two days later, Wilson picked up another report on the radio. A four-engine airliner had left the capital and disappeared. On a clear blue afternoon, it had taken off to fly down the Valley of the Volcanoes and then had disappeared with fifty-four people on board. The next day, the radio supplied three new rumors. The first was that the plane had fallen into the caldera of a volcano and the people were all alive but trapped in a land that time had forgotten, a land complete with dinosaurs. The radio announcer interviewed a university professor about dinosaurs. Another rumor was that the plane had been caught in the ray of a UFO and the passengers were all alive but trapped on another planet. The announcer interviewed a psychic medium who had contacted the pilot. The third rumor was that the plane had been hijacked by Colombian drug runners and made to fly to Colombia. It was being used to fly cocaine into the United States and the passengers were all alive but being turned into slaves to labor on a marijuana plantation.

The villagers believed all three of these rumors.

"This same thing happened before," they said, "three years ago. And those fifty-four passengers are still gone too."

That precipitated a thinking club discussion on the consequence of numbers.

"Why did both planes have fifty-four passengers?"

"Maybe that is the number of seats," I said.

"And what is the significance of that number equaling the number of weeks in a year?"

"There are fifty-two weeks in a year," I said.

"So far," they acknowledged, "that has been the case, but that figure is arbitrary, is it not? And numbers are arbitrary and, thus, capricious. Just look at the lottery."

"The lottery is random," I said. "It has nothing to do with anything human. Arbitrary, capricious, or personal."

"Tell that to the fifty-two people on that airplane," they said. "Tell that to the devil on the day you die."

"People who die on Sunday," Jesus politely warned me, "do not always go to heaven."

The next day the radio announced that the United States Air Force had sent an aircraft to assist in the search for the missing airliner. The plane was equipped with sophisticated sensors which could detect the wreckage of the plane beneath the snow on a volcano summit or beneath the canopies of the jungle trees.

This was the report that really disturbed the villagers. "Is this so?" they asked me. "Can this plane see through the trees? With what? With secret rays?"

This time the villagers took refuge indoors, inside the few buildings with tin roofs, which they hoped would shield them from the rays. They kept Jorge's radio on a cardboard box just outside the cantina, and the cantina became the scene of a Drinking and Thinking Club marathon, a forty-eight-hour symposium which discussed and dismissed as hopeless although interesting almost every problem known to man. Santiago assured me he did not believe in any danger, but he said the situation had its good aspect, the gathering of so many fine minds for such an extended time.

Wilson had been hurt on his motorcycle, which Hector had mysteriously gotten back from the soldiers. Now Wilson wanted to sue the Army for damaging his motorcycle, which had led to his accident, which had led to his swollen ankle.

"You need a lawyer for that," Jesus told him. "And all the real lawyers are in the capital city."

"Fine. He'll go," Napoleon said. "Wilson will press for his rights."

"He will need proof he was hurt," Blind Jorge pointed out.

"I have my ankle," said Wilson, and he took off a black rubber boot and displayed his injury. His ankle was black and green.

"Such evidence is circumstantial. You need an affidavit from a certifiable physician. And for that you will need an autopsy."

"How much does that cost?" Wilson asked. "Can I get it free from the Peace Corps lady at Huasipungo Pass?"

"Autopsies are never free," Wilson was told. "Otherwise, they wouldn't stand up in court. The widow Palos has an autopsy for her dead husband, Pedro. It is framed on the wall of her house. It has more government stamps than a letter to Lima."

"Perhaps I could use her autopsy," Wilson said.

"Not a chance, dear Wilson. The widow does not know what an autopsy is. She thinks it is a letter of condolence and honor from the erstwhile President of the Republic, who is now under the government's convenience of a house arrest. She would never part with it."

I told them that autopsies were performed on dead people, to determine what had killed them. They looked at me as if I had missed the whole point of the discussion.

"Thank you for the clarification," they said politely.

Santiago interceded and guided the discussion toward philosophy. "If autopsies are performed on dead people, we must ask, Why?" he said. "And why aren't they more logically performed on living people, to determine what is keeping them alive?"

"It is hope," Jesus said. "They say that hope cannot be found with a surgeon's knife. A dead person has sometimes died through the process of releasing hope, albeit involuntarily. People have seen this hope releasing. It is colored blue."

"Why blue?" Blind Jorge asked.

On the second day of the death rays, Napoleon left the cantina to help Angelina provision her canoe. She drifted away on another scientific expedition, with a group of British scientists who looked at us as if we were fools.

"Santiago," said El Brinco, "your daughter is extraordinarily brave."

At this, Lieutenant Hugo stood up. "Gentlemen," he said. "The time for defense is past. The first barrage of killer rays is over. It is time now to leave our bunker and find our airliner ourselves. Our country for our countrymen. Our dead for likewise. Our duty for the love of our mothers. Now, who volunteers to join in the official search and rescue?"

Everyone looked straight at Hugo and no one said a word. Hugo took this as if he had expected it. He turned to me. "You. I want to believe I can trust you."

I jangled my handcuffs. "Go ahead," I said. "Trust me."

"It is accepted military procedure to allow prisoners to regain their honor on dangerous missions. We march at dawn."

They all looked at one another and then cheered and called for beer. El Brinco ran out of beer that night, and we left the next day in the late afternoon to an absolute absence of fanfare. Hugo's announcement and the big party afterwards somehow made the villagers forget all about the killer rays. By nine in the morning, everyone who had to get out of bed had done their few chores and had gone back to sleep.

Hugo insisted on wearing my Gore-Tex boots. I got him to take off my handcuffs first. He wore my six-pocket pants and my Grateful Dead T-shirt. He had found a jungle ranger's campaign hat whose brim snapped up on the right side. He whistled every time he adjusted the hat. He appropriated my wide nylon belt and stuck his burned navy revolver into the top of his pants. Hugo looked like an Arab terrorist on vacation. I looked like the most destitute of the North American homeless. I wore black rubber boots, gray sweatpants, and a Seattle Seahawks T-shirt. Hugo shouldered my oversized nylon backpack, empty except for a papaya and a sack of animal crackers, and I followed him as he marched out of town.

To my surprise, Hugo marched right up the trail Hector had used to get to his watcher's blind and to show me the buried Inca gold. We climbed the lava flow, turned off onto the bench, and plunged into the jungle.

"Wait a minute, Hugo," I said as we were about to pass the spot where Hector and I broke the divining rod.

Hugo stopped and turned. We had climbed without rest for two hours. His face was wet with sweat and gray with exhaustion.

"Slow down," I said. "Where are we going?"

"To find the airplane."

"We have to slow down," I said. "We have to slow down and look if we want to find it. We have to find a place where we can get a better view, a rocky outcrop or something."

"The airplane's in here," Hugo said, and he turned into the jungle.

One hundred yards farther, we came upon the wreckage.

"God damn. What's this?" I said.

"Manifestly," said Hugo, "it is a crashed aircraft."

I could swear I heard music, the effect was so weird and powerful. There under the high vaulting canopy of the jungle trees, where light stabbed down in opaque shafts and hanging lianas held whole islands of vegetation suspended like green chandeliers, a massive tail section from an airplane rose thirty feet into the air. The airplane had crashed at a steep angle, its tail lifted like the tail of a breaching whale. The hatch at the base of the tail had blown open on impact and the fuselage had become a pool, brimming with dark, still water. Thirty yards beyond the tail, the cockpit lay tipped on its side, like the severed head of a fish thrown out with the garbage.

"Damn it, Hugo," I said. "This plane crashed years ago."

"Two years ago," he said. "But obviously, this is where planes do come to crash." Hugo sat down on a section of wing.

The craft had been a military transport. It was olive drab, its markings disappearing beneath the engulfing vegetation. On the side of the tail, the markings of the Air Force of the Republic still could be seen: a bull's-eye target of red, yellow, and blue. All around, under mud and vegetation, parts and pieces of plane and cargo littered the jungle floor. I walked up to the cockpit. Crude crosses had been placed in the remains of the seats of the crew.

"This plane carried contraband," Hugo told me. "It was overloaded with Yankee refrigerators for the wives and girl-friends of generals in the capital. And a Chevrolet station wagon and two golfing carts. Hector says the Chevrolet is still inside the airplane, underwater. The pilot got lost in the clouds until he found this ridgetop. An Indian found the plane six months later. He told Hector, and Hector told me so I could find it officially. I assembled an Indian crew to secure the remains. We buried the crew over there, with military honors, and I sent a Polaroid to navy headquarters. One would think such an achievement might get me a ship. But the government did not want the airplane found because of embarrassment of the contraband. I was directed to lose it.

"So I lost the airplane and the government expunged my report. But they accidentally expunged all my service records. I didn't get paid for an entire year. This is the first time I have been back here since. It is the scene of my greatest accomplishment. And my greatest indignity."

I realized we were not going to search for the airplane that had just crashed. I sat down next to Hugo. "Let's go back to the village," I said.

Hugo gave me the only friendly smile I ever saw him smile. "Yes," he said. "Tomorrow."

"Tomorrow? Why tomorrow?"

"For the desired effect. To create my opportunity. We'll take a few pieces back. You'll see."

"Don't tell me you're going to tell people you found the plane?"

"We did find the plane. It doesn't matter which plane. Such tragedy. Such heroism. There were no survivors."

"It's a lie."

"It is not a lie. It is a recognition. There will be no report to headquarters this time, only my unofficial and gentlemanly query. Perhaps the government needs an airplane to be found this time? If they need one, I have one. I am politically astute. Regardless, the effect for you and me is the same. In the village, you'll be a hero and I'll be your leader."

"You'll get caught on this, Hugo. Someone will know."

"Only Hector knows, Daniel. And a few dumb Indians."

"Hector will expose you."

Hugo gave another smile, not friendly this time. "This was Hector's idea," he said. "But what Hector does not know, Daniel Cooper from the United States, is just how much he has helped me."

The daylight failed. I gathered what dry firewood I could find. We spent the night on a piece of wing underneath the tail's horizontal stabilizer. I was totally miserable. The humidity rose and put out my fire just before it began to rain. When the rain stopped, the mosquitoes came out.

"This is stupid and horrible," I said to Hugo.

"This is exquisite suffering," said Hugo. "This is like my whole life compressed in an evening. You are honored to share it, Daniel the gringo. And tomorrow, armed with my distinction, I will conclude the greatest stratagem of my life. Tomorrow I claim Angelina."

I took the papaya and animal crackers out of my pack and handed them to Hugo. I lay down on the wing and stuck my head into my backpack to try to escape the mosquitoes.

"Go to sleep, Daniel Cooper. Disappear. Pass away. Allow me to savor my fate. My fate, *my fate*, is to marry Angelina, and to be happy."

In the morning, I awoke with one eyelid so stung by mosquitoes that it had swollen shut. My upper lip was swollen too, and the mosquitoes had ravaged my neck behind my right ear. Ants had found the crackers and fruit and then they had swarmed all over my body. I had to take off my clothes and shake them.

Hugo lay curled beside me on the airplane wing, his head resting on my Gore-Tex boots. His face was so gray that he looked dead. He awoke disoriented and I had to tell him where we were. I explained what the airplane was and why we were there.

Hugo shook his head and reached down to feel his left ankle. "Look!" he said.

Between his ankle and Achilles tendon were two black marks and the scabby traces of dried blood.

"What? A viper?" I asked.

"No-o-o-o," Hugo whispered. "No. A vampire!"

"Vampire? A bat?"

"The same," said Hugo. "Oh-oh-hhhhh . . ."

"This is serious."

"This is."

"You could get sick."

Hugo nodded. "I could lose my leg like the gimpy Brinco. I could lose my life, or at least come close. On the other hand, in service to my country, I am wounded, and gravely. How grand."

"How stupid, Hugo. Let's get out of here."

"Yes. We can go now."

Hugo carried back evidence that we had found the airliner. He limped into the village, dragging a steering yoke, and I followed him at a distance. That evening, in his dress whites, with his ankle bandaged in linens, Hugo presented his story to the thinking club. He had told Santiago to bring Angelina.

The thinking club members accepted Hugo's account without question, but without much comment either. They listened as Hugo described the scene of the crash and the night in the jungle and they looked at his ankle when he pointed at his vampire bite. El Brinco said, "So what? You've done what a cow does every night, get bitten by a bat. At least you still have an ankle."

No one seemed to want to press Hugo for details and no one asked me for corroboration. Hector was there. He watched from the steps to my room.

When Hugo finished his presentation, he took a deep breath. He said, "Something else happened last night. Something beautiful. Something incredible. A once-in-a-lifetime event. At the very worst moment, when everything looked grim—when the night was darkest, the North American was moaning, and I was nearest despair—truth appeared to me in all its glory."

"In what form, Hugo?" Santiago asked. Santiago had his arms crossed in front of his chest.

"In the form of a vision, Santiago. As a revelation. I realized as I lay there with my life slipping, slipping away that I . . ." Hugo paused. "How do I say this? How do I put this into words?"

El Brinco interrupted. "Try a pantomime, Lieutenant."

"Speak, Hugo," Santiago said. "Get it out."

Hugo breathed deeply. He savored the moment. His eyes were glowing with satisfaction and conviction. "I realized, Don Santiago, that I was not dying. Rather, that I was afflicted . . . infested . . . beplagued . . . with love. For whom? For whom? For whom? For your daughter, Santiago. For Angelina. Your daughter. Your daughter, Angelina, Santiago. I . . . love . . . her."

The members of the drinking club shifted on their benches. Santiago hugged his chest tightly. He shook his head.

"I claim her, Don Santiago," Hugo continued. "I claim her with this, my declaration, and I honor her with this, my public adoration and my lifelong devotion and worship."

Angelina was watching me. Hugo stood before her, with one hand held gallantly behind his back. He followed her gaze over to me. "Ah, yes. The North American," Hugo said. "For his service we grant him his freedom and bid him adieu. Adieu!"

Hector clapped slowly from the stairway. Angelina shook her head.

Blind Jorge loudly cleared his throat, and everyone turned to him to hear him speak. He spat. "Angelina is the honor of the village," he said.

"Of course she is," said Hugo. "I honor that honor."

Now no one spoke.

"Of course," said Hugo, "our engagement will be honorable. Honorable duration. Honorable intentions. Honorable everything."

Hugo stood still a moment and then shuddered violently. Angelina kept watching me.

9

When the America Direct Wilderness Exploits tour bus arrived in Los Puentes Caidos, the influence of the Rambo movie had almost run its course. But the first person off the bus inspired the villagers to new heights of jungle fashion. He was William B. Bodean and he wore a camouflage sweatband, a pair of glazed glacier sunglasses, a USMC T-shirt, a belt made from a nylon cargo strap, camouflage jungle pants with one dozen pockets, and Vietnam-style boots of black leather and green nylon.

This was the only time in my stay in Los Puentes that I saw villagers try to buy something from a tourist. The young men and boys brought out moldy mounds of sucres and soles and shoved the money at Bodean. They pointed at his belt and plucked at his sunglasses.

Bodean took a Swiss Army knife from a secret pocket and threatened the boys. Then he laughed and showed them its

seventeen blades and tools. From a long pocket along his left
thigh, he produced a telescoping fishing rod. He extended the
rod and cast a bright spinner into the cantina. Next, he took
out a signal mirror and blasted his admirers' retinas. Then he
pulled the unlit cigar from his mouth and he spat.

"Cerveza, compadres!" he roared, and three youths ran into
the cantina and plundered El Brinco's propane refrigerator.

Bodean took a Pilsner Grande from the first boy to reach
him. He took some money from another boy and paid for the
beer. He spat again. "Che Cerveza and Ronald Reagan!" he
toasted, and he chugged down half the bottle.

Around him, the young men of the village were already
beginning to spit.

Bodean finished his first half liter and reached for another,
while behind him, the other tourists debarked from the big
Mercedes bus. These tourists were more like the usual. They
were healthy and tanned retired engineers with video cameras,
young married couples in matching Banana Republic outfits,
and a few middle-aged women schoolteachers on sabbatical. For
a sum of several thousand dollars, America Direct drove them
around South America in a Mercedes bus and let them pitch
their tents in the dirty squares of villages. The tour company
provided a driver and a tour guide to show them the local sights.

"They're a bunch of sissies," William Bodean told me later.
"Especially the women. I've got to cover them every minute."

That night it rained on the tents in the square. The next
morning Angelina took a few of the schoolteachers to hunt for
butterflies, and Hector took others to video naked Indians. Half
the tourists never left the village square. They brought out folding aluminum lawn chairs and sat in tight circles facing each
other until the bus departed for the mountains again.

The following morning, two tents remained in the square.
To the villagers' delight, one of the tents was the base camp of
William B. Bodean: an eight-by-ten freestanding dome tent with

a camouflage rain fly and a sign that read "Trespassers will be violated." When I came out of the cantina that morning, he and Lieutenant Hugo Rios were sitting in front of his tent on folding campstools, looking at Bodean's topographical maps.

The other tent was not really a tent. It looked like a body bag, lying alone in the square. It was a navy-blue bivvy sack just big enough for a mummy bag to slip inside it. Its occupant had not yet risen, and a yellow dog was sniffing it and growling.

The camper within was a twenty-three-year-old New Yorker who told me, "I'm not from anyplace, really. I am traveling." His name was Danny Greenfield. Danny reminded me a lot of myself when I had traveled in South America as a youth. He was open-eyed and miserable. The big difference between Danny and myself was that Danny knew why he was in Los Puentes Caidos. He was there to see Hector Tanbueno.

Danny Greenfield wanted an Indian *brujo* to take him on a hallucinogenic vision quest. "I took a lot of anthro courses at City College," Danny told me. "I wanted to be an anthropologist like Carlos Castaneda and study the other side of reality. Then I realized I was fooling myself. I didn't need to be an anthropologist. Anthropologists are like faking themselves out all the time. They surround themselves with explanations for things before they experience them. They prefabricate reality and they never really know. They can't know, you see, because they blind themselves with their objectivity. They think they know what they're looking for. And their objectivity tricks them."

"Don't do it," I said.

Danny Greenfield had curly black hair, and his glasses kept steaming up. He was a skinny kid and it looked as if he'd had a lot of diarrhea lately. Besides his sleeping bag and bivvy sack, he carried mostly books.

"Forget all this and eat only bananas and beer for a week," I told him. "Hang out on the beach and eat cheese from the capital. Go back to the capital and hang out in the cafés."

"Is Hector around here?" he asked.

Hector was sitting beside me.

"No," I said. "Hector left."

"Hey, dude!" Hector said to Danny. "Want to have a generally jungle experience?"

"Is this Hector?" Danny asked me.

"You want to see some totally naked Indians?" Hector asked.

Danny looked at me.

"I'm not going to have anything to do with it," I said.

Hector rubbed his hands together. "Let's get down," he said. "Let's party."

Hector had Danny Greenfield pay for the beer and tell him all about the hallucinogen ayahuasca and vision quests, about the Yaqui way of knowledge of Castaneda's Don Juan, and about several other realities.

"There are multiple universes," Danny told Hector.

"Multiple choices, Danny. We call them *bejuco bravo* down here, and they knock your head off." Hector then told Danny that Danny was stupid and too objective. He paraphrased everything Danny had just told him about *brujos* and anthropologists.

"Reality is like multiple choice," Hector said. "You take your pencil and you take your pick. Don't hesitate. Don't fake yourself out. Go for it. This will cost you money, big money, Danny boy, but afterwards, you will thank me."

"I need a return ticket back to the States," Danny said.

"On silver wings, dude," Hector said.

Hector took Danny Greenfield to the Indian village that afternoon. I went with them. I thought my presence might keep something bad from happening to Danny. The Indian village was a half mile up the little river, and it was not really a village but a collection of huts. I had walked by it before, but I had left the Indians alone. The sight of them made me sad.

Hector whistled loudly before we arrived, and I'm sure that was the signal for the Indians to take off their clothes. When we got there, five naked Indians stood in a row, ready to pose for pictures. The little girl held a toothbrush. The young boy held a Popeye doll. The woman wore only a rawhide thong around her waist. Her body was hairless. The younger man had combed and parted his hair in the Western style. The thong around his waist was tied to his foreskin and it held his penis erect. He too had no pubic hair, and his genitals looked like a dead featherless bird. He rocked his head as he watched us.

All three adults had their earlobes pierced and stretched. The young man's and the woman's earlobes hung nearly to their collarbones. The old man wore bright red disks in his earlobes. His teeth were black and filed to points. His body looked young but his eyes were old. He looked as if he'd seen us before.

The old man spoke to Hector.

"He wants to know where your cameras are," Hector said. "What will you pay them for if you don't take their pictures?"

"Tell him I want to experience ayahuasca," Danny said. "Tell him I hope I am worthy."

Hector said something to the old man. The woman giggled and the two children ran off to play. The young man smiled with an open mouth and I realized he was brain-damaged.

Danny held his hands out, palms up, ready for inspection. The old man crossed his arms and hooked his thumbs into his ribs in a way that reminded me of Ed Sullivan. He stuck out his lower lip and studied Danny Greenfield.

"Should I take off my clothes?" Danny asked Hector.

"Of course," Hector said, but when Danny began to pull off his pants, the old man looked so horrified that Hector told Danny to stop. "Later," Hector said. "You can take off your clothes later. Do you want to pay me now or later?"

"Now," Danny said. He pulled out his passport wallet. "Do you take traveler's checks?"

"American Express or VISA. I prefer American Express."

Danny gave Hector one hundred dollars. The old man turned

to me and said something. His language was high and chirping. Hector said, "He wants to know why you haven't come here before."

I apologized, but Hector did not translate. "Let's get this over with," he said to Danny. "Do you want your mind blown or what?"

I watched everything, but I saw nothing happen. It all took place in Danny's head. The woman used a Bic lighter to build a fire on the ground. The old man brought out a pouch made of woven fibers and from it he took some pieces of vine. He pounded the vine on a flat rock until he had a pasty powder. He scraped the powder into a basket made of green leaves, he added water, and then he had the woman hold the basket on a stick over the fire. The water began to simmer and the old man stirred the mixture with an old and dirty toucan feather. He muttered under his breath.

The preparation took more than an hour. The sky clouded over and turned dark. Danny watched the basket and didn't say a word. Hector went into a hut and brought out a dirty pillow to sit on. He smoked a cigarette and blew smoke rings at the fire and at Danny. He winked at me. The old man said something and Hector lit a cigarette for him and placed it between his lips. The old man chanted and coughed on the smoke. I got restless, but Danny was reverent. The fire reflected in his steamy glasses.

After a long while, the old man took the basket and set it beside the fire. He took a plastic cup and dipped it into the potion. He pursed his lips and breathed deeply and rapidly, hyperventilating. Then he held his breath and drank off the cup. He shuddered, and handed the cup to Danny.

Danny filled the cup and imitated the old man by breathing fast and hard. Then he drank and gagged. He regurgitated the liquid all over his T-shirt and legs.

"Oh, God!" Danny sputtered. "I'm sorry!"

"Try again," Hector said. "Try again. Help the Lord help

those." Hector was now lying on his back with his head on the pillow. He blew smoke rings into the air.

Danny dipped another cupful. He took a deep breath and forced down the liquid. I could see his throat working as he tried not to vomit.

"Have another cup," Hector said.

"But the *brujo* only had one."

"You need more, dude."

Danny looked at me. "Do you want to try some?"

"I'll have to give you your money back," Hector said. "You insult the *brujo*. Drink!"

Danny filled his cup and drank it down.

"Drink!"

Danny drank another cup. He shuddered and sputtered, but this time he said, "It isn't so bad."

"It is poison," I said. "That's how it works."

"Life is poison." Hector said, and sat up. "It makes me puke." He looked around as if he were bored. He fished out more cigarettes for himself and the old man.

"Hang on and get down, Danny," Hector said. "Hold on. Get ready for some big shit."

The old man muttered and began to shake.

"He dreams he is a jaguar," Hector told me. "He always dreams jaguars. I dream fucking. I always dream fucking. I wish I could dream fucking jaguars. Who knows what evil will bring tomorrow?"

Then Hector got up and walked away down the trail. Danny and the old man did not move for hours.

Sometime in the middle of the night, the old man growled. That was when Danny started screaming. I tried to comfort him. The old man growled and Danny kept screaming, for hours. I held Danny down to keep him from running away into the night.

When day came, Danny Greenfield was conscious but he had not recovered. "It was a dark tunnel," he said. "Like the

Lincoln Tunnel. And these roaring cars kept running me down."

"That was the old man," I said. "He was growling. He thought he was a Jaguar."

"The cars were horrible. Horrible."

"It was the old man."

"I was back in New York!"

"I'm sorry."

Danny was a stinking mess. We walked down the trail to Los Puentes Caidos and he got a fresh set of clothes from his pack. Someone had rifled his belongings.

William Bodean was watching us. He had set up a camouflage sunscreen over his tent. He sat there on a campstool, wearing camouflage pants and a sleeveless white T-shirt. "It was that short guy with the big chest," Bodean said. "He said you owed him some money. Don't worry, though. I stopped him. You know, I can show you how to booby-trap your gear real good. But, hey, what the hell happened to you?"

Danny looked at him, but he couldn't talk.

"He got into some *bejuco bravo*," I said. "Some bad vine. But he'll be all right."

"That was him screaming?" Bodean regarded Danny. "Your body is your mind," he said to Danny. "It *is* your mind. People think we think with our heads, when we don't. That is a major mistake of civilization. Don't never mess up your body.

"You'd better burn his clothes," Bodean told me.

Hector Tanbueno and several villagers were watching us from the cantina steps. They came up to us now. Mama Cuchara came over too, from her hotel. Several children came with her.

"You owe us money," Hector said to Danny. "You kept the whole world awake with your screaming. Now you owe the people for their sleep."

Santiago came out now from inside the cantina. El Brinco hopped out alongside him.

"Look, Hector," I said. "This man is tired and sick. Lay off him. Leave him alone."

"This man is leaving," I said, in Spanish, to the villagers. "He is going away. Let's be good people and let him go."

"He is a hippie," Hector said to the villagers. "He is a drug addict. Look at him. An addict."

"He is a student," I said. "An anthropologist. Let's let him go home."

"And who are you?" Hector said. "A gringo too. What is going on here? Three gringos at the same time. With chairs. This is not good. We know what gringos do to places."

"These people are tourists. There are always tourists here. They are harmless."

I saw Mama Cuchara bend down, pick up a rock, and hand it to a five-year-old boy.

"Don't try it!" William Bodean shouted at the boy, but the boy reared back and threw the rock wildly.

"Stop it!" I shouted, but another child threw a rock. This one hit Bodean's tent.

"Give us some money, quick," Hector said.

Now Santiago spoke. "People," he said. "What are we doing? Here these good people come to our village and spend their money. So what do we do? Throw rocks at them? That is not civilized."

"It is not civilized," said El Brinco. "And I'll murder the next boy who throws a rock."

Mama Cuchara stepped forward. "He is a hippie," she said, pointing at Danny Greenfield. "Look at him. Filthy! Filthy! He stinks up our village. Smell him!"

Danny could not understand the Spanish, but he understood he was in trouble. He stood closer behind me.

Now Hector stepped in front of Mama Cuchara. *"Bueno,"* he said. "This is a mess. Here is the situation. The hippie leaves. He leaves us his money, to pay us back for our inconvenience. Let us be fair and give us our money."

Hector looked at me. "And don't talk, gringo," he told me.

"I will talk," Santiago said. "Hector, you are a vermin."

I heard someone in the crowd say, "Yes!" And all the villagers turned and looked at Hector. Hector felt their regard now
and he seethed with indignation.

"And you," Hector said to Santiago, "you are dead." He
looked around at the villagers to see if they had heard.

"And you are dead too," he said to me. "You are all dead."

We took Danny Greenfield down to the river crossing and
put him on a bus to Huasipungo Pass. We asked the driver to
introduce Danny to the Peace Corps volunteer there.

I realize now that things in the village were changing fast.
In fact, everyone seemed anxious to change. William B. Bodean
taught the villagers to spit before they spoke. Bodean also taught
the young men of the village to grab their crotches and say,
"Unhhhhh . . . nuh! . . . Nuh!" to emphasize the negative or
ridicule the world.

"*Idiotas,*" he'd say, when he watched their imitations.

The young men loved Bodean. They began to call themselves
los idiotas bravos, the brave idiots of the world.

Bodean spoke Petrolero Spanish, the argot of the oil fields.
Petrolero uses only the present tense, with auxiliary words like
"yesterday" and "tomorrow" indicating the time of action. Bodean said that a man who spoke English and Petrolero had all
the communication skills he needed. With Petrolero, he could
express any desire and certify any threat. He said that if they
would only speak Petrolero in the United Nations, then everyone
in the world would suddenly understand everyone else and all
holy hell would break loose.

"This world only gets along," he said, "because no one
understands what everyone else really wants."

Bodean liked the drinking part of the thinking club, and
once he had drunk enough, he liked to pay for everyone's beer.
This made him patron of the cogitative arts and the hero of El
Brinco, who began to give Bodean his first four beers free.
Bodean did not join in the discussions, but he listened and made
rude noises of both assent and dissent.

"*Afirmativo*," he'd growl.

"*Negativo*," he'd grumble.

He'd fart, and laugh. "Heh. Heh. Nuh. Nuh."

At first, some of the members addressed their comments to Bodean, but once the men realized they would get their beer anyway, the Thinkery resumed its tradition of expansively free speech. Santiago still supplied the lemons. He moderated the discussions and watched Bodean. Concerning William Bodean, as concerning any other topic, Santiago remained polite and perplexed. Once, Bodean showed us a photo of his ex-wife, naked. "She's a natural blonde," he said to Santiago. "I've got fifty of these snapshots. It gets me through checkpoints." Later, after Bodean's influence resurfaced, Santiago said to me, "That man from the military was never a gentleman."

During the thinking sessions, Bodean liked to sit next to me, which made me feel guilty by association, and he ordered me a fresh beer whenever I had a quarter of a bottle left. "Don't drink the dregs," he said. "We'll never drink the dregs again."

When the debate raged impassioned or comical, Bill Bodean laughed. "I pity these sons of bitches," he said. "They don't know how lucky they are."

William B. Bodean knew how lucky he was. He got five checks a month, deposited in the First National Bank of Miami and converted into gold—into bullion, not certificates or cash equivalents. He said he had it all figured out. He was U.S. Marine Corps, retired; Los Angeles Police Department, disabled; and two traffic accidents, hugely compensated. "You should see me on the witness stand," he said. "My lawyers should have paid me. I was the picture of pain and suffering, emotional anguish, and mental distress."

He still was. He had uneven ears, wide-set long-gone eyes, and a broken nose that outdid Santiago's.

"And then, I always had my secret weapon. I can make my neck vertebrae creak." The jury could hear his neck creak from across the courtroom.

"I rest my case," he said. "I was the victorious victim. And soon I'll be the sole survivor. Want to be next to last?"

Bodean had moved from L.A. to the northern California coast, where he outfitted a farm to survive the nuclear holocaust. He buried a thousand-gallon diesel tank and converted a barn into a bunker.

"And then I got antsy waiting," he said. "Ever wait on the end of the world? It's fun getting ready, but then . . ." He grabbed his crotch. "Unhhhhh . . . nuh! . . . Nuh! I'm telling you. You realize those fuckers in D.C. and the UN make their livings off this muddling through. So I got out."

Bodean received his fifth monthly check from the San Francisco Bay Area alderwoman to whom he sold his survival farm. The alderwoman wanted Bodean to leave the booby traps he had rigged around the farm's perimeter. "When I started to tell her about them, she put her fingers in her ears and said, 'I can't hear you. I can't heeeeeeear you.' She was smart. She wanted the defenses, but she didn't want the liability."

To me the Amazon often seemed like an Eden, like a new beginning, but to William Bodean it was the refuge from Armageddon, and a new and better ending.

"It's even better than that," said Bodean. "I researched the hell out of it."

Bodean said that only the Amazon would survive the nuclear winter. "The Amazon creates its own weather and then it keeps it. It sits right here on the equator, so it's between the two hemispheres and out of the global circulation patterns. It's out of the loop. It won't get hit by the nukes to the north and it's out of the way of the ozone hole to the south. In fact, it's even safer. It's in an ozone sinkhole. It creates one sixth of the earth's oxygen and then it inhales it itself. That's slick. And the upper Amazon is the best part of it. It has more species diversity, more genetic abundance, more weird science than anywhere in the world. That's why there may still be dinosaurs here."

After he said this, Bodean looked at me and grabbed his crotch. "Nuh!" he said. "Don't give me any shit. I don't believe in dinosaurs either. I just use them to make my point. They could be here and no one would have a clue.

"I've got everything I need, man," he said. "And what I don't need isn't here. I like that part."

Lieutenant Hugo worried about Bodean's paramilitary inclinations, but he didn't have to worry long. William Bodean and Hector Tanbueno soon got together. After a few days of preparation, Hector guided Bodean out into the jungle. Three days later, Hector returned alone, wearing Bodean's sunglasses.

"Don't worry about him," Hector told me. "I hiked him around in circles for two days, and then he got tired and he went back home. Unhhhhh . . . nuh! . . . Nuh! Heh. Heh. Heh.

"Believe me," Hector said. "Nuh! . . . Nuh!"

10

One day, while I watched Angelina lecture French tourists on the kinds of butterflies near Los Puentes Caidos, malaria struck me down. I was drinking coffee and a sudden chill shook me. It made me suck in my breath and hold it, shivering. Tears flooded my eyes, and around my vision of Angelina, a silver halo formed. My lips drew back and my teeth chattered. Inside me, my bones bent and ached. I felt my entire skeleton turn to ice: from my shoulders down my arm bones, from my shoulders down my backbone, down my leg bones to my frozen feet. The floor hurt my feet. My clothes hurt my skin. My hair hurt. My brain contracted inside my skull. The back of my skull began to cave in and a darkness caved in with it. Across the soccer field, the image of Angelina hurt me, swimming in my icy tears.

It was all physical, all terrifying. I thought I was dying. The chills strengthened. I tried to stand. I managed to pull myself up off the porch and, holding to benches and tables, move toward the ladder to my room. I passed Brinco and Consuelo, who seemed frozen at their table, looking at their hands of cards. I began to crawl up the ladder, which bowed and wobbled and threatened to throw me to the ground. I crept up it rung by rung into the icy painful air of my room. I curled up on the floor next to my bed and hugged my knees to my chest. Pain hammered me until I broke into pieces.

When I woke, I was lying in my bed, naked. I was surprised to feel well, to feel good, to have a fine, clearheaded feeling of possessing no mass, no inertia, of being used up and all gone away. Consuelo sat next to me on the bed. She wrung a wet cloth in her hands, waved it in the air to cool it, and laid it upon my chest. It felt wonderful, and I felt like the cloth, wrung out and wonderful, cool and transforming into cool water vapor, transpiring into the air. I breathed and felt the cool air on my tongue. Only my teeth still ached with cold.

I remembered being in the pain, but I could not remember the pain. The pain was gone and the full presence of Consuelo took its place. Consuelo existed as a cool happiness. She smiled sweetly and she hummed some sweet Andean song. The light from the window illuminated her face, and her full lips shone wet and her teeth glowed white and translucent. Her large eyes were dreamy and half closed. She wore a white linen sack dress with embroidered roses. She had a red ribbon tied into her dark hair, and a crucifix hung from her neck. The crucifix was tarnished silver. She hummed and dipped the cloth in the water, wrung it, and pulled it across my chest. It made me breathe deeply.

Consuelo looked into my eyes. "Can you see me this time?" she asked, looking into my head, looking into the back corners of my brain, which were as empty as caves.

"Are we here yet?" she said. "Don't go away, my little saint. I am with you now. Don't leave us now."

"Hello, Consuelo," I said.

"Ay! He is here. The saint awakes. Oh, now. How good. There I was, washing you, imagining you were lovely and dead. And here you wake. What surprises lives are. Such a still, sainted body you were, such skin, such handsome eyes, so closed for eternity. If you ever die, Danielito, I want to wash your body. I want to wash your corpse. I want to light the candles around your body and sit by you for three days."

I felt fully alive and totally relaxed. My mind was clear as it had never been. It had been emptied and unburdened. I could smell the jungle flowers. I could smell that the little river was high and its water was clean and golden. Outside the cantina, monkeys were screeching at children, and children were screeching at monkeys. I thought of Angelina now and I wanted to tell her I loved her.

Consuelo kept washing my body. She swabbed it with slices of lime peel. She dipped the cloth into the water and pulled it down my chest and my stomach. She pulled back the sheets and washed my genitals. She washed my legs and my feet.

"There," she said as she finished. "You are clean and sleek and pink as a river dolphin. You could have any girl in the village right now and the fathers would wait outside and understand. They would smoke their cigarettes and shrug. They would say, 'What can a father do?' They would drink aguardiente until they fell down. The mothers would bless you and make you drink chicha of pineapple and cinnamon. Which daughter would you like? the mothers would ask you. Which daughter would please you? But please take only one mother's daughter, Danny-ito. Only one. Take mine."

Consuelo smiled and I realized she was the sweetest woman I had ever known. I thought about Angelina and Angelina's distance and how close and good Consuelo was.

"Let me wash you, Consuelo," I said.

"I will never say no to you, Daniel, although I know you

love Angelina. Every man here loves Angelina, the virgin woman scientist, and they always make love to me. You may wash me, Danny, but quietly, please."

Consuelo's body was beautiful, dark and full. I washed her. I massaged her. I rubbed her skin with lime. I kissed her breasts and her lips and I made love to her—I fell into her—into her clean, hot silence, and then we washed each other again.

She said, "I will look forward to doing this again."

I said, "This could not happen again, quite like this."

"It will happen again, Daniel. Just like this. Once this happens, it happens forever. As long as you love Angelina, I am the one who gets loved. It happens with all of them. Besides, poor dear one, you know you have the malaria now. You will sicken again and again and again. And I will watch you and save you and wash you each time. Malaria can be a wonderful disease. It will teach you all about time."

We came down the stairs and found Hugo and Hector sitting at a table. When he saw us, Hector stuck out his lower lip and raised his eyebrows. Hugo took out a notebook and stubby pencil and scribbled something down. Between them, at the end of the table, stood Mama Cuchara. She had lost weight. She looked up and smiled at me the first smile I ever saw her attempt. It was ragged but genuine. She had three teeth, one above and two below. She was holding an aluminum pot on the table and she picked it up by its wire bail and advanced toward me.

"*El guapo!*" she chirped. "The handsome gringo!" She waddled over to me, her flat feet slapping the splintered floor, and she lifted the pot up under my nose. It appeared to be filled with garbage. A tin can, an orange rind, and a banana peel floated in the yellow liquid.

"What is this?" I asked.

"Chicha, *patroncito*. Pineapple chicha! Drink some and celebrate!" She reached into her pot and scooped out some liquid with the tin can.

"Celebrate what, Mama?" I looked at Consuelo.

"The birthday of the Virgin Mary, *patroncito*. She will be two thousand years old in just a few years now. Drink! Drink!"

"I can't drink that. I've been sick."

"Very well. I'll ask you again. Drink!"

"He can't drink that, Mama," Consuelo said. "He can only drink Seven-Up."

"There is Seven-Up in this!"

"He has to drink Seven-Up pure, out of the bottle."

"What pities! What then can I feed you, *gringuito*? Bananas. Cinnamon. Pancakes? Coca-Cola!"

"Only pure Seven-Up, Mama. For his health. And out of the bottle."

"How pure! How good! Imagine! Seven-Up!" Mama Cuchara's tongue stuck out of the gaps in her teeth.

"You should drink some of it, gringo." Hector called out. "You should drink more of it, Lieutenant," he said to Hugo.

Mama Cuchara snapped her tongue between her teeth and went back to their table and dipped the can for Hugo.

From then on, it was more than Angelina who kept me in Los Puentes Caidos. It was Angelina and Consuelo and the malaria. I don't know whom I loved more. Angelina was distant; Consuelo was immediate. The malaria was an intermittent, dependable hell.

I found myself bolder around Angelina. I followed her around the village and stood close to her down at the beach as she lectured groups of tourists about to set off on day trips to hunt butterflies. I began to help load her canoes, fuel the motors, and push the canoes out into the current. Napoleon and I worked as a team. Napoleon's short arms and legs were tremendously strong, but his long back was weak. I realized that I was now physically weaker than when I had arrived in the village. I blamed it on the food. I was more like a villager now. I was skinny and slow. I wore cutoffs and black rubber boots. I tanned darkly, and my blond hair was bleaching white. In my mirror, my teeth and my eyes got whiter, the blue of my irises paled, and the whites of my eyes took on a blue tint. Some of the tourists began to address me in Spanish.

Consuelo teased and flirted with me less. She hummed and whistled happily. More strangely, mean old Mama Cuchara acted as if she were in love with me. Some days, she waited for me outside the cantina and followed me around for hours. She stood beside me, patting my butt. I thought she was going crazy. Santiago thought she was trying to atone for her lifelong crankiness before she died.

All of this made me feel like a part of the village. Every few weeks, the chills and fever would take me down and I would wake up to love Consuelo.

11

"Imagine how it would feel, Daniel," El Brinco said to me. "Imagine how it would feel to be kicked to death by a one-legged man."

That was the only mention that El Brinco ever made to me about my affair with his daughter, Consuelo. It didn't scare me, although I knew that if he ever got me down, he could probably break my neck. El Brinco's one leg was built like a piston, but it didn't scare me because I didn't scare so easily anymore. That was another benefit of illness.

El Brinco made the statement during one of the Thinkery's philosophical discussions. They had been discussing death: what it was, whether it lasted, if life had anything to do with it, or if life and death were not complements but opposites, so far apart in the spectrum of reality that only man could see them both at the same time and think that they were connected. Only man could do this because only man was so confused.

"A little knowledge is a big confuser," Jesus said.

"That's why we have specialists," Blind Jorge said. "That's why the government is in the thrall of technologists."

Santiago asked, "But what is knowledge and what is understanding?"

"I have the understanding," Jesus said, "that to be kicked to death by a one-legged man would indeed be a great irony, but it would make sense."

"Isn't irony supposed to make sense?" said Santiago.

"Only afterwards," Jesus allowed. "And only considering that, as Jorge says, a one-legged man is a specialist. Death without circumstances is not an irony."

"But practically now, why would he kick you to death?"

Then everyone looked at me and there was a pause of silence in which everyone realized I was sleeping with Brinco's daughter. There was suddenly a lot of knowledge and no confusion. And Brinco had done all he needed to do. Just like that, I was married, in an unspoken, uncommon-law kind of way.

"Everyone becomes a specialist," El Brinco said, and he smiled. "Each in his own way."

"A blind man is certainly a specialist," said Jorge, pointing his face in my direction. "And furthermore, to be kicked to death by a one-legged man would be more ironic than to be shot to death by a blind man, which has happened."

"As we all well know," Jesus said.

"Consuelo!" El Brinco called. "More beer for everyone. This round is on the father of the house."

Consuelo served the beer. Santiago passed around lemons. Consuelo happened to be wearing white: a white blouse and tight white Colombian jeans. I was also wearing white: a pair of white shorts and a white T-shirt that said "Bay to Breakers. Beat Your Heart Out."

Before me, Consuelo had slept with Hector and with Hugo and with others, I'm sure. But her father had chosen me as her husband. Perhaps Consuelo had chosen me too, but I believe Consuelo had so much love she could have given it to everyone.

I felt more a part of the village. I realized that almost no one there was officially married, either by the Church or by the commandant of the army garrison up at Huasipungo Pass. Navy lieutenant Hugo Rios would have been within his authority to perform a marriage ceremony in a dugout canoe under his command on the open river, but that would have been seen as with little foundation in Los Puentes Caidos. And the Drinking and Thinking Club could have debated: Is a wedding on a river reliable?

Consuelo's love was as free as love gets. It even made Angelina seem less distant. I could still love Angelina as an object of longing and desire. I could love Angelina as my mistress if she would ever have me. I could even marry her in church. I could see Santiago as a kind of father.

Because I had gotten sick, things had gotten better. My malaria made time itself start over and over. The future was imminent and unpredictable, and all I could do was entertain expectations—of the best, of the worst, of the most bizarre. The way Mama Cuchara was now following me around and the way Hugo was becoming so charged with enervation made me feel that something phenomenal was about to happen and there was no way I could get ready for it.

That night in the cantina, I bought the next round of beer. I had not treated the house before because I had felt I would be buying the other men's regard. Now the thinkers all toasted me. They called me *el gringo duradero*. The gringo who stayed.

The Thinkery continued the discussion of death by irony. Being drowned by molten gold as the Spanish priests had been by the Incas was indeed ironic, but it was an advertised irony and the better ironies should not be seen coming.

Finally Santiago's drinking and thinking club decided. The least ironic of deaths would be nuclear annihilation, because everyone says it's going to happen. The most ironic of deaths could not be foretold, because that would ruin the final pleasure of realization. The most ironic death would be so ironic that you would die from the shock of the irony before your assassin could finish killing you.

"That would ironize the killer, too," Jesus said.

"He might have to kill himself," Jorge suggested, and everyone savored that irony.

Lieutenant Hugo was there that night. He was pacing the cantina and refusing Consuelo's offers of beer.

"Death by irony is never a pleasure," Hugo said now. "The most pleasurable of deaths is the death for honor, open-eyed and squarely shouldered, the death of release from a moral obligation, the death of an ethical redemption."

"Well said!" exclaimed Jesus.

"Do not shout!" Hugo commanded, and Jesus shut up. Hugo was wearing his blackened revolver.

"That most pleasurable death is by violence!" Hugo shouted.

"O.K., O.K.," said Jesus.

Hugo shivered. Since our night together suffering in the jungle, Lieutenant Hugo Rios had turned more and more apprehensive. His nerves, he said, now felt like wires. Not like electric light wires but more like telephone wires, and no one was answering the phones.

"Listen, men. Something's going to happen," Hugo said. "My skin feels like it wants to jump up and answer the phone. My skin rings and rings. It rings when I touch water. It rings when the slightest breeze touches me when I sleep. Do you see? My nerves are waiting for an emergency call. What's the problem? Is there a state of national exigency? How would we know? What is it? Is the Republic in trouble? By whom? Why? What is it? Something's got to stop."

Now Hugo controlled his shivering and he saluted us. He put his hand on the butt of his revolver and looked away, over his shoulder. "I have to go check to see if anything evil has been happening down at the beach." He walked out, holding his arms away from his sides.

"If there ever were a telephone in Los Puentes Caidos," Consuelo said, "I am sure the first phone call would be a long one, a full hour of bad news. Dead relatives. Dead babies. Debts. It is a hard dark night, Daniel, the kind of night something bad could happen down at the river. Hugo has no flashlight. He could stumble. He could drown. He could be murdered by someone very bad coming down from towns in the Andes."

"Or Colombians," Jesus said.

"Go with Hugo," Consuelo said to me. "Take your fancy flashlight and go show Hugo that nothing bad is happening."

"I don't want to go down there," I said. "Hugo has got a pistol."

Before the navy office had burned, Hugo had kept the revolver as shiny and symbolic as his ceremonial saber. No one thought he would ever use either of them. Now the saber and the revolver were scorched black and they seemed septic and evil. The plastic plates of the revolver's handle grip had melted away, making the gun look skeletal. The way Hugo wore the revolver now, stuck into his trousers, and the way he was always grimacing, pulling back his lips and baring his clenched teeth, began to frighten everyone.

A few days later, a man walked into the village. It was the tour guide from the tour bus that had first brought Bodean and Danny. He was a Valalto Indian and he wore his black hair in the traditional long ponytail, but he had adopted a Western costume: imitation Adidas running shoes, shiny black polyester pants, and a Hawaiian-print shirt showing pelicans lounging with martinis. He carried a black plastic briefcase and he told us he was looking for William Bodean.

"You all know him," said the tour guide. "The North American who spit on the ground and who thought that no one could see him. That survivor in camouflage. Where is he? Invisible?"

He told us that when William Bodean and Danny Greenfield stayed behind in Los Puentes, the other American tourists on the bus became alarmed. They contacted the United States Consulate and demanded an investigation. Danny was located at Huasipungo Pass. He had become a volunteer to the Peace Corps volunteer there, and he was now teaching potato farmers how to grow potatoes. But William Bodean was still gone. The schoolteacher tourists on sabbatical threatened to stage a hunger strike until Bodean was found, so the tour company sent the guide back to Los Puentes to find him.

"I had to pay my own money and take a lousy *transportes*," the tour guide said. "And the issue is all a dead monkey anyway. Those teachers went home when I said I would look for him. But the chief is such a *Sí señor, chi cheñor,* that I had to come back for this idiot Bodean. So where is he? I need him to sign a pink piece of paper with stamps all over it, pledging his continued existence."

He looked around at the thinking club members gathered in the Cantina Caida. The members all looked at one another, pleased at the opportunity to discuss such a weighty matter. Then the tour guide sighed like a man who knew that he didn't know just what he was getting into.

Hector was there, and although it was night, he was wearing Bodean's sunglasses.

"*Bueno*," Hector said to the guide, from behind the twin mirrors. "Can you describe this—how do we say it?—this *desaparecido*?"

The tour guide was from the capital, and he was in no mood for Hector. "He doesn't look like you," the tour guide told Hector. "And manifestly, he's not wearing his glasses. Where did you get them? And where is he?"

Expressionless behind the lenses, Hector switched to English. "Hey, butt ho'," he told the tour guide. "The dude is gone, hokay? Cool out."

The tour guide's face took on a look of long-expected disappointment. He looked around for help from someone else.

"A man can go where he wants in this country," Jesus said, "except on election day, and then he must go to his place of birth to cast his birthright ballot. El Brinco must go back to the coast. Wilson must go back to the mountains. And Jesus must go all the way back to Bethlehem."

Jesus laughed at his joke. He had been born in the village of Belem on the southern coast, where all the boy babies got the name of Jesus.

"Señores," the tour guide said. "Tell me now. Where is this gringo type, this man named Bodean?"

"Good sir," Santiago answered. "The person in question could be anywhere. Is it not that life allows us many directions and everyone has free will?"

"No, it is not," the tour guide said. "This guy paid for a round-trip ticket. He has got to go back or I lose my job."

"Please, good sir," Santiago said. "Sit down. You have come a far distance to the end of a bad road. We do not know where your object may be at this moment, but perhaps through discussion we could arrive at a proximity, in the manner of Sherlock Holmes, the distinguished detective Englishman."

Consuelo came up with a beer and the tour guide sat down, obviously thirsty. Santiago led a rhetorical search for William Bodean, which relied on the definition of survival. The tour guide drank two *grandes* of beer, shaking his head to everyone's theories. During his third beer, I could see the alcohol hit him. He sat up straight and looked around at all of us. He left the cantina and stepped into the hibiscus grove. Then he returned and sank into a slump.

No one mentioned Hector's involvement in Bodean's disappearance, but the tour guide kept watching him. Finally the guide finished his beer and pulled a bottle of Jack Daniel's out of his briefcase and set it on the table.

Jesus whistled when he saw it. "Whew! What is that?"

"American whiskey," the tour guide said. "Thirty American dollars per bottle."

"Is it good?" Jesus asked.

"Thirty American dollars per bottle."

Jesus whistled, and then confided, "Hector Tanbueno took the American survivor out into the jungle and left him there."

"I thought it," said the tour guide. He looked at Hector. "Where did you take him?"

"On a botanical experience," Hector said.

"Where did you leave him?"

"I left him alone."

"Under whose authority?"

"His own, as a citizen of the world. In fact, he begged me to let him go."

"Do you have a guiding license, señor?"

"No. Do I need one?"

"Have you paid your dues to the tourism association? Have you studied tourism and the commercialization of indigenous cultures at the national university? Have you taken the certifying vow of the accredited tour guide?"

"I don't need to. I studied creative writing at Hobb High School in Cleveland, Ohio. I excelled in interpersonal relationships, lifetime skills, and consumer math." Hector stuck out his lower lip.

"You are educated then," the tour guide said. "So, good. Do you know this whiskey?"

"I studied that whiskey in the United States."

"Do you want some?" the tour guide asked.

"Yes," said Hector.

"Yes!" said Jesus.

The tour guide poured whiskey into Hector's glass.

"Where is this William Bodean?" he asked.

Hector drank down the whiskey and pursed his lips. "The

possibility has been established," Hector said, "that perhaps this William Bodean is dead."

"Perhaps he is. Where is he, perhaps?"

"Perhaps I don't know. He was not a man to share information. And he was not dead when I last saw him, but it is always a possibility, no? People die. I can show you."

The tour guide closed his eyes. He was getting into something he did not want to hear, but he had to hear it. He was also drunk and he seemed to know it. He opened his mouth and licked his upper lip.

Now he looked at me. "Are you with the government of North America?" he asked me.

"No."

"Are you with the government of this republic?"

"No."

"Do you want some whiskey?"

"No."

"Good." He poured himself half a tumbler of whiskey.

"Where did he die?" he asked Hector. "Will you sign papers to that effect? Is there a notary nearby?"

"We have a navy lieutenant," Jesus said.

"Pffft!" Hector said. He poured more whiskey for the tour guide and more for himself. The rest of us watched the two of them.

"Where did you kill this North American?" the tour guide asked Hector.

At that moment, Hugo appeared.

"Here is the lieutenant!" Jesus said. He reached for the whiskey bottle but the tour guide held it away.

Hugo did not look like a naval lieutenant anymore. He was far too sick. He looked like an AIDS patient or a concentration camp prisoner. He was gray and hollow-cheeked. His nose was sharper and his eyes were yellow. In a slow, repetitive nervous tic, he kept stretching back his lips and baring his teeth. "Ggghggg-gggh," he said. His head rocked back as he did this. He wore a pair of my cutoffs and my black Grateful Dead T-shirt with the skeleton dancing on roses. His scorched revolver projected from the waist of the cutoffs.

"I can't eat," Hugo announced to us all. "I can't drink water. And I am tormented by those obligations."

The way he held his hands out away from his sides made him look as though he was ready to draw for his revolver.

"Sit down and relax, Lieutenant Hugo," Santiago said.

"I can't sit down. Furniture hurts me." Hugo glared down at the tour guide and pulled back his lips in a tight, cadaverous grin.

Hector now smiled behind his mirrored glasses. He looked small and fat next to Hugo. "The lieutenant is the law in this town, señor tour guide. He is the law and the order of the Amazon. Pffft!"

"My dear lieutenant," the tour guide said to Hugo, "good evening to you. This man here may have killed a North American."

Hugo looked at Hector. "That may be against the law," he said.

"Of course it is against the law," the tour guide said.

Hugo's eyes were dull and burning. "We don't know that," he told the guide.

"We don't know that?"

"We are waiting for the arrival of my new code books. What are you doing here?"

The tour guide repeated his story.

"Did my code books come with you on the bus?" Hugo asked. "Do you have a permit to hunt for foreigners?" He took his black revolver out of his waistband and set it on the table.

At this, the tour guide took a deep breath. He looked down at his own hands and then put them on his briefcase.

"There may be rules, limits, seasons," Hugo said.

Hector spoke. "I believe that the foreigner William Bodean told me he was a Nazi."

"There may be regulations concerning the hunting of Nazis," Hugo said. "Perhaps only Israelis can hunt the Nazis. There is a world order now, a definite protocol. We are all connected. The UN, the OAS, the World Bank, the Kennedys, all of us. We are all waiting for my code books." Hugo looked out into the darkness. Then he shivered and blinked. "And I think I need glasses."

"Would you like a drink?" the tour guide offered. "This whiskey is very rare."

"Yes. Drink it, Hugo," Hector said. "It is fire."

"Maybe I can drink it," Hugo said. He took the glass from the tour guide and sipped at it carefully, but he had to swallow with his mouth open and his lips stretched back. The whiskey threw him into a painful convulsion. His teeth chopped together like blocks of wood.

"Wah! *Madre!*" he whimpered. "Why?" He grasped his elbows but that hurt him too, and he let go of them, holding his hands out as if they had been burned.

The tour guide took the opportunity to open his briefcase and remove a pistol. The sight of the second gun made the whole drinking club gasp. It was a tiny, chrome .25-caliber automatic. The tour guide held it without speaking. Hugo looked at it as if he did not recognize it as a gun.

"Hugo," Santiago said. "You are ill."

Hugo nodded.

"Are you in a delirium?" Santiago asked.

"Are you in a delirium?" Hugo echoed, shaking his head. "No. You are in too much clarity. Don't look at me like that."

I have never seen a man with harder edges. The hard white light of the gasoline lanterns made Hugo stand out like a cutout against the black jungle night.

"I am in too much pain," Hugo told the tour guide.

"Of course you are," the tour guide said. "One can see that."

Consuelo came up to Hugo. "Huguito . . . ?" she began.

"Woman! Don't touch me!" Hugo drew away from her and hissed through his clenched teeth.

Unconsciously, several of the drinking club members mimicked his hiss. Hugo glared at them. Santiago looked stricken. I felt that time had stopped and death was trying to break out and happen.

"More of this whiskey then," Hugo said. "More of this talk of dead North Americans." He looked at me. "More of all this fire." He drank down a tumbler.

He shuddered. "Imagine!" he said. "I cannot swim in water and I can only drink fire! Indeed, I am changing."

"At last, Hugo!" Hector said. He snapped his tongue against the roof of his mouth. He smacked his lips and grinned broadly.

"Now things are more equal," he said to the tour guide. "Frankly, I was worried for you before."

The tour guide waved his little pistol. "This is the strangest place I have ever been in my life," he said.

"Yes. We are in the Twilight Zone," Hector told him. "That is a place on television in North America, where nothing goes the way you think it will go. Isn't that right, Daniel?"

The tour guide looked at me. "Are you in on this too?" he asked me.

"No."

"Or yes," Hector said. "Every question has multiple answers. Watch!"

Hector picked up Hugo's revolver.

Hugo did not notice, but the tour guide stiffened. None of the rest of us moved.

"This is going to be so simple," Hector said to me. "Like my guidance counselor in the high school told me. You don't need to know the answers, Hector, only how to take the test. That is life, my guidance counselor told me."

Now Hector and the tour guide each had a gun. They faced each other across the table. I sat to one side of the tour guide, Santiago sat next to Hector, and Hugo stood at the end of the table. The tour guide was now drunk in a bad way, pride showing in his eyes. He was watching himself in William Bodean's reflecting sunglasses, set on the nose of Hector Tanbueno.

"Perhaps the survivor is dead," Hector said to him. "Who cares what happened to the survivor?"

"Perhaps his mother cares," said the tour guide. "Perhaps I care."

"Well, I don't care. Perhaps he is where he wants to be right now. Dead or alive, it's a free world."

"It is not a free world. The man paid for a round-trip ticket and he disappeared before completing his trip. The chief says to come find him and I come. Where is he?"

"Pfffttt . . . !" Hector said. "As this old goat Santiago will tell you, each man has his own free will."

"To do what? To die?"

Hector's face lit up behind the sunglasses. "Sometimes to die. Exactly!"

Santiago leaned forward across the table, spellbound. Hugo watched us all dully. He looked demented, like a drugged Muammar Khaddafi. His eyes burned like translucent shells. A dull yellow light burned behind them.

"Hector," Hugo said now, quietly, lisping. His voice was quivering and thin. "Hector. You know there is no such thing as free will."

Hector dismissed him. "Sure thing, Lieutenant."

"There is no free will. There is only fate. Some call it gravity, but I know better."

Now Santiago spoke, as if he were consulting an oracle. "How, Hugo? How?"

Hugo looked at Santiago dully. "Poor Santiago," he said, and shivered. Pain was burning him up inside. "Poor old daft Santiago. Your fate is to die from asking old questions. My fate is to marry your daughter, the glory of Angelina, and—I realize it now—my fate is to be unhappy."

"You've got half of it right," Hector said.

"How, Hugo?" Santiago asked. "How do you know this?"

"I know fate," Hugo said. "I can see it. I can see it just before it happens. I know that fate is like the gravity of the earth and we are all falling off cliffs to its center."

"Not me," said Hector. "I push people off the cliffs."

"You are all crazy," the tour guide said. He covered them with his little pistol.

Hector took off William Bodean's sunglasses. His large, heavy-lidded eyes were drooping, one eye staring slightly away. He breathed deeply, his huge, Indian rib cage swelling. "Are you a man, señor tour guide?" Hector asked.

"As much as you," the tour guide answered.

"Then do you believe in fate? Or do you control your own destiny?"

"Of course I control my destiny."

"And William Bodean, the dead survivor?"

"I was hired to be his tour guide. I was hired to control his destiny until he was delivered back to the capital."

"You are too proud and too confused," Hector said, "but I will clarify things for you."

Hector cracked open the cylinder of Hugo's burned revolver and emptied the cartridges out into his palm. He slipped one of them back into a chamber. He slapped shut the pistol and spun the cylinder. "I have a test I call Free Will or Fate. The Russians call it roulette. The Americans call it *Wheel of Fortune*. Whatever it is, it is multiple choice. We give fate its choice, and fate takes a guess. Or of course, we use our own free will and refuse. Sometimes, obviously, a coward has more free will than a real man does. Do you understand? Sometimes a real man has no choice. A real man has to do things."

Hector pulled back the hammer on the pistol. He held the pistol muzzle to his temple, and with no hesitation, he pulled the trigger. The hammer clicked down.

"Like that," Hector said, and shrugged.

The drinking club gasped. Hector smiled to his audience.

"I feel like I like this game," he said. "I played it in Cincinnati with the North American high school boys, and I haven't lost at it, yet."

He slid the revolver across the table to the tour guide. "You cannot spin the cylinder. If you decide to play the game, your chances are now exactly one in five. You are almost certain of winning this round. If you don't play the game—then what? What, Santiago? What is the tour guide who refuses free will?"

Santiago looked muddled. "What?" he repeated.

"Alive!" I said, and everyone looked at me.

"No, gringo. If he refuses to play, then he is a coward," said Hector. "Although, I grant you, alive."

The tour guide picked up Hugo's pistol and hefted it in his hand. Then, with his little .25 pointing at Hector, he put the revolver to his head and pulled the trigger. The revolver clicked.

No one spoke, until Hugo said, "Hmmmmm. *Bueno*." Then he reached forward, picked up the revolver, cocked it with two thumbs, and set it to his temple. He arched his eyebrows, closed his eyes, stretched back his lips, and pulled the trigger. The revolver clicked.

Hugo did not move. Hector stood up and pried Hugo's fingers away from the gun. "Round two!" Hector announced. His nostrils flared. His huge chest inflated. He put the gun to his temple and smiled.

"Don't you love it?" he said to me in English. "Round two. Round two."

He pulled the trigger. The revolver clicked.

Hector smiled again and handed the revolver to the tour guide. "This is the most wonderful game in the world," he said. "It's fifty-fifty-fifty now. You can play it and live. You can play it and die. Or you can run away."

The tour guide hesitated. He put down the revolver and drank off the tumbler of whiskey. He licked his lips, and he picked up the revolver and hefted it again. He looked at me and smiled with his lips. His eyes did not smile. His teeth chattered. I could not face him and I looked away to Hector, who was watching me now. Hector glared at me as if he had me where he wanted me too.

The tour guide lifted the revolver and placed its muzzle against his temple. I got ready for the explosion. The cantina was bright, bright against the black night. There was a radio playing Colombian salsa music, I was sitting on the bench right next to the tour guide, and he was jabbing at his temple with the gun barrel.

"Don't do it!" I said. I gritted my teeth and fixed my eyes on Santiago. Santiago watched the tour guide.

The revolver clicked.

The tour guide lowered the revolver.

"Magnificent!" the entire drinking club whispered. "This . . . is . . . magnificent!"

Santiago slowly let out his breath. "This Russian roulette uses too many bullets."

The tour guide swallowed and almost vomited.

". . . is idiotic," he said.

"That's not what Bodean said," said Hector.

"Bodean . . . ?" the tour guide began.

"Bodean didn't have a gun," I said.

Hector looked at me sadly. "You don't understand probabilities," he said.

Now, still staring at me, Lieutenant Hugo Rios reached down

and picked up the blackened revolver. He raised it to his temple.

"Hugo!" I said. "Don't do it! This one is it."

Hector laughed. "Is it?" he asked. He shook the cartridges in his hand.

"There are no bullets in that gun?" I asked.

"I'm asking you, dude. Do you understand probabilities?" Hector shook the cartridges.

Hugo stared at me and pulled back the hammer. The cylinder rotated one chamber forward.

"No. Don't do it," I said. "Hugo, don't do it. Don't do it. Don't do it."

"You are free, Hugo," Hector said. "Man, you are free. This once in your life, you are free."

Hugo's mouth moved. "I know. I am destined. To marry," he said.

"That's right," I said. "So, stay alive."

"But I hurt," he said.

"You are sick, Hugo. Stay alive!"

"I am already unhappy."

"Hugo, you are free," said Hector. "So, do it. Pull the trigger. Be free."

Hugo closed his mouth and twisted the muzzle of the revolver into his temple.

"Do it, Hugo."

"No," I said. "No!"

Hugo opened his eyes so wide his eyelids disappeared. He drew back his lips, opened his mouth, and then slowly lowered the gun. He leaned toward me. "Are you going to marry Angelina, too?" he whispered.

Hugo began to turn the revolver toward me. His eyes were empty. He leaned toward me, swinging the gun around. I grabbed the tabletop and started to stand.

Then the tour guide's head exploded.

It blew out against me. It hit me with bone and hair, and

the hot gas from the pistol muzzle burned my face. It knocked me back over the bench. My head hit the floor and I rolled over and jumped to my feet, ready to run.

But the scene had frozen. Everyone sat frozen in his chair. Jesus looked horror-stricken, Santiago looked amazed, Hector was still smiling. Hugo, who still held the gun, had closed his teeth on his tongue. A trickle of blood ran down his chin. A cold blue snake of smoke coiled up from the barrel of his black revolver.

"Oh boy, oh boy. Oh boy! Huguito!" Hector said. "I am a-*mazed!*"

The tour guide lay dead on the floor and now every member of the Drinking and Thinking Club stood up.

I left the cantina. I was spattered with blood and brains and so nauseated by my fear and the gore and the bright lanterns that I stumbled out through the strip of jungle between the cantina and the little river. I staggered through the deep dry litter of dead leaves and I ran across the beach, peeling off my shirt and shorts. I dived into the black river. The water hit cold and hard. I scrubbed my skin with sand until it burned, and then I pulled myself into a little pocket of still water dug out at the river's edge.

I floated in a place where the current had gouged a small cove into the bank. It was a bright moonlit night and the jungle was black and invisible. I felt anything, any person, any fear, could walk out of that blackness and get me. I got up onto my knees and washed my face again, pulling the water back over my head. The sound of the gunshot still rang in my ears. My jaws clenched and my temples ached. The water was cold and loud behind me as it rushed around the great black rock in midstream. I shook and shuddered. I still felt the man's hot, wet brains on my face. The stinging shrapnel of his exploded skull still ripped at my throat. I filled my mouth with water and gagged it out. I slapped at the water with the palms of my hands.

I rolled my head around on my shoulders. Then I looked up and saw Hugo standing above me.

He was a skeletal silhouette. On his chest, the Grateful Dead skull shone in the moonlight. His eyes shone dully. Hugo looked down on me from the bank. He still held his pistol in his hand, huge at the end of his bone-thin forearm.

"A tour guide who did not believe in fate," Hugo said. "That man did not. No. Why not? Was it his choice to die? Is it our choice to die?"

"No, Hugo," I said.

Hugo's eyes flared at me. "But I want to die. I choose to die. Do you believe in choosing to die?"

"No, Hugo."

"I want to choose to die."

Hugo grinned his death mask grin. His whole body vibrated like a puppet on a wire, but his head was as still as if pinned in space. "You are in water," he said. "You could be a fish. I cannot touch water without catching fire. That makes me a . . . what? What am I?"

"A man, Hugo."

"No. I am a ghoul."

"No, Hugo."

Hugo looked up at the moon. "I am no man. I am obsession. Obsession! You hear me? A joke! A flaming, crying, ghoulish joke!"

He looked down at me. "And you, fish. Do you love Angelina?"

I didn't speak.

"You are a lie. A lying fish. A swimming, talking, English-speaking, pink fish that lies. We should have known about you all along. Did you know about yourself? I am going to marry Angelina and die."

"Yes, Hugo."

He hesitated. "I am?"

"Yes."

"You pink, lying fish."

He pointed the pistol at me. "Do not splash me, fish. Water is gasoline. I am dynamite. Dynamite to kill you and every fish like you. Do not splash me, I warn you."

"I won't, Hugo."

Hugo paused and pulled back the hammer of the pistol. I was sure there were no bullets in it. I did not think that Hugo could think clearly enough to have gotten bullets from Hector before he came after me. I stared up into the pistol's muzzle.

"You pink, naked, lying, fornicating fish," he said. "Do you believe in free will?"

"Yes," I said.

This shook him. It took him seconds to get the pistol pointed at me again. "And do you love Angelina?"

"Yes."

This shook him like a blow. He sobbed and he got the gun pointed at me again. "I am not even sorry, man. Not now," he said.

The pistol hammer slammed down.

"There!" Hugo said.

I ducked beneath the surface and pushed out into the current. I let the water carry me downstream, bouncing me along the river bottom. I held my breath until I reached the shallows where the strand came out to separate the two rivers. I surfaced, took a breath, and looked back upriver. Hugo was still standing by the bank, pointing the pistol at the river.

I walked up the strand to the village. When I got to the cantina, I covered myself with my hands and walked through the crowd standing around the corpse. Upstairs, I dressed in long pants and a jacket and wrapped myself in my sleeping bag.

Hugo was a murderer now and mad, and everyone told him to go into hiding to escape the investigation that would certainly come. He stayed at the cantina for the rest of that night. I think he remained standing the whole time, hovering over the body like a ghost. When daylight came, the people all returned to stare at the body and they crowded around Hugo and shouted at him to leave. They surrounded him and waved their hands. For the first time, I noticed that Hugo was a head taller than most of the men of the village. He was tall, translucent in his paleness, and almost Christlike as he looked at me above their heads. He resembled the Christs in medieval paintings, already dead and on his way to heaven.

"I thought I killed you, too," he said to me, and now I saw that he was dying. Hugo seemed as dead as the man who lay at his feet. He was so pale and light he appeared to float. Hugo held his hands up above the bobbing heads of the people as if he were holding them above a rising flood of water and he could not let them get wet. "Don't touch me," he breathed at the people. "Don't touch!"

His eyes were round, dark and lidless, with large purple shadows beneath them. He held his mouth open and tried to swallow, but he could not. "Water! Water!" he whispered.

The sea of men parted for him and Hugo floated out across the soccer field. As the men watched him, several of them waxed religious. "This is a miracle," they said. "This is biblical. You'll see. Soon we will all be witnesses to a revelation."

Mama Cuchara intercepted Hugo in the center of the soccer field. She held her pail of chicha up to him and Hugo screamed. Hector Tanbueno had disappeared.

Hugo went into hiding, but he did not go far. He skulked in the jungle just beyond the village until the next afternoon. Then he came completely apart. He burst into people's houses and knocked kettles off their stoves. He stuck his head in through their bedroom windows and he screamed "Fornicators!" at the top of his lungs. He climbed trees and screamed "Fornicators!" at the sky. He cursed the sun and the sky for hurting his eyes. He cursed the branches and the breeze for hurting his skin.

He screamed, "Angelina! I hurt! Angelina! I hurt! Oh! Fornicators!" from the treetops. He hung in the crotches of tree
limbs and cried for hours. "I am on fire!" he screamed. "I will
marry you, Angelina!" His cries drowned out the shrieks of the
chicharras and made the whole village stop talking.

On advice from El Brinco, I moved up the hill to Santiago's
house and for one night I lay under the plank table in the small
kitchen without a roof. I did not sleep, knowing I was in the
same house with Angelina. She lay a few feet away, beyond the
thin partition of the bamboo walls.

Santiago snored and rumbled, but Angelina made no sound.
I imagined her with folded wings, surrounded by her dead butterflies. My eyes were pinned by her beauty to the wall. I felt
like Hugo, and I felt Hugo in the jungle outside.

We ate together that next evening, Santiago, Angelina, and
I. Hugo hung somewhere above us in the trees, screaming for
Angelina. I asked once, "Do you want me to stop him?" and
Santiago said, "How? By shooting him with that tour guide's
pistolito?" Someone had taken the bullets out of the tour guide's
pistol and given it to the children of the village to play with.
The children had gone around shooting people with imaginary
bullets, and one of the older girls wrote down the name of
everybody who was dead.

On the second afternoon after he shot the tour guide, Hugo
screamed from the top of the balsa tree that spread above Santiago's house, "I want you! Angelina!"

Santiago looked up. "That man is mad," he said.

"More," Angelina said. "*Él es rábido, Papá*. I believe that
Hugo is rabid. The bat that bit him at the crashed airplane must
have given him the rabies."

An expression of horror crossed Santiago's face. He looked
at me.

"I feel fine," I said.

Hugo died in the fire that night. For a long time afterwards,
whenever I slipped into the fever of my malaria, I had the same

red, fiery dream. I became Hugo Rios on the way to his wedding.
I carried a gasoline lantern so bright that I saw nothing but its
white-hot mantles, all ablaze and incandescent. I followed my
lantern up the hill to Santiago's house. I was coming for Angelina. The lantern burned my hand. Its brightness burned my
vision. I stood in the center of Santiago's bamboo house and I
cried out. *Angelina!* Butterflies papered the walls of the house
with their glistening, flaming wings. Moths filled the air in the
room with their enormous blind eyes and their burning, burying,
suffocating dust. My skin burned with the reflection from the
butterfly wings. My lungs burned with the dust of the moths.
My teeth and tongue caught on fire; they snapped and chattered.
Angelina's name burst into my brain and set it aflame. *Angelina!*
I screamed. I bit. I gnashed. *Angelina! I hurt! I want you!*

Then the butterflies took flight. They caught fire and flew.
They circled me once and attacked. I struck at them with the
lantern until I burned them all. I set the world on fire.

We were all asleep when Hugo exploded. Angelina and
Santiago escaped the flames. They pushed through the split-
bamboo walls and took cover in the jungle. A crowd gathered
in the soccer field below the house and watched as the house
blazed. I was asleep upstairs in the cantina. I heard the crowd's
loud murmur and I came down from my room. I saw the crowd.
I saw Angelina's house on fire and I panicked. I pushed through
the people and scrambled up the hillside to the inferno.

"Angelina!" I screamed. "Angelina!"

The bamboo house blazed white hot. I could see its dark
skeleton, and inside it, I saw a black, flame-shrouded figure
slumped to the floor.

"Angelina!" I screamed. I looked around for a plank or board
to shield me as I went in.

Then I saw Santiago and Napoleon and Angelina back in
the jungle. Her eyes were wide and white. I stood there with
the heat from the fire baking the back of my skull and reflecting
off the face and eyes of Angelina. Suddenly, I felt as if I were

still asleep. I felt as if I were in a dream trap set by Angelina. She looked directly into my eyes.

"Angelina," I said.

"Yes," she said, nodding. "Yes?"

Then the people all screamed and I turned around as the house evaporated and the whole scene twisted into a fiery spiral that spun into the sky.

The next morning the villagers found Hugo's burned corpse in the black ashes of the house. They carried it down to the cantina in a blanket and laid it out on the table, next to the body of the tour guide.

"There is no evidence that this charcoal is Hugo," El Brinco said. "But we will treat it as if it were he. Otherwise, he might come back again and set the whole village afire."

Consuelo set candles around the charcoal corpse. For a day it smelled of burned meat and then it began to rot. Its blackened shell cracked and pale yellow juices oozed out. Big spots soaked into the blanket and soon iridescent green flies encrusted the spots like jewels. I moved over to Mama Cuchara's, but the stench filled the village. To fight the vapors, Mama Cuchara had lit candles in broad daylight and she was wadding up pieces of newspaper, setting them on fire, and tossing them out into the road. She was so happy to see me that she stopped her exercise and began to fill a three-gallon aluminum basin with river water to make me more chicha.

"*Tóme, patroncito*. Drink!" she hissed, and threw a pebble into the pot.

Consuelo honored Hugo with a circle of candles, and El Brinco hired two Indians to carry the table onto the soccer field and wrap the corpses in blue plastic. They buried Hugo next to the tour guide in the sand by the big river. Out on the soccer field, El Brinco poured gasoline onto the table and set it afire. The table was already impregnated with diesel and insecticide, so it spread a sticky black smoke through the village.

Everything changed now. Tourists still arrived, but they took one look around and climbed back into their buses. Hugo's relatives never came because nobody told the Navy that he had died. No word went out about the dead tour guide either.

Then the big river rose suddenly one night and dug up the bank and washed away both corpses. The villagers were relieved, although now everyone was afraid to venture downstream and the men stayed in the village and drank. The ghosts of Hugo and the tour guide and probably of William Bodean were waiting for them downriver. When another man from the tourist agency arrived to look for the tour guide, the villagers told him that he had gone off with the navy lieutenant and that thought frightened them all the more. Now the night scared them and so did the hissing gas lanterns. There was a rumor that all the lanterns were conspiring to explode, just before the earthquake. The earthquake was back on everyone's lips. We had lost our electricity; now we gave up gas lanterns. By candlelight, the thinking club discussed strategies for confounding ghosts. "They are unhappy. Ghosts are unhappy," became the consensus. "That is why happy men never see ghosts."

These were practical matters, beyond philosophy, and no one followed Santiago's leads. Discussing philosophy had become bad luck. Philosophy brought ghosts and unhappiness.

"Perhaps philosophy is happiness," Santiago said, but the men crossed themselves and ignored him.

The villagers had dug the two graves right next to the big river, and once the river had washed away the loose soil, a breach was opened and the river began to erode a bigger and bigger hole in the bank. It looked as if the big river was going to dig a new channel across the soccer field and into the little river and then Los Puentes Caidos itself would wash away.

"What can we do?" the villagers asked.

"Fill the breach with rocks," I said. "Get the Army to bring a bulldozer down here and build a seawall."

"No. The river is navy business," they said. "And we don't want to tell the Navy that Hugo is dead."

"Hugo died of obsession," Santiago said. "Perhaps the Navy would understand, because the Navy understands obsession."

"No," the villagers said.

I agreed with Angelina. Hugo had died of rabies. He had contracted it when the vampire bit him during the night we spent at the crashed airplane. When he got no modern tranquilizing treatment, he had to go mad like a dog.

"Hugo did not die of rabies. He died of obsession," Santiago told me. "You saw the fire. And now the whole village has it. He was screaming for my daughter, Angelina. I can close my ears and still hear him scream it. He is infecting her name with his obsession, his obsession that killed him."

"He was sick," I said. "He had rabies."

"And whom did he bite? Did he bite you, too? Did he bite me? Did he bite everyone in the village? Now I am afraid the whole village will get sick and be screaming for Angelina."

Santiago looked at me and shook his head. "And now this dust. If we don't get some rain soon, this dust is going to explode."

The village had just realized, with a collective start, that it was in a drought. There had been no rain in three weeks. The rivers would rise five feet in the night from storms up in the Andes, but still we saw no rain. In a drought in the jungle, the dust is unbelievable. It is a fine vegetative powder, as fine as fungal spores. The dust coats everything, and at night, when the humidity rises, everything blossoms with mold.

12

The drought did not survive the people's notice. A few nights later, it rained. It started raining past midnight and it rained hard until dawn, when it stopped as if the sun turned it off. The rain left the soccer field under one inch of water, which reflected the sky and made it look as if people were walking on a mirror. Children played at skidding on pieces of plywood, and the village dogs nipped at their bottoms.

Finally the world was fresh in the morning. El Brinco called up to me to come down and have coffee. "Or beer and orange juice!" Brinco shouted. "This rain makes me thirsty. My God, how good it is that everything bad is over."

The village looked good now, and it smelled good again. The dust was settled, the jungle was washed, and the rivers were high. The big black rock in the center of the little river was all but underwater. It was a Saturday, and there was supposed to be a market, but the rivers were so high that none of the downstream Indians and homesteaders would come up to the village with their produce. They were too busy floating through the tree branches and picking fruit from their canoes.

Then word came down from Huasipungo that the pass had been closed by a landslide. The potato trucks from the mountains would not be coming either. "Too bad the landslide is on this side of the garrison," El Brinco said. "We won't get any soldiers. I could sell them all of my beer."

The soldiers were good customers but bad drunks. El Brinco was not that disappointed. "And I wouldn't mind if Hector did not come back either," he said. "We need some rest here in the village."

Hector, he said, was probably staying in an Indian village, far in where the rivers meandered. Hector was probably stuck there for now, until the waters receded.

"When is that?" I asked.

El Brinco shrugged. "Tonight?" he suggested. "But Hector may stay longer. He makes the Indians wait on him, hand and foot."

Everyone dressed in good clothes that Saturday, and we all hung out around the Cantina Caida and enjoyed one another's company. Santiago came down from the abandoned house that he and Angelina had moved into and I had helped thatch. He said Angelina had gone up on the mountain to replenish her insect collection.

"There are incredibly ugly insects up there," Santiago said. "They live in the fog forest. They appear only after the rain that occurs after a long dry spell. It is like a magic formula, don't you think? I think they are half salamander and half beetle, caught at the moment they are trying to change from wet amphibian to dry insect to survive the drought. It's hard to believe because it doesn't make sense. But the German pharmaceuticals will pay a lot of money for them."

Santiago and I looked around at the villagers. I had forgotten how many babies there were.

"I think things are better now," he said. "How are you feeling?"

"Fine," I said.

"You should eat," he told me. "Get Consuelo to make you some rice and green bananas. Drink some beer, my son. Put some fat on your bones. Only desperate women make love to broomsticks."

"That's not true," I said.

Santiago watched the villagers with their babies. "Evidently," he said. "Well. We'll get the philosophers together and we'll talk."

The village enjoyed its day alone together and everyone went to bed early. An hour after dark, Consuelo came up to my bed.

"It's about time for you to have another episode," she whispered. She took off her clothes and lay down on top of me. "Are you feeling well?" she asked.

"Fine."

"I don't think so," she said. She had doused herself in a cheap gardenia perfume that took away all the air in the room.

"Here, let me help you," she said. "Let me help you feel better."

At about three that morning, we all heard the croaking. Later, people said that it was such an odd, penetrating sound that it woke them out of deep sleep. To me, at first, it sounded like a cat whose wailing ended in a rattle. But as I listened, the sound took on such a range of tones that it became almost human. It called out, and it answered itself, and it always ended in a croaking rattle. I could not tell where the sound was coming from, and I lay in bed and listened. I later heard that it woke the whole village, but it was so strange, so otherworldly, that no one got up to investigate. Later, the villagers said they thought it was many things: Presidente Wilson dying on his radio; an

albino river dolphin calling all the village wives to come out
and make babies with him; jungle trees coming alive and discussing their tremendous burdens; a UFO lost, out of gasoline,
or looking for human babies.

Consuelo woke after I did. "What in God's grace is that?"
she asked.

"It sounds like an animal," I said.

"It does. It's a river dolphin. I know it is. They sound like
that when they die. They croak. I've heard them. It is the saddest sound. Who would think they could die? Won't anyone
help him?"

"Not me. It is too dark."

"That's when they die," Consuelo whispered. "That must be
when they die. When it is too dark and no one will help them.
Ay! What a thought. Daniel, don't die. Turn on the light. Where
are you? Here I am! Where is your Yankee flashlight?"

"Shhhh, Consuelo. I'm here."

The croaking would stop for several minutes and then com-
mence again. Consuelo and I lay awake and talked. It was so
dark that our voices hovered above us in the air.

At dawn, we heard the screaming of the village's two oldest
women running back from their morning bathing. "He's here!
He's here! He's here!" they screamed.

"Who's here?" we asked them.

The two toothless women stood in their wet slips, clutching
their towels in front of them. "He's here! He's here!"

"Who is here?"

They looked at each other with their mouths open. "Who?"
they asked each other. Then, "He's here!"

We went down to the little river's beach and saw him, a
miniature man, standing on the rock in the river. He was the
smallest, saddest sight I have ever seen in my life. He looked
old, incredibly old, and he was so incredibly white that he looked
blue. He was wet to the bone, and he was naked. He stood on

the rock facing us, holding his arms out in front of him. His eyes were large, and his mouth was open. The old man tried to speak, but all that came out of his mouth was a pained, pitiful croak.

"Who is it?"

"It is a dolphin!"

"It is!"

"It is no dolphin. It is a man."

"Who is he?"

"He is Wilson."

"He is not Wilson."

"He is from the UFO."

"He is not. He is human."

"He is Lieutenant Hugo!"

"No."

"No. Look, he is a poor old man."

"He is. Oh! *Pobrecito!*"

"Well, somebody save him, whoever he is."

"I know him!"

"Who is he?"

"He is . . . He is . . . He is the American survivalist!"

"Ay! Ay! Yes! And just look at him! What has happened?"

"The jungle has taken its toll."

Napoleon Elefante pulled a canoe up along the shallows and floated down to the rock and retrieved the old figure. When he got him ashore, everyone had to touch him. He looked impossibly old and he was so thin you could see the outlines of his abdominal organs. He had pale blue eyes and a wisp of transparent hair.

"He looks like a ghost of you, Daniel," somebody said.

"He looks like an angel. A very sick angel."

"Have you come here to die?" an old woman asked. "Are we all going to die?"

The old man looked at her and opened his mouth. He croaked at her and then closed his mouth.

"Oh, my God, he is speaking English," the old woman said.

We took him back to the cantina, wrapped him in beach towels, and fed him chicken soup. All the villagers came down to see him. The sight of him upset everyone—everyone except some of the old people of the village, like Mama Cuchara, who reacted to the sight of him with joy.

The rumor evolved on one side of the cantina that the old man was William Bodean, the American survivalist whom Hector had guided out into the jungle. Hector had not killed Bodean but had left him out there and Bodean had survived in the jungle on nothing but a safety pin and a piece of mirror. Out in the jungle, all alone, he had aged forty years in forty days.

"Like Jesus in the wilderness," someone said. "What else can you think?"

"Nothing else," came the answer. "It is the survivalist."

"Of course, I don't believe it," Santiago told me. "But it does make a horrible kind of sense."

"It's not Bodean. It's just an old man," I said.

"Of course," said Santiago. "But why does he speak English?"

"He doesn't. He's not speaking any language."

"No," said Santiago. "Not French, at any rate."

The old people of the village adopted the old man. They took turns spoon-feeding him while the younger villagers asked him questions.

"Why have you returned? Are you going back to the tourist agency?"

"Are you going to kill us? Are you going to kill our babies?"

"Have you seen the future? Are we going to have an earthquake?"

The old man looked acutely at everyone who spoke. He scrutinized them so profoundly it unnerved them. Some women went away crying and came back with gifts and flowers. The old people attending the old man would then take the gifts and give them to others in the village. I was given spoons and cloth and a white plastic crucifix. The gift giving multiplied. Everyone was so upset by the old man's visitation that they began to bring more and more household items down to the cantina. The old people took them and redistributed them throughout the village. The old people became like disciples to this castaway, who did not say a word that anyone understood. The old people stood around him and smiled toothless, beatific smiles. I looked out on the soccer field and I saw Mama Cuchara. She was all alone in the middle of the field. She held her arms out in front of her as the old man had done on the rock. She held her arms in front of her and she stumbled around in an awkward circle. It looked to me like she was dancing.

Inside the cantina, the speculation continued.

"The old ones really think he is Jesus," Napoleon said.

The villager named Jesus heard this. He walked up to the old man. "Well, are you?" Jesus asked.

The old man examined Jesus, and croaked in his face. Jesus turned to us with a disgusted expression and said, "We should not mix this with religion."

Finally, in the afternoon, Santiago sat down in front of the old man. "*Compadre*," he said, "I have one simple question. Perhaps, where you come from, they know the answer. My question is this, and you may answer it simply: What is the meaning of death?"

The old man gazed at Santiago for what seemed an eternity. Santiago sensed that some great insight was coming and he leaned toward the old man expectantly. The old man blinked meaningfully and opened his mouth. We all waited, listening, waiting, until I realized that the old man had died.

"He's gone," I said.

"At last," said someone. "He had seen so much."

"He answered you, Santiago!" somebody said.

Santiago rocked back on his bench. "I asked the wrong question!" he exclaimed. "The idea of death has killed him!"

"No," Napoleon said. "It was Hector who killed him. Hector took the survivalist out into the jungle and then Hector killed him. The survivalist just came back to tell us."

"He came back as a ghost. He was dead all along!"

The old people of the village gathered closer around the old man's body. They all reached out and touched him and stroked his blue skin.

"Maybe he was Jesus," Jesus said. "Maybe we will never know."

"If he was," someone said, "he has died again. We had better put him into a cave and wait for the angel. Who has a Bible? What happens next?"

"Just get him out of here," said El Brinco. "Get him out of my cantina. Bury him, burn him, throw him in the river. This is bad. This is very bad for us now."

I lifted the old man in my arms. He weighed nothing. I carried him out onto the soccer field and only the old people followed me. I passed Mama Cuchara, who was waltzing alone. I carried him down to the bank by the big river and buried him there in the sand where the river had taken away the other bodies. I knew that the river would take away his body, and that seemed the right thing to happen. I felt something now I had never felt in my life. I felt dread. I soaked up cold dread from the air in the village. The warm sand felt good as I buried the body, even though the sand jumped with fleas.

Napoleon and I checked the grave in the morning, and sure enough, the old man's body was gone.

"This is bad," Napoleon said, and he crossed his short arms high on his chest and looked away down the river.

After it took the old man's body, the river kept rising. Rain had not fallen for two days, but the big and little rivers both became torrents. We watched whole islands of trees and debris float by, and the villagers called these "Noah's boats" because many had animals clinging to them. One enormous raft of flotsam swept by on the morning of the second day. In the middle of it stood a small pinto horse with a man on its back. This caused a great commotion in the village and everyone ran down to the bank and waved at the man, but he was either dead, asleep, or so deep in despair that he had ceased to look around. We watched him ride his horse and his island into the sunrise, and it made even me feel that this was some kind of omen.

None of the village men would take their canoes to go rescue him. "You go up to a dead man like that and touch him and he explodes with putrefaction," they said.

"What if he isn't dead?" I asked.

"What if he isn't? Then he asks you what the hell you want. 'Can't you see I'm in a hurry?' he says. 'Can't you see I'm going somewhere?' "

"We don't want another survivalist," the people said. "It is his island. Let him have it."

The big river continued to eat away at its near bank until Mama Cuchara's hotel fell into the river, pulling with it the ruins of the telephone shack. Mama Cuchara never noticed or knew about this. She was so involved in her dance by this time that we all thought she was insane. She had been waltzing away every waking moment since the old man had appeared from the river. She held her arms in front of her, her palms turned in, her fingers almost touching, and she shuffled a slow, rocking sidestep, a slowly repeating circling dance. She always smiled, she seldom ate, she danced like this for hours, until she collapsed, and then, hours later, after she woke, she would struggle on the ground like a dying parrot until someone came out and helped her up and she would start the waltzing again. A few of the old men of the village would go out and try to lead her indoors, but they ended up being led by her. They danced a slow minuet around the square.

The other old people now spent a lot of time watching her. They nodded to each other and smiled. Until now, the old folks had remained in their chairs in their children's homes, tending their smallest grandchildren and passing time. Now they seemed to fill up the village. Most of them now acted the way Mama Cuchara had acted before she started dancing, when she followed me around with her pineapple chicha. The old people kept taking other people's things and giving them away and asking all of us how we were. They were as relentless as beggars and as thorough as thieves. I began to shout "No!" at them and push them away. They kept climbing the stairs into my room and throwing my books and toothbrush out the window.

When I yelled at them and went out to pick up my things, they all gathered to help me and they piled my arms with my own and others' possessions. My anger made them swarm around me like flies.

"*Pobrecito,*" they said to me, stroking my arms. "*Patroncito.*"

"*Patroncito,*" the old folks said to all us younger people. "*Viejito. Mándeme. Dígame.*" Little old one. Order me. Tell me. "What can I do for you?"

"*Nada!*" I yelled at them. "Nothing! Go away!"

As the raging big river, the Norona, worked away at its bank, a gaping hole, eight feet deep, ate up over half the soccer field, and I thought the whole village was going to be washed away. But then one day, the water rose so high that it broke through the banks on the other sides of both rivers and it flooded the jungle to the east and the south. The waters spread out over such a wide area that the current slowed to a halt. It now appeared that the village floated in the middle of a stagnant sea and that trees grew out of the water.

"Now!" Santiago said to me. "Now what?"

He waited for my reaction. "Well?" he said.

Then he held up his palms and I shrugged.

The rivers stalled, slack and stinking, but their surfaces hid powerful undercurrents. Once every few hours, a great tree

would cruise by, out in the middle of the big river's old channel.
Beneath the still surface, the invisible current held the tree's
branches and pulled it along. The tree trailed a wake behind it
that washed against the bank below the village, and it looked
as if the tree moved under its own power. Most of the villagers
saw this as an evil sign, but the old ones stood on the bank and
applauded.

Then it started to rain again, a light drizzling rain in the
village and certainly more up in the Andes. The dappling waters
rose so high that the whole square disappeared, and the men
waded out and retrieved their canoes from the vanished beach.
They tied the canoes to the poles supporting their houses, or
they came by the cantina for curb service and floated in their
canoes and got drunk.

Mama Cuchara continued to waltz, calf-deep in the waters
of the square. She had been dancing for days.

"She is crazy. Go out and get her," I said to the people.
"Go out and get her and tie her down if you have to."

But the people saw no reason to. "She's doing better than
the rest of us," they said. "Just look at her dance."

Now many other old people stood out in the rain and watched
her. Old men were waiting to waltz with her, and old women
were beginning to bob their heads, picking up Mama's rhythm.

Finally, when I wasn't watching, Mama Cuchara took off
her clothes. I looked out into the square and there she was,
dancing with an old man who wore only a wet undershirt. Their
wasted skin hung in folds from their hips. I waded out and cut
in and picked up Mama Cuchara and brought her into the cantina. She was a wet leather bag of jerking bones. We cleared
away tables to make a dance area for her in the middle of the
floor. I pinned my beach towel around her. The towel had a
picture on it of a dinosaur eating a palm tree. Consuelo tried
to feed her some soup, but she was only able to follow her
around with a bowl and spoon and spatter my towel with chicken
grease.

Angelina came back down after her time on the mountain, carrying with her examples of the strangest beasts—insects that looked like human fingers with legs, beetles like steam shovels, a queen ant the size of a child's foot, and a quart jar full of a viscous yellow fluid, which Angelina said was a single animal: a giant, wandering slime mold.

This was her prize. She said that when the slime mold fruited, it would spread out thinly enough to cover a half acre and then grow a forest of furry orange spikes a half meter high that could suffocate a man with their spores. Angelina said a German pharmaceutical company would pay her one hundred dollars for the jar. They would make powerful medicine with it. It would cure some dread disease in Germany, France, and North America and finally, later, maybe twenty years later, the drug would be obtainable in South America.

Angelina was standing ankle-deep in water as she told me all this. She crossed her arms and talked on, standing in the rain but paying no attention to it. Almost everyone but I had stopped noticing the rain or caring if he was wet. Angelina had been up in the fog forest for a week, and it looked as if I could scrape her clothes off her with a spatula. Her pretty face was covered with insect bites, but she kept her hair up under a campaign hat and her teeth were white and clean, and her lovely mouth moved beautifully as she spoke.

Although it kept drizzling in Puentes Caidos, the waters began to recede. Over a week's time, the rivers sank back to their banks and the flood left us with mud, ooze, and stink. The surface of the village square was black as tar, and small writhing creatures under the surface made the earth jiggle with their squirming.

The squirming earth lasted one day. Overnight the creatures metamorphosed, and in the morning, we rose to find the village invaded by frogs.

Or they were toads, or salamanders—I never knew exactly. They resembled slugs with legs, or leeches with legs. When I first looked out that morning, I thought the mud had bloomed with algae, but then I saw them move. These amphibians were one inch long. They were colored a dark, mark-free green, their black eyes covered most of their heads, and they were always moving, incessantly squirming. They didn't hop or crawl, they writhed, and they could not move without rolling over. They squirmed past and over each other in all directions. The males latched onto the females and the females tried to scratch off the males, and the coiling pairs trailed yellowish strings of eggs behind them.

The children loved the frogs. They carried them in their hair and their armpits, and they stuffed them down into one another's pants. They would run up to me with their mouths full of frogs and spit them at me and run away. The old people reacted more strangely. Caught up in their craze of gratuitous grace, they went into everyone's home looking for table scraps and moldy rice, and then they scattered the food to feed the frogs.

The rest of us could not stand the frogs. They climbed to the tops of the posts of the cantina, leaving a slug's trail of slime. They slid along by glue or suction out into the middle of the ceiling and then dropped onto our heads. I had never seen an umbrella in the village, even during the longest rains, but now umbrellas came out of nowhere, and people sat in the cantina under their umbrellas while frogs bounced off the nylon. All the umbrellas were black and white with pictures of giant pandas. I was told they were gifts from years earlier, from a visiting Chinese cultural legation.

The villagers had seen these frogs before, but never in such profusion. They called them *zapatitas*, "little shoes," and that first night the *zapatitas* started clicking. They sounded like metal heel taps on a cobblestone street. *Click. Clack. Clack.* Together the thousands of frogs created a thunder of millions of marching shoes.

The thinking club gathered the next night to discuss the

newest emergency. Blind Jorge was the most upset. The racket drove him to distraction, and the feel of the squashed frogs under his bare feet bothered him so much that he made two men carry him to the cantina. "This scourge has to end," Jorge said, covering his ears. "As the world dries out, these monsters must die."

"Oh yes," said Jesus, "and then imagine the stink."

"Diesel and a match," said Jorge. "That's our combination. We'll cremate the little fuckers."

"Jorge," said Jesus. "Please watch your language."

"These little fuckers deserve my language."

"Diesel fuel would burn down the whole village."

"Maybe it's time. And maybe it's time. Maybe it's a sign for the end of time. I don't know. These fucking, fucking frogs."

Now Presidente Wilson rose to speak. He was the oldest member of the Drinking and Thinking Club, a good ten years older than Santiago. And as he spoke, he wore on his face an expression of surprise and happiness. "Brothers! It is indeed a sign," Wilson said. "It is a sign of abundance, of better things to come. We have had more water than we want. Now we have more frogs than we can possibly use. What's next? Food? Money? I have eaten these frogs. They are good. They taste like bananas, or raw fish. On rice, their eggs are like soy sauce, salty but not so picante."

Around the cantina men groaned.

Wilson continued. "Perhaps we can sell them to the Japanese or North Americans, the way we sell them stuffed piranha and shrunken heads. As we know, there is a market for everything."

"Exactly," said El Brinco. "Like when that Indian sold you the electric eel so you could jump-start your motor scooter."

The frogs were still dropping from the ceiling and Consuelo was sweeping them outside.

"Little old Wilson," Brinco said to him. "You have joined the little old lady, our *mamacita* Cuchara. You have gone insane like the other old people. These slimy monsters are more than bad. They are dangerous and poisonous. They have poisoned your very small, very little old mind. Go out and dance, Wilson. Go out and dance like Mama Cuchara."

Presidente Wilson looked outside. There were eight or ten old people out there shuffling and dancing, several of them all or partially naked. Wilson shook his head. "Perhaps I will soon. I am beginning to feel a little like dancing. But I do know something because I have been talking with all my old brothers. Have you noticed how happy they are? They are back in Eden. They credit the old man who appeared on the rock—you know, the ancient and aged North American survivalist? The sainted Bodean? The one who would speak to us only by croaking? My old brothers say that he predicted this day of these creatures. By his croaking! And here they are. Remember how kind the old man was? How gracious and kind? How different?

"If he was the ghost of the North American survivalist, can you see how much he had changed? If he was the Christ child himself, our good little teacher, our sweet little *Jesusito* rearisen, returned to bless us and all our desires, base as they may be, can you see how good, how kind he was? Everything is wonderful now. It is! Or so the old people tell me. And I'm beginning to believe them. I feel good about this. I do feel like dancing. I feel like taking off my clothes. They tell me they are extremely, exceedingly, immeasurably happy and they want us to be happy too."

"The old ones are too happy," said Jesus. "They took all my comical novels."

"They want us all to go crazy," Jorge said. "They steal everything from my house and give it to my neighbors. Now they are giving my food to slugs! I think we should kill all the old people, too."

"We can't do that," Jesus said. "Can we?"

Presidente Wilson smiled. "Go ahead, my good and blind

gentleman and friend, Jorge, and all my good and blind gentlemen friends like Jesus. The old ones will only smile and forgive you."

"This is too much," said Jesus. "Somebody get me a gun."

Blind Jorge could sense Wilson's smile and he hacked up
some mucus and spat. "That tasted like one of those slugs," he
said. "Would you like to eat it, Presidente Wilson?"

Now Santiago spoke. "Gentlemen," he said. "Is our intelligence reduced by our contact with amphibians, these evolu-
tionary slackers? Are we not smarter than they are? And have
the frogs hurt anyone? Killed anyone yet? Have they done anything but coat us with their sickening slime? Or made us gag
in our sleep and vomit ourselves awake? No. Not yet anyway.
And there is good in anything. Who knows? This may make us
waterproof! That's a joke, obviously, but who knows? I am saying
this: Who knows? This may not be a sign, but perhaps it is a
test. A test. Yes, that's it. It's a question on a test."

"Like Hector's tests," said El Brinco. "All multiple choice."

Santiago shook his head. "The question asks this: What does
this all mean, gentlemen philosophers? What's important in
life?"

"You always ask the same questions, Santiago. Me, I want
fewer slugs!" Jorge said. "And fewer choices. And fewer
people."

"Perhaps the gringo survivalist was right," Jesus said.
"Maybe it's right to be the last one left."

"The survivalist is dead!" Napoleon said. "And if he comes
back, I will break his neck."

"The American Express man is dead now too," one man
said. "Hugo did that. And we know that Hugo died in the fire.
We can count on that. Perhaps Hector is dead too. I hope so.
Who knows? But certainly Bodean."

After this, there was no more conversation. El Brinco
claimed he had run out of beer and the men found no cause to

keep reasoning. They all agreed that they hated the frogs. Consuelo ran around with her broom, sweeping out the little green monsters, and we all sat there, disgusted, and agreed.

The next morning, someone found Mama Cuchara dead in a heap of squirming amphibians. Her hair was matted with frog eggs and slime. Her body was disjointed and slack.

"It looks like we're getting our wish, Jorge," Jesus said.

There was a sense of relief that Mama Cuchara was gone, and a further easing when people noticed the frogs dying too. But as the sun rose, the frogs swelled in the heat, their skin turned transparent, and their bodies popped like fetid soap bubbles. Fly maggots writhed inside the tiny corpses. By early afternoon, a swarm of wasps invaded the village and they began to lay their eggs in the scraps of frog carcasses. These wasps had big stingers and oversized mandibles. They ate the frog corpses and the writhing maggots, and their buzzing sounded like hungry growling as they shook their prey like little bulldogs.

As news spread of Mama Cuchara's death, people came down to the square. There was no funeral or wake; they just stood around. They watched the old people shuffling and dancing as Mama Cuchara had danced until she died. They danced her same slow, circling waltz and touched their fingertips together and smiled.

"What do you think it means, Daniel?" Santiago asked me.

"I think the old ones are sick," I said. "A disease is making them do this."

"A dancing disease? Or a social disease?"

"It's a brain disease," I said. "Look at them jerk. Look at their eyes. They are out of it, Santiago. They're sick."

"Then what should we do?"

"Send for doctors. Many doctors."

Santiago shook his head. "A plague of frogs. A pestilence of flies. An invasion of wasps. And next, an epidemic of doctors? What will the doctors bring? Lawyers and lawsuits? They always come next. Judges and jails? They always come next. Priests and hell? Always next! We are caught in a vicious circle, Daniel. Perhaps it is better to let events stop themselves. Perhaps it would be better if we all went away and came back later."

The wasps mated, and the females ate the males and then flew away, leaving their consorts' carcasses in the square. A child stepped on a dead wasp and was stung. Her foot swelled up until the skin split. The villagers now swept and shoveled up all that was left of the frogs and wasps and dumped them into the chasm the river had dug into the soccer field. Following Jorge's advice, they poured diesel fuel onto the mess and set it all afire. Then everyone was seized with the desire to keep the fire going and they went around and gathered up every spare scrap of lumber: boards left over from Santiago's house and from Mama Cuchara's hotel and the telephone and navy shacks. By evening, the village was considerably cleaned up. It was also diminished. Los Puentes Caidos was disappearing.

The next day Hector Tanbueno appeared, not from downriver but on a bus from the capital, with a French TV crew. Hector was dressed in a white polyester suit and a Panama hat. He smoked little cigars and affected sophistication by pinching his lower lip as he talked. The French were all dressed in baggy, pleated khaki trousers and tight tank-top T-shirts. They parked their bus just outside the village and walked around the big hole in the square. They immediately began filming the old people dancing.

"I brought some business," Hector said. "What the hell is going on around here?"

The French had brought with them laser equipment. Their idea was to find a group of primitive jungle Indians, show them the lasers, and then film their reactions to modern wonders.

"I'm going ahead to Titupini," Hector told me. "I'll get the Indians to take off their clothes and hide them. They're all brain-damaged anyway because of the manioc. These French will think they're original aborigines. I'll send them downriver and let them rot. Why did the old people take off their clothes?"

The French director came up to me and said, "The Amazon is ruined. What are you doing here?"

He looked around at our village. "What is this place? Civilization has destroyed everything. I filmed the same thing happening in Borneo. What are you doing here? You have ruined this place. This place should be made into a universal park and only be visited in the daytime."

Then the director saw Angelina.

"You must be Brazilian," he told her. "You are too beautiful to be from here. Do you want to be in the movies? I see you're wearing clothes. I can make you a star."

"I have a jar full of slime mold," Angelina said. "Would you like to see it?"

"I would be enchanted," said the director.

Angelina left to get the jar. The director turned back to me. "Who is that woman? What does she mean by slime mold? Really now. What do you think you are doing here?"

"Mildewing," I said.

"I will film you, too," he said to me. "You are a universal type. I see you everywhere I go, in every innocent community. There's the lone modern man, the American man. He comes from any nation, England, Holland, Germany, even France. And now Japan. But he is American, a type. He's infecting the people like he's a virus. And why? He has no reason to be there, but he's there. He's a Coca-Cola colonist, a cultural common cold. He's there, and just by his being there, the community rots. Look at this place. It's rotting. Have they no clothes? I'm lucky I can frame my shots."

The director watched for Angelina. He pinched his lower lip. "Is she coming back?" he asked.

"Do you do television?" I asked. "Or movies?"

"I do truth, you cretin. Where did that woman go?"

"She's getting you your slime."

"Why are these people dancing?"

"They are sick. Do you have doctors with you?"

"We have that one in the bikini, but this is his vacation. They are sick and they're dancing?"

"Things are different in the tropics."

"Listen. I have film from Indonesia of people eating their parents' brains. I have film of Kalahari boys burning their circumcised foreskins."

Angelina returned without the jar.

"Hello, starshine," the director said. "Where is your creature? I would like to film it."

"I decided not to bring it. You would not be interested."

"I am interested in you and anything about you. You are the light of the world in this very dark place."

This made Angelina look at me. "What do you mean?" she asked the Frenchman.

"Listen to me, my splendid one. Everywhere I go, I search for light. As the world gets darker, there remain a few rare, shining people who protect the light, who illuminate joy and beauty and truth. I have come all the way from Paris, by way of Sumatra, around the globe, seeking that light. I found it nowhere, until I found it here. In you."

"What do you mean?" Angelina said.

"But you are light," he said. "You are life. You are love. Look at you. You radiate. You illuminate. All the rest is just your shadow."

"How do you know?"

"I can see it. I can feel it."

"Feel what?"

"What? But love," said the Frenchman. "*Amour. Amour.* I love you. I love you."

"You say it so easily."

The Frenchman bit his lip. "Easily? But it kills me. Still, I could say it one thousand times."

"Not now, please," Angelina said.

"No-o-o-o." A wave rolled through the Frenchman's eye-brows. "But soon?"

Angelina looked at me.

"This guy burned his foreskin," I said.

"But why?" she asked the Frenchman.

13

Old people died. They turned happy and they danced. They danced until they dropped in their tracks and they died. If it hadn't been for the fact that all the dancers were old—and happy—everyone would have panicked.

One morning, we got hit by an earthquake that sounded like a series of giant doors slamming shut underground, beginning under the big river, crossing under the village, and heading up the road out of town. This quake was all noise; the ground hardly shook. We all stood there with our arms outstretched, waiting to be knocked down, as we listened to the earthquake go under us. It was a cool morning, and immediately after the earthquake, a heavy mist sprang up from the ground.

After that, Santiago told me we had to leave, he and I. He said we would go visit his father in a village high in the Andes. Santiago had not seen his father since he left the village with a group of young emigrants from the Altiplano region over forty years before. He and his father had been arguing then, about fate, and Santiago had gone away angry and confused. Perhaps now it was time to pay his respects to his father and reestablish conversation.

"I have rethought the existence of fate and free will," Santiago said.

"And what do you think now?" I asked.

"That they both can exist, but not at the same time. And it depends on how you consider them. Before or after. Before something happens, you can feel your free will. This is ignorance, of course, but the ignorance frees you. After you screw up, you can see it was fate. We all have free will until all is too late. Hugo's death taught me that."

"Perhaps your father is dead too," I said.

"Not Papa," he said. "He is a very healthy man. Besides, where he lives, the people do not die of disease. They die of accident, murder, and finally of old age, but they do not get sick in order to die.

"Let's go," he said.

"And what about Los Puentes?"

"What will be, will be. Finally."

We got ready to go. We carried nothing but two of my jackets and some of my money, but the jackets made it obvious that Santiago was leaving the jungle. Before we could drink a last beer and step out of the cantina, people had gathered in the square.

Jesus asked, "Where are you going, Don Santiago?"

"Up into the sierra to look for my father."

"You're too old to have a father, *viejo*."

"I have a father. You know the whole story."

"It's a story, Santiago. You have never gone to see him. You never leave Caidos."

"I do. Many times."

"Not after an earthquake you don't. Or just before."

"That," Santiago said, "is a coincidence."

Blind Jorge was there too. "Exactly, old friend," he said. "That is why people are worried. It is like with a murder. Someone is killed and we don't know by whom. Then someone else is gone and we don't know why. But the coincidence remains in the village and it changes the place. Life is a coincidence here."

"Life's a fluke!" said a woman. "It is a shame, also."

"It is wonderful," Consuelo said, and she smiled at me. She looked very happy that morning.

"Santiago," said Jesus. "What do you know that we don't know?"

"I've never known anything that isn't there for everyone else to know," said Santiago.

"We all know that," said Jesus. "You taught us that. That is why we are worried. Things are more obvious now."

"Yes, we all know there was an earthquake," the woman said. "And that was the first fog that ever put out my cookfire. If that's a coincidence, what happens next?"

The people stood shoulder to shoulder, blocking our way across the square. The French TV crew noticed the crowd, and I could see the director telling his men to ready their cameras.

"Good people," Santiago said, "I am merely going up toward the volcano to look for my father. I want to ask him something and come right back. Nothing will happen while I am gone."

"What do you mean by that?" Blind Jorge asked.

Santiago looked at Jorge quizzically. Jorge continued, staring at a point above Santiago's head. "Exactly what do you mean by 'nothing,' Santiago?"

Santiago's shoulders slumped. "Most exactly, my old friend, I mean nothing."

El Brinco was standing next to me, leaning against a post. Now he hopped down into the crowd and he pivoted on his one leg, shouting to the people. "Exactly!" he shouted. "Exactly!

Nothing! We want nothing to happen, neither here nor to Santiago. But how do we guarantee that? That nothing will happen? Well, of course, I know. We will throw a *despedida*. We'll have a great big going-away party. *Bueno!*"

El Brinco widened his eyes. " '*Bueno*,' did I say? Did I hear someone say, '*Bueno*'? Yes! Someone did. So that nothing will happen to our dear Santiago, I myself will treat my friend gratis to his part of the celebration. Likewise, so that nothing may happen to this village in his absence or worse, our Santiago, in his graciousness, will entertain the village, gratis also. That is to say, free. Financially compliments of his daughter, Angelina, who is up on the mountain gathering monsters."

"Creatures," Napoleon corrected.

El Brinco whistled. "Creatures. Hey, Napo! Beneath Consuelo's bicycle! Dig up the treasure I have buried there."

Napoleon Elefante grabbed a shovel blade with no handle and got down on his knees to start digging for beer. Some of the people entered the cantina to begin the *despedida*, and others went home to prepare holiday food and put on better clothes. The French brought their cameras over to the cantina. That left the square empty again except for four old people waltzing. One old man was as naked as a bird. Santiago watched the old people dancing and he shook his head.

"We must get out of here," he said.

A few hours later, the whole crowd was back. Some men had gone out with their *escopetas*—matchlock shotguns that shoot pebbles and glass—and they had killed three woolly monkeys to roast for the dinner. Now they made a fire pit out of the hole Napoleon had dug. They built a fire in it and burned off the coats of the monkeys, until the air stank with scorched hair. Hairless, the three big monkeys—two *machos* and a female— looked like two miniature men and a woman.

El Brinco noticed my disgust. "Almost cannibalism, no? But wait until you taste one. Sweeter than pig. They travel with the howlers and they live on fruit and bamboo shoots. And the males are great lovers. That's certain, you can see. Especially that one who looks like me." El Brinco pointed to the larger male, who had a big sad face and a round, muscled belly. "They look like men, but just before you kill them, they cry like little babies."

I looked from the monkeys to Brinco.

"Of course, it can be manly to cry," he said.

Women brought aluminum buckets heaped with fruit and bamboo shoots and other buckets full of pineapple chicha. They pounded a paste out of manioc in a child's dugout canoe. Children brought down their pet guinea pigs to be spitted and roasted with the woollies.

Hector got back from Titupini just at dark. "Did you get that earthquake I sent you?" he asked.

The French TV crew set up their cameras and lights. Soon their Honda generators were purring away. The director came up to me and said, "You stay out of the picture. Stay out of the way. I warn you. We will cut out everything you say."

Except for Consuelo, all the women took turns crying about Santiago's departure. They took turns serving food and being brokenhearted. The men drank beer and they all got emotional. They took turns sharing testimonials of Santiago's wisdom.

"Well, one thing is obvious," Napoleon said. "Santiago taught us that all is not as it seems."

"Especially not here in Los Caidos," said Jorge.

"And one does not have to travel to the capital city to get run over by an accident."

"It can happen right here—it's the truth. One can find anything."

"To thine own self be truth," Napoleon added.

"That's right," Jesus said. "It can happen to you. It can happen to us. How close we have come in our many discussions. But we never seem to quite get at it, do we?"

"The truth? Near misses, Jesus. That's almost as good."

"Perhaps it is the nature of logic," Santiago said, "to be nearer to truth but never quite there. The best arguments are circular in form, perhaps. They keep circling and circling around the truth, like the vultures that ride the air above our village. They rarely land. No, there are too many dogs. But they are curious up there and they would like to know us."

"You mean they would like to eat us," said Jorge.

"Not while we live," Napoleon said. "We wouldn't allow it."

"Then there is my argument," Jorge said, and he waved a monkey arm bone. "We are woollies without wool. We would taste just like this."

The monkey meat was slippery and stringy. Everyone shut up for a few moments and enjoyed the meal. Then Jesus said, "Let's face it. We're in a hell of a state here now, aren't we?"

"Cut!" the French director shouted.

As the director jumped up, a flood lamp swung around to illuminate Hector, who sat on the railing under the eaves. Hector closed his eyes against the brightness and smiled.

The director rearranged his equipment. "This is wonderful. Beautiful. I can cut anything that does not fit. But I want the American to shut up. Christ, I wish Angelina were here for this. She'd be like Jane Goodall among chimpanzees—wild and free. She'd be like Sally Ride among astronauts. Absolutely weightless. Absolutely. I'll get her later and splice her in. This will get us an Emmy! This will win me an Oscar!"

"Are we going to see a movie?" Napoleon asked him.

"You *are* a movie," the director said. "You are becoming art. Just keep it rolling."

"And with all the lights," Napoleon said.

"I can feel them," Jorge said.

"I can too," said Brinco. "You don't have to be blind."

Consuelo brought more beer and spoke to us all. "Remember that Beta movie we saw here in the cantina?" she said. "Remember Rambo? What a handsome man."

"I remember," Santiago said. "I remember that the people did not do well with the movie. They forgot it was pretend."

"That was the problem!" someone said. "First, the dead pig."

"Then the navy office burned."

"Then Lieutenant Hugo went mad. Wasn't he bit by a bat while he was watching the movie?"

"People should know better," Santiago said. "They should not be so gullible. They used to be wiser. They used to be wary. When any outsider brought in some gimmick, the villagers were always critical."

"That's right!" said El Brinco. "I remember it now. Once a man pulled a covered wagon in here, with big signs advertising an elephant. But when he took off the cover, the people all said, 'That is no elephant!' "

El Brinco stood up to continue his story.

" 'It is so an elephant,' the man said to the villagers.

" 'It can't be,' said the people. 'Elephants are big.'

" 'This elephant is big,' said the man.

" 'But elephants are colossal,' the people said.

" 'What's colossal to you?' the man said to the people. 'The trouble with you is that you've never seen an elephant.'

" 'And we certainly aren't seeing one now,' said the people."

El Brinco laughed. "And then we all demanded our money back."

The villagers laughed and clapped their hands.

"But we never got our money back," said Jesus.

"Of course we didn't," El Brinco said. "The man said if he couldn't keep our money, he would have to leave his elephant right here with us and then the elephant would eat all our houses."

"An extortionist elephant with an appetite," said Jesus. "That was the problem."

"You're forgetting one thing," Santiago said. "Remember now. You all said it wasn't an elephant."

"Whatever it was, it was big and hungry."

Napoleon now asked, "What did you think it was, Santiago?"

"I said at the time that we couldn't be sure."

"That's right," Jesus said. "And then everyone started guessing what the elephant could be. Of course, none of us had the slightest idea. But people started guessing that perhaps this creature was a mix, you know, the issue of two animals who got together and screwed when they shouldn't have."

"This is wonderful!" Consuelo said. "What did people guess?"

El Brinco and Jesus looked at each other.

"A whale and a mule."

"A mule and a dolphin."

"A mule and a manatee."

"A dolphin?" Napoleon asked.

"Now I remember the rest of the story!" El Brinco said. "Remember? That elephanteer told us the story of the nine blind men and the elephant. How each blind man felt a part of the elephant and declared it to be something different. A tree trunk. A rope. And so forth, you know. A boa constrictor. And several other items of household use. Remember, everyone? Then what did we do?"

Blind Jorge spoke up proudly. "You went and got your own blind man to come to see the elephant."

"Indeed we did. Our finest hour."

"And what happened?" I asked.

"Shhhhh!" the director hushed.

"Well!" said Brinco. "Well, let me think. Blind Jorge came out and he examined the elephant. With his hands, of course."

"Yes. I felt it all over. I can still see it now. I felt its nose, its tail, its deep genitals."

"And what was it?" asked Napoleon.

"It was an elephant, Napo. It was a young girl elephant. With smaller ears than I expected. It was sadder than I expected, too. It had tears in its eyes. Big, thick tears that stuck to my hands. They smelled like hair lotion, like *Brillantina*."

"It was an elephant?" said Napoleon.

"Clearly," Jesus said. "And the man left with his elephant to cheat people elsewhere. We never got our money back."

"We never do," Brinco said.

"But we learned something, didn't we?" Santiago said. "And that made it worth it."

"I remember this much," Blind Jorge said. "I remember that shortly after the incident of the elephant, my young friend Napoleon Elefante was born. Remember, Napoleon? You were named after that elephant."

Napoleon looked surprised. "I was?" he said. "Why?"

"Well, because of your unusual shape, of course. You know, your short arms and legs. Your long intelligence. Things like that. Your father put two and two together and he remembered the elephant."

"But my mother said if I am anything, I am dolphin."

"Part elephant, part dolphin," Jesus corrected.

Napoleon looked hurt.

"Part human," Jesus said. "The better part, dolphin," he hurried to add. "You are a noble addition to our community."

"Why would a dolphin mate with an elephant?" Napoleon asked.

"Because that's what we had just seen."

Napoleon Elefante looked down at his body. He held out his arms and compared them to the other men's. Consuelo went to him. "You are beautiful, Napito," she said. "And wonderful too. I have often thought that your body was perfect. It is so much like a saint's."

"Cut!" the French director shouted in English. Then, in Spanish, he said, "That was beautiful. This is great. We'll get tape of naked Indians. We'll get us a priest. That's great. This is beautiful. What I need now is a series of testimonials, to open

my program, or close it. I want your impressions, gentlemen,
your philosophies. Give us a moment to rearrange our cameras.
Arrange your thoughts, because this is delicious. Damn, I wish
that Angelina were here. I'll get her yet. Gentlemen, one moment
and we'll begin again. One by one, this time. Film profiles,
gentlemen."

The crew rearranged the cameras again, and this time they
set up small black-and-white monitors, one for each of the three
cameras, in positions so we could all watch them.

"You first," the director said to Blind Jorge. "Please sit
here, old man. Now tell us. How is it different, being blind
here rather than elsewhere?"

Jorge turned his face up to the lights. "Hotter here," he
said.

"No. I mean in the Amazon."

"I have never been elsewhere."

"Then, I mean, how does your handicap help you? How does
it help you to *see*, as it were, see things in a different way?"

"It doesn't. I am blind."

"I mean, what powers do you have that sighted men do not?"

Jorge turned his face from one lamp to another. It seemed
to me that for the first time, perhaps because of the heat from
the lamps, Jorge was feeling attention paid to his face. His face
had reddened.

"Old man," the director said. "What do you hear that other
people cannot hear?"

"Well, last night," Blind Jorge said, "I heard splashing in
my heart."

"Excellent! We'll use that. What else? Tell us anything. For
example, how do you dream?"

"I don't. Do I?"

"Damn it," the director said.

Santiago leaned in toward the lights, looking back and forth
from Jorge to his TV images. "Jorge," Santiago said to one of
the monitors. "What does truth look like to you?"

Jorge opened his eyes wide. It was one of the few times I had seen him do this. His eyes were river-blinded, and gray. They looked as though spiders had spun webs across them, but in the black-and-white monitors, they shone like silver coins.

"I don't know," he said. "I'd have to be more than blind. I will always regret I never learned to read."

"Cut!" the director said. "Very good. Next!"

Next was Jesus. He waved away the director. "I know how this works," he said. He looked straight into one of the cameras. "Hello, Mother," he said. "This is your only son, Jesus. Try to get to a television so you can see me."

"Cut!" The director looked around. He saw that Hector had come over from the railing. "O.K., you," he said. "Hector, come here. And please, keep everything in Spanish."

Hector took Jesus' place on the bench. *"Bueno,"* he said, and he observed himself proudly from the three points of view. First, he stuck out his lower lip. Then he rubbed his chin. Then he got serious and put his eyebrows together. He lowered his voice to that of a Latin radio announcer, booming his *b*'s and rolling his *r*'s. *"Este es su Hector,"* he said. "Welcome to Hector's television show, brought to you tonight by Hector. Hector—"

I laughed.

"Cut! You, shut up! Hector, Hector. We'll get you later, downriver with the Indians. So save it, O.K.? Next!"

The director looked around. He spied Consuelo. "You."

"Not taking off my clothes," Consuelo said, smiling.

"Of course not. Of course not. We just want philosophy." The director paused. "But then again, why not? This is French television, after all, where French women show their breasts all the time. Where fashion is fashion as a statement of liberation."

Consuelo looked over to her father.

"This is French television," the director said to El Brinco. "It's always in good taste."

El Brinco nodded. "Surely. Go ahead, daughter. You have my permission."

"No way," Consuelo said.

El Brinco looked at me. "Can she have your permission?"

"No way," I said.

"Thank you, Danny."

"My pleasure, Connie."

Consuelo laughed. This was the first time I'd seen her drinking beer.

"Just who are you?" the director asked me.

"A long story."

"You'll ruin this place," he said. He turned back to Consuelo. "O.K., good. Now, woman, what is your philosophy?"

"Try to stay healthy and try to stay sanitary. Change my underwear. Try to read one book a year." Then Consuelo smiled a great, beaming smile.

"Wonderful!" Napoleon and Jesus applauded.

"Good for you," the director said, and he shook his head. He looked around the room. "You. Santiago. Your turn now."

When Santiago got on camera, he appeared not to know who it was on the monitors. Then he recognized himself, and his face filled with humor. He looked quickly from monitor to monitor, as if trying to catch himself in the act of moving.

"Santiago," the French director said. "You are known in the jungle as the village philosopher. People come from miles to ask your opinion. Now people from around France and the globe are watching. They are asking, 'What is this wise man's philosophy?' "

Santiago smiled as he considered the question. "*Bueno*. Because you ask me, let's say I don't have one. A philosophy, that is. Philosophy has me. *Fi-lo-so-fí-a*. You hear it? Like that. Let's say it like that. *So-fí-a*. Like a lover. She likes to tease me with tantalizing questions."

I watched Santiago move in the monitors. He looked rested and happy, his broken nose had character, and he enjoyed the production so much that I thought he would make a good TV weatherman back in the U.S.

Santiago looked quickly from one image to the next.

"Who are we?" he asked.

"Where did we come from?" he asked.

"Where are we going?" he asked.

Then he laughed and looked back at the first image. "Hah! Caught you!" he said.

"Cut!" the director said. "Enough of this."

The director looked around the cantina. He looked at me and he shook his head. "Ruined."

Then he noticed Napoleon, who was entranced by the televisions. "You. Boy," he said.

Napoleon turned to him.

"It's your turn, boy. But here, please, I want you to be standing, to maximize your physique. You are very interesting, visually. You know that? That's true. Fascinating, really. Come here."

The director moved away the bench and table and he had his crew move the three cameras so that they had Napoleon in a full-face, a profile, and a full-body shot. He sent two men to set up lights out in the square, to give some dimension to the background.

"There!" he said. "Perfect. Now, what is your name?"

"Napoleon. Elefante, it appears."

"O.K. Elefante. Here is the scene. This is your body talking, understand? Your grotesque, dwarfish, but interesting body. A body with a story. And language of its own. And what does it say? Think about it for a minute. We have all the time in the world. This is your statement, Elefante. Now, everyone! Please. All quiet on the set."

Napoleon stood there and said nothing. He watched the full-body monitor intently. The director looked down at his wristwatch and nodded at the seconds passing. He glanced at his cameramen and back at his wrist. Then Napoleon began to move.

He pulled off his T-shirt and dropped it to the floor. He held his short arms straight out, then touched them over his head. He watched the monitor. He ran his hands across his chest. Then he bent over and pulled off his shorts. People gasped. Napoleon stood naked before the cameras, with the shorts slung over his shoulder. The director sat forward now and signaled a cameraman to do a slow circle around Napoleon. The rest of us stopped watching Napoleon himself and we watched him on the TVs. Napoleon's body was smooth and hairless. It was prepubescent, although he must have been more than twenty years old. With his large head and short limbs, he looked as if he were three years old and yet he was as tall as I. On the monitor, in black and white, he looked like a statue.

The camera circled him twice. Hector came over and stood behind me. "I don't believe it," he said into my ear.

"Hey," Hector said to the director. "I can get you real Indians with no hair."

"Shhh," said the director. "This is magnificent. We can back this with music. He looks like a Michelangelo, like the *David*. But a giant dwarf of the *David*. I can't believe it. What a comment this is, here in this jungle. On the modern age. Technology, civilization, art. All dwarfed by nature."

"It sucks," Hector said.

"Television is all image," the director said to him out of the side of his mouth. "If you can image it, you can get it. You can get it and I've got it."

The villagers were overcoming their shock.

"Put on your clothes, Napo," El Brinco said.

"You're embarrassing the women," Jesus said. "And me."

"Don't listen to them, Napo," Blind Jorge said. "You are doing fine."

"You're doing fine, Napito," Consuelo said. "We love you, *grandito*."

"We've always loved you, Napito," the women said.

"Now I too wish Angelina were here," Santiago said to me. "What a *pueblo* this is. Watch the people, Daniel."

In the bright TV lights, their hair and skin shone. Their eyes reflected rows of lights.

"Just great," Brinco said. "Why don't we all take off our clothes."

"No, Papa."

"I didn't mean it, Consuelo. I mean, look at this. We are really, really sick."

"You've got that right," said Hector.

"Well, me, I feel refreshed," Santiago said.

"Me too," Blind Jorge said. "I've got the idea."

Napoleon Elefante then looked away from the television monitors. He looked out into the village square where the lights had been set up. There, in the brightness framed all around by night, five elderly villagers were waltzing. One old man was naked, too.

Napoleon let go of his shorts and strode out of the cantina. Consuelo and half of the women followed him immediately. El Brinco said, "Damn it," and grabbed Napoleon's shorts. He chased the women out into the square and forced the shorts into Consuelo's hand. Consuelo stepped up to Napoleon, who had begun dancing alone. Napoleon graciously accepted the shorts and stepped back into them. Then he and Consuelo began to waltz. Now most of the villagers left the cantina and went out to the square and they began dancing. Jesus brushed aside the hands of several women and waited his turn with Consuelo.

"With what music?" the director asked himself. "Classical. Beethoven? Or the New World Symphony." He and his crew gathered their equipment and moved into the square. Hector followed. He walked through all the dancers and into the night.

I stayed in the darker cantina, watching the grayish glows fade from two of the monitors. One camera was still set up and I sat down in front of it. I watched myself on the monitor. No matter how I turned my head, if I kept watching the monitor, my eyes would never look back at me. It made me think of how my generation is more in love with itself than any in the history of the world. We were the first on earth to grow up with TV. Imagine Narcissus with a mirror that talked but never looked him straight in the eye.

Someone came back into the cantina and set up Jorge's shortwave radio. He tuned in a station from the Netherlands that played Golden Oldies American music. Out in the square, the *despedida* rolled on. People sent candle balloons up into the air. They carried Santiago and Napoleon around on their shoulders. "Our heroes!" they shouted.

Consuelo came into the cantina for more beer. "Come out and dance, Daniel," she said. "Everything is better." She took a swig from a *grande* and handed me the bottle.

Santiago came by once. "Everything," he said, "is desperate."

I listened to Van Morrison's "Brown-Eyed Girl," to Simon and Garfunkel's "Bridge over Troubled Waters," and to The Doors' "Light My Fire." I felt the music. Then I felt the chills. The malaria was upon me.

14

Three days later, after a great rain, I left with Santiago. We walked to the old river crossing and caught a bus toward the capital. We got off after two hours, in the mists of the fog forest, and we began to hike up a high vaulted trail that tunneled through the vegetation. The forest here grew by hydroponic suspension, taking its nutrients from the misty air. For a mile at a time, we could not see the sky. Everything grew green. The only flowers I saw were a dozen varieties of pale orchids with animal faces, and the only real animals existed solely as sounds. I heard things moving everywhere around me, but I saw nothing but tendrils, vines, branches, and boles. Once, when we stopped to rest, Santiago reached above his head and brought down a green mass that looked like a clump of grass. It was a sloth, its hair grown green with chlorophyll. The sloth smiled at us dully.

Although the trail was not steep here, we moved on all fours to keep our balance, reaching hand past hand from root to root, until we came to a cliff. I could see that the cliff rose straight above the trees up into the mist, and the effect was so powerful that I wanted to stay there and lie back and stare at it. It looked like a great living, breathing sponge and I had no idea how we would climb it.

But Santiago said we had to climb it, and soon. If we didn't, we would be caught by the night in the fog forest and that experience was always unpleasant. "There are poisonous centipedes here as big as your arm," he said. "They can sting you one hundred times. And if you sleep on the ground, the ground engulfs you. If you sleep in the vines, you are strangled."

"But where will we climb it?"

"Right here," he said. Santiago reached up and grabbed onto the mossy side of the cliff and pulled himself up. He kicked his feet into the vegetation to make himself footholds and he quickly, and quietly, rose up the cliff.

I took off my boots and hung them around my neck. I grabbed a handful of plants and began hauling myself up. The thick wall of the jungle brushed my back and made me feel that if I fell, I could reach out and catch myself in its branches.

I climbed two hundred feet and I broke out above the canopy. Here, the slope veered off vertical and I was able to put on my boots. Santiago was out of sight ahead of me, but the trail was apparent and I began to clamber. I was soon above the clouds. The volcano rose above me. The sun warmed the sweat on my neck and the wet vegetation gave way to grasses and rock. I came across Santiago at the entrance to a cave that opened out toward the jungle.

"This is it," he said. "Just as Angelina told me."

The cave had once been a bubble in molten lava. It was shaped like an egg sliced lengthwise and its walls were obsidian smooth. Its ceiling hung with rose crystals of quartz.

Santiago pointed back out over the jungle. The sun was

setting behind the volcano, and the arrow-shaped shadow of the volcano was gliding away from us across the cloudtops toward the heart of the Amazon. Beyond the clouds, I saw dark green forest, meandering rivers, and the occasional half-moon of a sandbar. At the far edge of the jungle, the horizon curved perfectly. Above the horizon, the moon was rising, banded by the heavy atmosphere. Never have I had such a strong sensation that I was standing on a world in space.

Santiago went out to look around. Angelina had stocked the cave with moss from the jungle, and the moss had dried to a soft green carpet, in places a foot thick. It was getting dark fast, the planet tipping into night, so I gathered dead branches and I used some of the dried moss as kindling. I built a small fire at the mouth of the cave and waited for Santiago.

I was starving, and we had not brought food. Santiago came back with an armload of rocks. They were spherical and hollow, their interiors lined with rose crystals, just like the roof of our cave.

"Thunder eggs," Santiago called them. "Every time one of these breaks—boom!"

"We can't eat thunder."

"No. But look at this one."

He handed me what looked like a black piece of lava. When I touched it, I dropped it. It was alive.

I kicked it over. It was black on its back, and on its underside, it was a bright orange, the Day-Glo orange of an emergency banner. It was a toad.

"They're all over out there, making love. Still hungry, Daniel?"

"They're probably poisonous."

"We don't know that."

"You eat it then."

"I am not the hungry one."

The toad flipped itself over and disappeared. Santiago squatted on his haunches and built a small cairn with the thunder eggs.

"When we first met," he said, "not so many years ago, after the so-called miracle where everyone didn't die, it was then I changed from being a wonderer to being a questioner." Santiago waved a hand out toward the black jungle. "Now it's hard to come up with a good question when you see something as big as all this."

"It's big," I said.

"It's big, Daniel. And we are small. But sometimes I think it's all my fault—what's happening in the village. Sometimes I think I ask too many questions. And God or someone keeps throwing answers at me. I'm not quick enough to catch them and the answers keep coming, flying right by me. Do you know what a good question feels like, Daniel? It feels like an elevation. I feel lifted up on my toes by a feeling of *What?—What's that?*—as I try to look over a wall."

Santiago looked at me over the little fire. "Do you know what an answer feels like?"

"Food?"

He nodded, and then asked, "Whose business is this, philosophy? Whom has it ever helped?"

"Where I come from, the only discussions of philosophy are on government-sponsored TV."

"That's interesting, Daniel. What's in it for the government?" I didn't know.

"It must sound better, coming from a TV?"

"I don't think so."

"Well, tell me then. What do North American wise men talk about, instead of philosophy?"

"Economics," I said.

"Money? I see."

The flaming moss showered us with miniature sparks that did not burn. I pointed to the little cairn Santiago had built.

"What are the stones for, Santiago?"

"Economists, apparently."

Before we retired, Santiago told me the myth of Los Puentes Caidos.

This myth was brand new, as mythologies go; it was one generation old. But it had all the qualities of the world's great stories: creation, destruction, great cycles, and mystery. The mystery interested Santiago the most.

"Happiness used to be the least of our worries," he told me. "We never had time for it except when we dreamed. Now with this dancing, we are sick with happiness. The whole village may die from it. What does it mean?"

Santiago and most of the old people in Los Puentes Caidos had been born in the village of Santiago's father, a place called Ingabamba, not far now, nearer the Guaguaruca volcano. Ingabamba had a peculiar reputation. The village itself kept dying, while its inhabitants seemed to live forever. The many deaths of the village were due to the volcano. Guaguaruca kept erupting, the earth kept quaking, and by ash or by shaking, the village was periodically destroyed. Its survivors lived on. And on. Ingabamba was one of those few places on earth where people commonly live to well beyond one hundred years of age. The Ingabambans joked that the main threat to their health was not disease and cigarettes but European scientists, who were always trying to stick them with needles to sample their blood.

Over and over again, Ingabamba disappeared beneath blank gray ash. During the eruptions, people hid their babies beneath overturned buckets, or put them into wicker baskets and set them adrift on the roiling water of the little river, hoping they would float to safety.

Far downstream, the water joined the Amazon. "Who knows?" Santiago said. "Maybe now those children are presidents of Brazil."

When Santiago's group of emigrants left the region, they

followed the river downstream. At the confluence with the muddy Norona, they found an abandoned village that would come to be known as Los Puentes Caidos. Its residents had recently fled. There was no food still cooking on fires or laundry hanging from the hibiscus, but there was something more forbidding. Before the people left, they had suspended all their furniture by ropes from the ceilings.

"We thought that was strange and it always bothered us," Santiago said.

The previous residents never returned, and the new occupants eventually cut down the furniture and took up housekeeping.

"It was funny about us," Santiago said. "We kept everything neat until we realized no one was coming back. Then we let everything fall apart."

But the legend remained, and everyone thought that either the original people would someday return or they themselves would someday leave the village and others would find it abandoned.

The next day I realized that Santiago had no idea of how to get to his father's village. I was hungry—he was bemused— and we walked west for hours across an iron-red plateau pocked with pools of sterile water. The great volcano rose from the far side of the plateau, a perfect, smoking cone. I kept us walking straight toward it. Santiago talked to himself.

At noon, Santiago stopped. He kept looking around and then down at his feet.

"Do you want to rest?" I asked.

He shook his head.

"It was right here," he said.

"What was?"

It was then we heard a horn honking. We stood in the black pools of our shadows and watched a bus drive straight toward us across the lava.

The bus was a typical Andean transport, a converted American Bluebird school bus, painted pastel blue and bedecked with ribbons. It drove right up to us and stopped. The driver opened the door. He was a boy of about seventeen.

"Hop on," he said. "We're lost."

Santiago and I looked at each other and got on.

"Where are you heading?" the driver asked.

Santiago didn't speak.

"Ingabamba," I said.

Santiago put his hand on my arm and shook his head. "I regret to tell you, Daniel. Ingabamba is here. Ingabamba was right here."

I looked back out the bus door at the endless plain of lava.

"The volcano finally got it," he said. "We are standing on Ingabamba."

The driver nodded. "That is not much help. So, O.K., where are you coming from?"

"Los Puentes Caidos," I said.

The driver squinted. "Never heard of it," he said. "I told you. We're lost."

He began driving south, weaving around the holes and spatter cones.

"I am sorry, Santiago," I said. "Perhaps your father got away."

"How?"

"Somehow."

We drove on. I asked the driver, "You say you're lost. But what are you doing here, lost?"

The boy smiled with bright teeth. "We stole this bus. All of us! We came in from Colombia, late last night. We have tons of contraband. Cigarettes and deodorants. Dandruff shampoo. When the real driver got off to talk to the border guards, we could tell he was selling us out. So we took over and skedaddled. The guards had no jeeps. And no bullets, maybe. And now that driver has no bus. All he could do was shout. In the middle of the night, we turned off the Pan-American to get good and lost. The sun came up and here we are. Does anyone know about this place? In Colombia, this would be a national park. Or a parking lot!"

The driver laughed. I looked back through the bus. It was half filled with middle-class Colombians, the women in dresses of solid reds or blues, the men in gray suits.

I drank a bottle of bootleg Heineken beer and ate a box of cookies shaped like Christmas trees. Santiago still didn't eat. In a few hours, we came to the edge of the lava flow and found a two-track trail leading to a muddy road which wound past haciendas and onto the Pan-American Highway.

Santiago and I got off at a town called Fuentes, a spa famous for its waters. I gave the driver some money. "Where do you think you'll go?" I asked him.

"Peru!" he said. "They have no catsup in Peru. They have no anything there. We've made it this far. And I've got all the driver's papers. All paid up! The union is international."

At Fuentes, Santiago accepted a hamburger. I said we should head back to Los Puentes, but Santiago said we had to wait.

"Perhaps something different is going to happen," he said. "And it will help if we're not there."

"Perhaps Angelina needs us."

"Of course she needs us. That's why I did not tell her we were going."

We stayed in Fuentes, where hot springs emerge beneath a cliff at the base of a horsetail waterfall. We soaked in the hot, pea-green water and showered under the crystal-cold falls. We waited, while Santiago watched the mountains and I read newspapers. It felt as if we were soldiers on leave from a war zone. Santiago seemed shell-shocked.

"I've noticed," he said, "that if the world's too still, if *something* isn't moving, then everything disappears from our minds.

Maybe that's why we blink and roll our eyeballs about so much—to keep the world moving in our heads. That's why the frog has to blink his eyes—to keep the world out there, in front of him. If I'm not there, seeing Los Puentes Caidos, maybe Caidos isn't there at all."

"If Caidos isn't there, then we're not anywhere, Santiago. Think about Angelina."

"I wonder if I am doing what my father would have done," he said. "Once, he said that lives are stories told over and over. The good ones keep getting better."

"What do you think?"

"What do I think? I think we have to think about it, Daniel. I've always thought that. And while we're at it, we have to think about thinking. We learn best by thinking, just as fish breathe by drinking." He paused. "Don't they?"

"No," I said. "Let's go back."

"Sometimes," Santiago said, "if something's confusing you, you have to go away from it and then come back."

"We're away. Let's go back."

But we waited in Fuentes. I kept thinking about the other time I had left Angelina, and how long I had been away. Finally I said, "I can't stand it. I've got to go back."

Santiago said, "Now! Now we go back!"

I hired a pickup to drive us to Los Puentes Caidos, but an army roadblock stopped us just past the Huasipungo garrison. The pickup turned around and we got off.

"Felicitations!" the lieutenant in charge greeted us. "I regret my colonel is not here. He was recalled for urgent consultations. You know how it is, what with the war and all."

"What war?"

"Well, the rumor of war."

He was eager to see my U.S. passport and visa. "I am not with the infantry," he said to me. "I specialize in chemical and biological warfare. That is why I am here."

"Why is that?" Santiago asked him.

"Because the village below here is under quarantine. Martial quarantine, under rules of war. The people are sick there. We don't know with what. I hesitate to implicate Peru."

Santiago raised an eyebrow. "What kind of quarantine is a martial quarantine?"

"It means the locality is militarily sterilized."

"What does that mean?"

The lieutenant smiled. "It means no doctors allowed. It means we shoot."

"You shoot bullets."

"Especially bullets."

"You shoot sick people."

"Sick people and doctors. We shoot the sick especially. The Republic, old man, is now a technocracy. Things will get better. Get used to it."

"But we have to go in there. We have family and friends."

The lieutenant nodded. "The armed forces sympathize. And we understand. You can go in there, old man. You cannot come out. Unless we shoot you first. Or until the quarantine is lifted."

"How long will that be?"

"*Cuarenta días*. By law, forty days. Minus the five days we have been positioned. Or until the epidemic finalizes itself. Whichever comes first."

"Has anyone tried to come through here?"

"Some North Americans waving handkerchiefs. We hit one of them and they ran away. That is when the colonel got worried and returned to the capital. And then later, three of the villagers came up from below. They smiled and sang. They tried to give our soldiers aluminum pans and flowers. A clever ruse. We shot them, too, of course. Because they were sick."

"You killed them?"

"Let us say they were casualized."

"Do their relatives know?"

"They were casualized, not classified. It will all be in my report."

"We're going in there," Santiago said.

"You may go in there. We'll shoot you when you come out. Or, if you prefer, you may come back and hide behind that big kapok tree, where my men cannot hit you. You may shout me information, for my report."

The lieutenant checked my passport again. "I am also a technologist," he said to me. "I would like to own a Macintosh. Perhaps we can talk about computers."

"*Vamos*," Santiago said to me.

"Forever in your service," the lieutenant said, and saluted. "Don't shoot us in the back."

"Don't worry. You are not sick, yet."

We hurried down the road.

15

The destruction surprised us. It looked as if the Army had attacked and left the village in ruins. Smoke rose from the remnants of one house, now a rectangle of ashes enclosed by spears of half-burned bamboo. Other houses, on the hillside, had been burned too, and their remains looked like craters left by artillery. The trees around the houses stood scorched and brown, and scraps of smoke seemed to catch in their branches.

In the middle of the village square sat a Mercedes tourist bus. It was blackened and gutted, its window glass broken and tires melted. Nearby lay the carcass of a yellow dog, its legs stiff and sticking into the air. Another dog was sniffing at the carcass from five feet away. When this dog saw us, it yelped and ran off. Then the dog I thought was dead got up and snarled at us. In front of the open store, four or five men, all villagers, lay side by side in the dirt. They all wore cutoffs and baseball caps. They all looked drunk, or dead.

Then we saw the cantina and the white parachutes. Many of these parachutes were strung from the cantina's eaves to form a pavilion of billowing tents. Others hung from a line extended from the cantina out to an African palm. Behind the cantina, toward the little river beach, more parachutes draped over the hibiscus trees. The visual effect was that of a carnival, or a battlefield hospital.

"Laundry," Santiago said. "Look at all the laundry."

He and I walked slowly toward the cantina and stopped in front of it. The interior of the building was hidden behind billowing nylon. Inside, someone was singing.

"Hello!" I shouted.

"Hello! Anyone!" Santiago called.

We heard bare feet walking across the bare board floor. The footsteps came closer, retreated, then came closer again. Then Consuelo slipped through the curtain, backward. She turned halfway toward us and stopped, looking over her shoulder. She was already smiling and she brightened when she saw us. She wore a short, togalike gown made from torn white parachute nylon.

"Oh, Danny!" she said. She held her fingertips together and curtsied.

"Consuelo, what's going on?"

Consuelo dipped and ran her fingers along her gown. "One hundred parachutes," she said. "One hundred clean air force parachutes brought by the Navy for the Army downriver. In all consideration for the national armed forces. Now to bury the dead."

"Tell us what's happening, Consuelo."

Consuelo curtsied again and did a slow pirouette. "Too wonderful," she said. She stopped turning around, but she kept twisting her shoulder to the right and dipping.

Santiago pointed to the store and the men lying in the dirt. "What goes?" he asked.

Consuelo looked at the men. Her smile left for a second but returned before she spoke. "One hundred cases of beer," she said. "One hundred parachutes and one hundred cases of beer. Such considerate numbers from a considerate Navy. Soon we will have one hundred cadavers."

"What do these parachutes have to do with beer?" Santiago asked. "And what cadavers?"

"The Navy knows. The beautiful, beautiful Navy."

"Consuelo," I said. "What's the matter, Consuelo?"

"I am happy," she said. "But I am so sick."

I chilled. Consuelo sighed and said, smiling, "The dancing and smiling frightened the Navy. But Lieutenant Hugo Rios del Rio would not have been frightened.

"Que no," she said. *"Que no. Qué lindo. Qué lindo. Lindo.* Oh, no. How beautiful. Beautiful. Beautiful."

"Consuelo!" I said. "What is wrong?"

"Everything is too beautiful." Consuelo turned around in front of us again. She looked beautiful, and happy. She looked more African now, thinner and darker, more like her father, El. Brinco. Her teeth were whiter. Her brown eyes were tremendous.

"I am sick!" she said. She held her elbows in her hands and she shivered.

I ran up the steps and held her.

"Oh, oh, one cannot stand it," she said. "Oh, oh, I cannot stand it. Tell me, Danielito, is this how you felt after your fevers?" She smiled and then shivered and dipped her shoulder. The convulsion was so strong it shook us both.

"Consuelo," Santiago said. "Where is Angelina?"

"Inside."

Santiago started to go in, but then he held back.

"Oh, I love you, Danny," Consuelo was saying to me. "I do! The feelings I have feel like they are going to kill me." A sudden spasm jerked her from me. She turned away, into the cantina.

I started to follow her, but Santiago held my arm.

"No," he said. "Wait. I cannot go in until I see her first. If she is sick or dying, I cannot go in. My own Angelina! What have we done?"

He led me around the corner of the cantina. He pulled apart some of the nylon and looked inside. I hesitated to see, but I wanted to, too much. I looked in over his shoulder.

Inside, we saw Angelina, looking like an angel. She was tending to people who looked like ghosts. The air in the cantina smelled heavy and sweet. Soft light shone through the white nylon. Sticks of palo santo, the incense tree, were tied to the posts and burning. Their smoke fell like slow water down to the floor.

Angelina stood facing us, looking down. She was draped in a gown of flowing white nylon. Braided cords of parachute nylon wrapped around her waist and then crossed between her breasts and rose over her shoulders. Her face was illuminated in the soft white light. Her forehead seemed to glow.

Six or seven villagers lay in the cantina, all dressed in white parachute nylon and all tied by parachute shroud lines into reclining blue leather seats from the Mercedes bus outside. Some smiled sweetly. One woman sang softly. Two kept turning their heads from side to side as if they were watching a parade.

"Ah! Ah! Hah! There you are!" one of them said when he noticed us. He continued to sweep the room with his gaze. "Ah! Hah! There you are," he said when he saw us again. "Ah! We have been waiting for you!"

It was Jesus. He was wrapped up in nylon, his head swaddled like an Arab's. He looked deliriously, stupidly happy. "Ah! There you are! We've been waiting for you!" he chanted. "Oh!" and he watched something invisible go by him.

Angelina looked up from her work and saw us.

"Ah! *Tú!*" she shouted at me. "Thou! Where hast thou been?" She had not called me *tú* in fifteen years.

"Angelina!" Santiago gasped. "My God! My daughter! Are you well? What has happened?" He threw up his hands and ran into the cantina. I followed him inside.

Angelina brushed her father aside. "At last!" she said to me. "And now! You! You would leave me again!" Angelina began to cry. "You couldn't! You couldn't!"

I went to her. I expected her to hit me, but she dropped her arms and she let me hold her. She leaned into me and gave a great, deep cry.

"What has happened here, daughter?" Santiago asked, hovering around us. "Why have you tied them down?"

"Because," said Angelina, "they will fly away. They will flit around like butterflies and I cannot watch them. I cannot feed them. I cannot find out what's killing them."

"What's killing them?" Santiago asked.

"Their brains!" she said. "That's all I know. The whole village is dying. Happily, giddily, joyfully dying! Or getting drunk and getting evil." Angelina pinched my arm so hard it hurt.

"And Consuelo?" I asked.

"Consuelo? She is different and she dies differently. She can still do things. She can sweep, in circles. She helps me, in circles. And I leave her free so I don't go mad."

Santiago held his hands to the sides of his head. He turned around and surveyed the scene. When he turned away, Angelina whispered to me, "And I've got it too. I think I am dying, Daniel."

"You're fine," I said.

At this point, Santiago staggered. He sat down on the arm of Jesus' bus seat. "I think I've got it too," he said. He put a hand to his forehead.

"No," I said.

"In that bus on the lava, I was going around in circles," Santiago said. "In my thoughts, circles. In my dreams, circles. And my conversations with you, Daniel. Hopeless circles. This world is an image of life in my head."

Consuelo came by and grabbed my arm to stop herself from turning. "*Dios*. Yes. This world," she said. "When I stop, it spins."

"You're sick," I told her. "Consuelo, sit down."

"I'll vomit," Consuelo said. "Will you dance with me? I won't vomit if you will dance with me. Make love to me, Daniel. Daniel, dancing. And I won't vomit, dancing."

Angelina hugged me tighter. "Daniel is mine now," she warned Consuelo. "I've got him now."

"Oh yes. You got him, at last," Consuelo said brightly. "We know!"

"We are all going to die!" Angelina whispered in my ear. "Are we all going to die?"

"We'll get help," I said.

"Are you in love now?" Consuelo asked Angelina. "How? So much? So finally?"

"We must get help," I said.

"It is too late," Angelina said. "These *pobrecitos* will be dead tomorrow."

"Does it feel good to you?" Consuelo asked Angelina.

"Does what feel good?" Angelina said.

"We have to get help," I said.

"Love, Angelina," Consuelo said. "Does love feel good? I love. I love Daniel and I feel sick."

All of the angelic villagers smiled. "Oh! Hah!" Jesus said. "There you are again!"

Santiago moaned. "How can it be that I am dying and I am the only one who does not feel happy?"

"We need to get help," I said. "I'll go to the capital for doctors."

"The Army," Santiago said. "They'll shoot you like a goat."

"I'll find a way."

Angelina squeezed me. "If you leave me again . . ." she warned.

"If . . . you . . . leave me . . ." Consuelo sang.

"Then come with me, Angelina."

She squeezed me. "I cannot go yet," she said. "And you cannot go yet. I will not let you."

"You cannot . . ." Consuelo sang.

Angelina did not look like she was dying. She looked tired and frantic, at her wits' ends. Consuelo looked like she was crazy, and sick, but not like she was dying. Jesus looked like his mind was gone. I could see that he was dying. His eyes were filled to the brim with nothing.

Santiago sat on the arm of Jesus' chair and held his head in his hands again. *"Este mundo,"* he said. "This world is unreal. And I feel . . . ?" He cocked his head and listened for an answer.

I did not know what all was going on, but Angelina was holding me now and I knew something had changed drastically inside her.

"It is I who will leave you," Angelina whispered to me.

I kissed her. She pinched my arm.

"Santiago," I said.

Santiago looked up. *"Sí, compadre?"*

"We must ask the right question now, *viejo*."

Santiago shrugged. "What is the right question?"

"The right question is always the same. What can we do?"

Santiago pursed his lips and raised his eyebrows. At that moment, he looked ancient.

"Perhaps nothing," he said.

"Something," I said.

I took Angelina's hand and I led her to the beach so we could talk. When we passed the hibiscus trees, I saw three bodies wrapped in parachute nylon. They looked like the larvae of giant ants.

"We roll them into the river," Angelina said.

Up the beach on the little river, we found Blind Jorge sitting in the sand. He held a palm frond over his head. Napoleon Elefante stood about three paces away from Jorge. Napo crossed his arms and stared away downriver. He wore a pair of tattered white briefs and he had wrapped a turban of parachute nylon around his great head to shelter his eyes.

"The situation is hopeless," Angelina said. "Jorge is hiding. He says he is invisible. Jesus is dying. He thinks he's watching a parade. El Brinco is drunk. Napoleon is sullen. Many are dying. Others are evil. Evil on purpose, terrible evil. Evil while they smile."

Angelina told me that when Santiago and I left on his quest, the epidemic exploded. Half the people in Los Puentes Caidos suddenly started dancing and smiling. Everyone took to the village square, either dancing the macabre stumbling waltz or chasing the dancers around the square and trying to tend to their loved ones. Nearly all the older villagers fell down and died. The younger dancers let them lie where they fell, and kept dancing and smiling.

That was when the bus with the American tourists arrived. They were four English professors, on a field trip to the land of Latin literature, the land of magical realities. The professors thought that the village was having a fiesta and the villagers were all drunk or passed out. So the professors danced with the delirious villagers and had their pictures taken together.

Then the navy pickup truck arrived, loaded with the usual beer for the garrison downriver and the illogical cargo of parachutes. The two sailors unloaded their cargo onto the beach and went looking for Lieutenant Hugo Rios. An ecstatic, delirious villager told them what had happened to Hugo, and what had happened to the North American survivalist, and what had be-

come of the last tour guide. Cheerfully, the villager described
the contagion of this strangest kind of happiness.

The sailors told the tour-bus driver, and after a short discussion, they all panicked. They jumped into the navy truck
and fled, stranding the tourist professors. The sailors alerted
the commander of the army garrison at Huasipungo Pass. The
commander imposed a quarantine.

The professors stayed in the village for another day. At first,
they were angry at the tour guide for deserting them, and then
they realized what was happening around them. The professors
held a meeting and decided not to panic. They would go speak
to the garrison commander. They worried because none of them
spoke Spanish and Angelina refused to go with them. But that
didn't matter because before they got close enough, the soldiers
shot at them and hit one of the professors in the elbow. Then
they all ran back to the village screaming and they demanded
that Angelina do something.

Angelina already had. She had confiscated their bus and
moved its seats into the cantina, which she converted into an
infirmary. Hector Tanbueno, who had been charging the professors to show them naked Indians, now offered to take them
away from the plague and lead them on a secret trail around
the roadblock. He would do it for all the cash they had on hand.
The professors voted. Two wanted to go with Hector. Two wanted
to wait for the U.S. Marines. But when the first two followed
Hector out of the village, the other two professors ran after
them. Hector stopped the procession and made everyone pay in
advance.

That was four days ago, Angelina said. No one had seen the
professors, or Hector, since.

"And Jesus burned their bus," Angelina said. "He burned
the bus and half the village."

"And where did Brinco go?"

"El Brinco started downriver to fetch the French."

"The French? The television people? Why?"

"What else could he do? He couldn't go upriver without getting shot. He said he would go talk to Jacques Cousteau. Daniel, listen to me. Everyone has gone crazy here. And so have I. Everyone who is not dancing and smiling is going crazy in some other way."

We walked up the beach past Jorge and Napoleon and we stopped opposite the big black rock. Angelina told me that after the sailors fled and Hector led the American professors into the jungle, the younger villagers began to die. Everyone now realized that the dancing was a fatal disease, and that kindness and happiness were all its symptoms. This scared everyone who was not already too happy. Blind Jorge got a revolver and tried to shoot himself in the eyes. Another man snatched away the revolver, and before anyone could stop him, he shot himself in the knee.

"And the others," said Angelina, "the big talkers like Jesus, they decided the only antidote to such kindness and goodness was evil. So they all got mean."

El Brinco broke into the Navy's beer and got the entire village drunk. Little Jesus picked fights with the bigger men and the bigger men beat him mercilessly. Between beatings, Jesus led gangs of arsonists who burned the bus and the houses.

"El Brinco got all worked up," she said. "And he slapped Consuelo. And when she laughed and kissed him and hugged him and told him she loved him, he broke into pieces and wept. Consuelo the gentle, the always kind Consuelo, had fallen ill with the kindness. El Brinco despaired. Was there no justice? He decided to go get the French. He thought that perhaps the Frenchman Cousteau, who saved the world's oceans, who was here in the jungle to save the Amazon River, could save the people of Los Puentes Caidos."

"That Frenchman is not Cousteau," I said.

"Daniel, that does not matter."

When El Brinco prepared to go downriver, Consuelo decorated his canoe with flowers. By this time, Jesus had fallen ill too. He stopped burning people's homes and gave away all his money, and in his happiness, Jesus kissed Brinco goodbye. El Brinco floated away in the morning, crying like a baby, beating his head with his fists, riding his raft of flowers.

"We all watched him from the beach," Angelina told me. "It was sad and beautiful. El Brinco drifted away sideways. Everyone was cheering, the sick and the well, and then something grabbed Brinco's canoe from below and the current rolled him over with all of Consuelo's flowers, and El Brinco nearly drowned. It was then that I realized how many people were sick, because so many people kept cheering."

El Brinco hopped back into town and those people who were sick kept dancing and dying and those who were well got drunk again and burned down more houses and started killing pigs and pets. And people.

"Almost everyone went crazy except Napo," Angelina said. "And most everything burned. Only the cantina is a refuge. So far."

Angelina amazed me. She had not talked so much since I first met her when I was a young drifter and lost.

"You know, Daniel," Angelina said, "before all this began, you were the one who looked crazy to me. Now you look like the sanity of the world." She looked deeply into my eyes.

"You look wonderful to me, Angelina," I said.

"I have watched you since you came back to Los Puentes Caidos. At first, I thought you came back here to go crazy, like gringos do. Why did you return? Did you come back because you loved me? Did you love me, Daniel?"

"Yes," I said.

"Then why didn't you tell me? Why didn't you tell me you loved me right away? All of this would not have had to happen."

Angelina turned away from me and faced the big rock. "This

is all horrible. Horrible. Why didn't you begin by asking me if I loved you?"

"I was waiting, Angelina. I wanted you to love me."

"But I loved you."

"Then I was waiting for you to show me."

"To show?" said Angelina. "To show you? Me? How does a woman of North America show a man that she loves him?"

She looked across the river. "I showed you I loved you, once, I thought. And you never once told me that you loved me."

"I love you, Angelina."

"Oh!" She put her hands over her ears. "This is too late!"

The jungle had not changed since the day I arrived, but everything else was different. Now no one was swimming in the river. No children basked on the black rock. The beach was deserted, except for the blind Jorge hiding beneath his frond and the great dwarf Napoleon, who looked like a genie just out of a bottle.

"I want to show you again," Angelina said. "Once more, for my own sake, and then that is it."

I reached for her, but she stepped out into the river. She turned to face me. "But first, you must say it again, Daniel."

"Say it? I love you, Angelina."

"Again."

"I love you."

"Again."

"I love you," I said, but it hurt me to say it.

"Fine," she said. "That's enough, Daniel."

Angelina fixed me with her clear green eyes. She untied the knot of shrouds at her waist. She gathered the white nylon of her gown in her hands and pulled it up and over her head. She dropped the material into the river and she stood before me, naked. The sight of her transfixed me. Angelina was the most beautiful vision I have ever seen. Her golden skin attracted the

sunlight. Her green eyes matched the jungle green. They reflected the golden sand of the beach. And the sand reflected
the sunlight up against the undersides of her cheekbones and
breasts. The roar of the river flowing past the black rock coursed
around her shoulders and wrapped in her hair. Her hands opened
and revealed her pale palms. Her ankles parted the water. Above
her breast, the blue birthmark of a butterfly flew toward her
throat. The river flowed behind her, moving in sunlight, and
beyond the river, the jungle darkened.

It shamed me, it hurt me, but I said it again. "I love you,
Angelina."

"That's enough."

"I love you."

"Stop it, I said."

Her white nylon gown, made from a parachute, drifted away
on the river. It passed Jorge and Napoleon, and Napoleon saw
it and waded out after it.

"I love—"

"Enough!"

Angelina smiled. She shook her head and smiled. "I would
drown myself," she said. "I was planning to—to show you. I
was crazy. Now I am free."

She was beauty. "I am free," she said. "I will leave when
I can."

Then she saw something behind me. She slipped away into
the water and swam out in the river.

Santiago came up beside me. He looked immensely sad.
"All is lost," he said. "And I don't have a clue."

Angelina swam into view from behind the black rock, but
Santiago did not see her. He noticed Jorge and Napoleon. "What
of the blind man and the dwarf?" he asked.

"Jorge is invisible," I told him. "Napo is watching him."

"Invisible from himself?" Santiago asked.

"I see him," I said.

Just then, Angelina climbed out of the river and stood on the black rock in the middle of the current. She was a perfect form, a beautiful human body. Her physical presence graced the world.

I waited for Santiago to notice his daughter. He did, but he didn't seem to recognize her. He sucked on his teeth and contemplated her seriously.

"Now that is magnificent," he said. "Who is that?"

"She is your daughter, Santiago. Angelina."

I waited for the realization to strike him.

"She is not sick, is she?" Santiago asked.

"No, Santiago. She is the healthiest human on earth."

Santiago took my hand. "She is yours if she'll have you," he said sadly.

Santiago walked down the beach without spirit. Napoleon saw him and ran to embrace him. Out in the current, Angelina spread her arms to the sun. I half expected her to fly away. It was too much to watch her, and I turned to follow Santiago.

16

antiago seemed broken. I decided to call a last meeting
of his drinking and thinking club, if only to engage him.

"It may surprise you," I said. "Maybe all is lost, but
if you quit now, you will miss the summing up. Listen, Santiago.
I will get your thinkers together. We will drink and we'll talk.
We will figure it all out. Then I am going. If you and Angelina
won't leave with me, I'll go and bring help from the capital."

Santiago considered this and then nodded. "We could put
our minds together," he said. He rubbed his forehead with both
his hands and he looked at his fingertips, as if to see if something
had rubbed off. "Yes. Well, yes. This may be the opportunity.
Perhaps this calamity will sharpen our brains and we will come
up with something." He looked at me hard. "Yes? Something
tremendous, do you think?"

"I do, Santiago."

"Then yes, Daniel. Then we must understand it all. It is at

times like these when we have most opportunity. The right question asked at the right time may possibly result in the answer."

"That's right."

"That's right. And as long as you still have your wits, Daniel, a last meeting of the minds might produce something big in you, too. Who knows? You might come up with something. You see, I've been wondering—Why else would our village, which prides itself on its thought, be attacked by a disease of the mind? Why the illogical? Why the unreason? Perhaps, at the least and at last, we could frame the right question, construct an answer, inscribe it on paper, and put it into a bottle to float away on the river. Then, Daniel, thus so well documented, thus so well finished, well . . . Well, we could die."

"Not die, Santiago."

"But we could find an answer!" He paused. "But who would read it, Daniel?"

"Who knows. Maybe somebody in Brazil."

That made him smile. "Brazil," he said. "I like that idea."

It was easier to resurrect optimism in Santiago than to find any regular thinkers left in Los Caidos. Two more people had died in the cantina, where Angelina was now back at work. I helped her wrap the bodies in parachutes and we laid them with the corpses under the hibiscus trees. Working so close to Angelina made me feel shaky. And the odor of death mixed in the back of my brain with the redness of the hibiscus's bright trumpets. Angelina was back to business as usual. After touching the bodies, she went down to the river and washed her hands.

Several of the drunks had wakened near the store. Other village men had joined them from elsewhere. El Brinco was there. While the others watched indolently, he and a man with a knife now fought a slow circling battle in front of the store. El Brinco was pivoting on his one leg and fending off the knife man with a wooden chair. The man lunged at El Brinco and

Brinco broke the chair over his head. The man collapsed to his knees and began to vomit.

As I approached, they all turned to me and some raised their eyebrows. El Brinco smiled in recognition.

"Hombres," I said. "Come to the cantina. Santiago calls a meeting. You have to decide what to do."

"What to do?" Brinco said. "Now that's rich. What to do. What's left?"

"A last meeting," I said. "For Santiago's sake. Come on. Let's go over to the cantina."

The village men looked at each other. "Why not?" the man who vomited said. "Let's go over to the shade. Somebody help me up."

Blind Jorge was already in the cantina, as was Napoleon Elefante, who sat with his hands squeezed between his knees. Napoleon's hands and knees were dirty from digging up a cache of El Brinco's beer. Consuelo circled around, setting out bottles. Angelina was tending to her remaining patients, who were all swaddled up like babies.

"Happy to see you," Jesus said to us. He was still tied to his seat. "I think I am getting sick."

The drinking session started out badly. The men snatched up the bottles and began to guzzle them down.

"No gargling, please," Santiago said to the men. "Please take your time. And sit down to drink. There is plenty refreshment. We will think and discuss in our usual manner, although I can see you are not the usual members."

The men took their places. "The usuals are dead, Santiago," El Brinco said. "Or worse, insane."

"Or gone. Many have run."

"We are the *un*usuals, Don Santiago. We are what's left over, the remains, the afterwards. We have small education."

"Or need of it, around here," growled the man who had vomited.

Santiago surveyed the men I had gathered. "Perhaps that's the natural progression," he said. "And perhaps for the better, for the anesthetic effect, to help us with the objectivity. So, sit and drink, good gentlemen. And tell me, what has been happening? What have you been doing?"

"Bad things," Blind Jorge said, shaking his head. "Very bad."

"Evil things," said Napoleon. "They fight evil with evil."

"Then tell me, please."

Jesus spoke up. "I burned down two houses! Then I burned down my own."

"I helped you, Jesus," said the man who vomited, "to burn down the house in which you were born. And I killed a pet dog, a family's pig, and my favorite cat."

"Manifestly," said Jesus. "And then I killed Presidente Wilson."

No one was struck by this but Santiago and me.

"You killed old Wilson?" I asked.

"I caught him laughing," said Jesus.

"Jesus got radical," El Brinco said.

"I can take the smiling. But laughing . . ."

"How . . . ?" Santiago began.

"Like this!" Brinco pointed down with his thumb. "What? Crrrrrk! Whoops! Dead."

"But you *killed* him, Jesus?" Santiago asked.

Napoleon spoke. "These men also killed some old ones, Santiago. Of course, some may have been dead already."

"But, Napo," said Santiago. "You say they killed Wilson?"

Napoleon held up his clasped hands and shook them as if he were strangling a doll.

"Some of the old ones may indeed have been dead already," El Brinco said. "But who knew, the way they'd been acting? And what does it matter? Who can tell about anyone these days? What is life? When is death? It was nip and tuck there for a while. Time has slowed now, but who knows about later? For a while it was all speeding up. Horribly so. Formidable, it was. And it was Jesus who caused the real terror. 'Let's hurry things up!' Jesus shouted. 'Let's hurry things up. It's the end!' "

"That was rich," the man who vomited said.

"Hurry up!" Jesus now said. "That's exactly what I said."

"In truth, some people have gotten better," said Napoleon. "But you should have been here when it seemed none would survive. Events! Such events. It was history, I tell you. History, all charged with events."

"It was the end!" Jesus said.

"Yes," Brinco said. "The whole village dancing and dying and killing for no reasons. No reasons! Your worst enemy becoming kind and caring and offering to give you your own machete, which he had just stolen to give to you, with a smile like you should thank him. It made you want to take it and hack him into infinitesimal pieces."

"What is to be said, Santiago?" Napoleon asked. "You know I would try, but what have we left to think? The end of the world came early to Los Caidos."

Napoleon spread his short arms wide and opened his big hands. At the same time, blind Jorge held out his hands, palms up. Santiago looked at me. The thinking club was foundering.

Now Jesus shouted, as clear as a bell. "That's it! I enjoyed it. I'm ready to go. Thank you for the patience, and please now, somebody go ahead and let me up."

"We need a sign from somewhere," Santiago said.

"Listen to me, Santiago," said Jorge. "We had the sign. When things went bad, for the first time in my life I felt really blind, actually, literally blind. The screaming was horrible. The laughing was pitiable. The smells of buildings and bodies burning, you can't get them out of your nose. Awful! Awful! The little children crying. No! Then I stopped listening and I realized—I had vanished!"

The man who vomited laughed. "No! You? How can you vanish? I can see you right now. You're an old blind man."

"Keep looking, friend," Jorge said. "I have heard from Santiago that if you stare at something long enough, it will disappear. The way I feel now, I can't see you and you can't see me."

Everyone stared at the blind man.

Jorge waved a hand in front of his face. "It's working, my idiots," he said. "I can't *hear* you. I can't *feel* you. You can't *see* me."

"Somebody!" Jesus cried. "Would somebody please let me go!"

Angelina went to Jesus, but no one else moved. Flies were filling the room. Some of the parachute nylon had pulled down when we entered the cantina and now the men squinted and waved their hands in front of their faces. Consuelo circled through with more beer for everyone. Everyone drank greedily, noisily. Santiago drank deeply. He looked small to me, and defeated.

I stood up. "That's it," I said. "That's it. I'm going."

"No!" cried Angelina. "I won't let you." Her eyes shone bright and fierce. "I will go first!"

The whole drinking club sat up and watched us.

"I'm going," I said. "Angelina, you said you loved me. You said you would show me. Show me now by letting me go."

"Love!" someone said.

"It's not unbelievable," Napoleon said.

"I cannot leave my father," Angelina said.

"Of course you cannot," Napoleon said.

"Yes, Daniel, wait," Santiago said in a small but brighter voice. "She cannot go now. You can see that. And we have not finished our discussion."

"We've had enough. All we've ever done is talk."

"That's not true, Daniel." Santiago's voice grew quavering and thin. "We were right on the edge. I was right on the edge.

I was thinking of something true. Wait a minute now. It's coming back." Santiago put his hands to his forehead.

I felt how much I loved him, but I said, "It is too late."

"That's not true, Daniel."

Then we heard the mocking voice of Hector Tanbueno.

"That's not true, Daniel," he mimicked, singing. *"That's not true, Daniel."*

Hector entered from behind a shroud. Several of the drinkers applauded when they saw him. Hector bowed theatrically.

"Still drinking?" he asked. "I'm happy to see it." He held up an Auruna Indian sack woven from plant fibers. "See what I have for you? Lemons! Lemons, Santiago, so you can drink and think in a Santiago fashion. Suck on a lemon, my honey, my sweet. Let the truth sting as you speak it. And pucker up, *compadres*. Think while your mouths are all puckered up and your brains are turned into crayfish seviche. And then tell me." He clucked his tongue. "What? *Qué pasa?* What's going on? You don't know?" He poured the lemons out onto the table. They wobbled down the plank and the men picked them up. "You don't know what's going on?

"Hey, dude," Hector said to me. "I see you came back. Too bad for you."

Hector was wearing clothes that weren't his: a pair of new Banana Republic six-pocket cargo pants and a red T-shirt with big white letters that read, "Nowhere Else But Stanford."

Santiago did not turn to look at Hector, but his expression drained further and his eyes dulled. Hector walked up to him and fished around in one of his pockets for another lemon and a jackknife. He squeezed the lemon into Santiago's beer.

"Think about it, old man," Hector said. "Drink this and think about it."

He pulled another lemon from his pocket and tossed it to me. "That one's yours," he said.

The lemon was soft and mottled. It looked rotten compared to those on the table. I tossed it over my shoulder.

"Pffft!" Hector said. "I'll get you a better one later. Well, boys, what's the subject today? Life? Death? Love? Money?" He pulled out a wad of American bills and traveler's checks and tossed them onto the table. "See? I know what I'm talking about."

A few of the men whistled.

"There's more where that came from. The U.S. of A. I know how to get there and I know how to get all we want. Airplane tickets. Credit cards too. You know about credit cards? They never need money. Hey, what's the matter? Why all the long faces?"

Santiago slowly drank down his beer.

"Hey, old man," Hector said. "Brighten up. This could be your last day. This could be your birthday. As a gringa once told me, 'Today is the first day of the rest of your life.' That's the gringo's creed. At least they say that it is. At least she thought so at the time.

"That was Cynthia," Hector said to me. "Remember Cynthia, Danny boy? I wonder whatever happened to her."

"She's fine, I'm sure."

"I disagree," Hector said. "And also her friend. The one who had the hots for you."

The men all squeezed their lemons into their beers.

"That's it, boys!" Hector said. "Let's pucker up to get kissed. By what? What is the question? What is the debate of the day today?"

"How about this?" one of the men asked. He looked as if he had just woken up. "How about, 'Is this really the end?' "

"Good," said Hector. "Is this really the end? That's really good. That's really true or false. I can answer that one. The answer is: true. Really true. This is really the end."

The men drank. Nobody spoke.

"That one was easy," Hector now said. "Ask me another. Make it harder this time. Make it a multiple choice, as they do in the U.S. The hardest kind of question. Is it A? Is it B? Bzzzzz! Time's up! Come on now, you geniuses."

I was about to speak, when Santiago said, "The question is this. What do we do? We must do something. What do we do?"

"Oh, Jesus Christ. It's too late, old man," Hector said. "It is too late to do. To do? It's done! I have done it already. It is over. *No hay nada que hacer*.

"Do. Did. Dead," he said to me in English.

"Daniel," Santiago asked me. "Is it too late?"

"No."

Hector laughed. "Yes! This time it is. This time, it is forever too late. Too late," he said, and he laughed again. "Well now. That test was easy."

"What do we do?" Santiago repeated.

"Too late, *viejo*. I have already done it. I claim the victory. This village is mine. You are mine. Angelina is mine." Hector pointed at me. "And you are dead, gringo."

At that moment, Jesus screamed, "Let me go!"

Hector shrugged, and he smirked, "Would somebody let the sweet Jesus go?"

One of the villagers went over to Jesus. "I think he is dead, Hector," he said.

"Dead? Well, good. Then he is food for God. He doesn't matter anymore. Has he started rotting? God works quick.

"See what I am working with here?" Hector said to me. "You don't have any idea."

Angelina checked Jesus for life and then came over to stand by me. She stood beside me but did not touch me.

Angelina looked Hector squarely in the eyes. "Go away, Hector," she said. "Get out of here."

Hector smiled and licked his lips.

"Daniel loves me," Angelina said to him.

"Ooooh?" Hector minced. "Oh? Now. Well? O.K.? So? That does not matter. Tell me something that matters."

"I love Daniel."

"Well, you won't. Because he's going away. He is a tourist, Angelina, a go-to-hell, gone-tomorrow gringo tourist. He does not matter at all. When he is gone, there will be no one left around us but us. So don't worry. First, I will take care of Daniel. Then I will take care of you. I will take you to the capital, Angelina. You will have a shop on the Avenida Amazonas, selling butterflies and expensive curiosities."

"When I leave, I leave on my own," Angelina said.

"And Daniel will not be with you," said Hector. "I, Hector, will be there. I will be there in the capital, on the Avenida Amazonas. I will sit across the avenue at the Englishman's Pub and I will take care of business. I will export imports. I will sell antiquities. I will be rich and famous. I will be a poet and a fine man."

"You are a bastard, Hector," I said.

"You are a gringo, gringo. Which is worse. As long as we understand each other. By the way, how are you feeling, Gringo Daniel? Dizzy? Giddy? Happy? Funny? Do you feel sick? Do you feel like dancing? Feel like smiling? Would you like to get sick? I'll see that your life is sweet and short."

"Go to hell," I said. "Where are the people you got those clothes from?"

"Home," Hector said, and he shrugged. "California, by now. And happy too, we must believe. They gave me their addresses, they were so delighted. They want me to visit them and swim in their hot tubs. 'Thank you,' I said when they gave me their addresses. 'You sons of bitches, thank you and God damn you. Now I know where your houses are, and I am coming to California to burn them all down.' "

Some of the men laughed. I turned to Angelina. "I am going to get help," I said.

"No," she said.

"How, gringo?" Hector said. "We are quarantined here. The soldiers will shoot you. I told them to."

"I'll go your route, you bastard. I'll go around."

"You'll never make it," Hector said. "You'll never find it."

Hector turned away from me and slapped Santiago on the back. "Drink up, old man. And think up more questions."

"Why?" Santiago asked.

"That's a good one, old fool."

Santiago's face faded. He looked older than ever. He shook his head and peered into the bottom of his glass. Then he cocked his head in that manner he had always had, of complete, consuming attention. But it looked to me that this time his attention was failing. I had to leave but now I could not.

"Drink up, brutes!" Hector shouted to the drinkers. "Let this be the drinking party to end them all."

Everyone's bottles and glasses went up. "Hear! Hear!" they shouted.

"Hear, hear, you bastard," El Brinco said to Hector.

"You've got it," said Hector. "Drink! Drink!"

The men drank.

"And choke on it," Hector said to me. "Hey, America. This Bud's for you." He took another bad lemon from his pocket and tossed it to me. I let it hit my chest and drop.

"Later," he said.

Suddenly, Jorge spoke up. He cleared his throat and he spat. "I'm back," he said. "I couldn't help hearing that the devil had arrived."

"In person, Blindy," Hector said. "Strike in any direction and you will hit him."

Hector closed his eyes and smiled like a cat, pulling his chin back into his cheeks. Then he turned on me. "Gringo?" he said. "I am going to—"

Then he stopped.

Hector half opened his mouth and took in a slow, deep

breath, his nostrils flaring and his eyebrows rising. "Oh, oh. Well now," he said. "Well, well!" And he smiled and began to count. "*Uno . . . dos, tres, cuatro . . .* Now!"

I smelled the decay and I thought, *Earthquake!* Then the world knocked out from under me and I was on my knees. The men on my side of the table struck their faces against the tabletop. The men sitting across the table all fell backward onto the floor. Santiago, at the head of the table, rocked far to his right and then straightened up again.

A smaller tremor rolled beneath us, going the other way, followed by a third, flowing back, stronger but fading. Still on my knees, I put out my arms for balance. Lemons rolled across the floor. Litter and chaff rained down on us from the ceiling.

The air still stank, but the earthquake was over. Consuelo came over and helped me to stand. Angelina went to her father.

The men got up off the floor.

"*Dios!*" they said.

"That was an odd one."

"With my compliments, gentlemen," Hector said. He hadn't been budged.

"There was something you can't take home," he said, and he stuck out his lower lip. "Pfffft! So!"

Santiago was shaking his head and kneading his leg muscles above his knees. He looked more dazed now.

"What was that?" he asked me.

"Earthquake, Santiago."

Blind Jorge felt his way back to his place on the bench. "That was a miracle, nearly," he said. "For a moment there I thought I was gaining my sight." He rubbed the back of his head where he had hit it against the floor. "That's what it would feel like, I'm sure. Like some bright . . . some bright . . ."

He stopped, and then shook his head. "Gone."

"There you have it," Hector said to me. "We're all fucked up, aren't we?"

Then Napoleon turned around and slugged him.

Napoleon hit Hector twice, both times in the face, with quick jabs from his short arms, and Hector was down.

"What's this?" all the men shouted, and Hector was back up. Like a crab, he had scuttled to a post and climbed up it to stand.

"Napo, you bastard!" Hector said. He held his hand near his face but he wouldn't touch it. "I'll get you."

"*Cabrón!*" Napoleon said back to him.

Hector's eyes flared at Napoleon.

Then Santiago shouted, "That's it!"

Everyone turned.

"What?" Hector said. "Who is talking?"

"We've got the answer," Santiago said. His face was bright, his eyes wide. "You see?"

Hector forgot Napoleon and rubbed his face.

"You've got nothing, old idiot."

"We do something," Santiago said. He looked around at all of us.

Hector's eyelids closed halfway and he stretched his lips into a wide, flat smile. "Oh, really now? I beg your pardon."

"We do something."

"Do something. Do what, old man?"

Santiago massaged his legs with his hands. Then he looked at all of us again, gave one long look at me, and smiled.

He looked down at his knees. "First, we stand!" he said.

He put his hands on his knees, he leaned forward, and he fell.

"Papa!" Angelina tried to catch him. She went with him to the floor.

Hector began laughing. "Ha, ha! Ho, ho! Oh no! Too much!" Then he drummed his barrel chest and let out the *whoop! tunh!* of a big howler monkey. "I had almost forgotten," he said.

"Santiago's drunk!" someone said.

Napoleon helped Angelina get Santiago back onto his bench.

"Interesting," Santiago said. "I was going to stand."

"You can't," Hector said.

"But I was going to. And then . . ."

I went to Santiago and put my hand on his shoulder. "You stood, Santiago," I said. "It's all right. I'll be back."

"You can't go!" Angelina said. "Look at Papa."

"I'm going," I said.

"Go," Consuelo said from behind me. Her voice was strong.

I patted Santiago's shoulder. It didn't seem that he felt it, but he turned and looked up at me. "Go!" he commanded. "I was going to go with you."

I went upstairs to load my pack and found that everything I owned was gone.

Angelina and Hector followed me to the edge of the village, each trying to dissuade me, Angelina saying that I could not go, that she would go first, Hector saying that I dared not go, that I would be killed—in fact, he would see to it. Then Hector decided it was a good idea for me to go, a very good idea indeed, and he went and got a machete and he followed me into the jungle. "Jesus gave me this fine machete," Hector said. "Where do you think he got it? Was it yours, perhaps, at one time in history?"

I strode ahead until the path got steep. Then Hector caught up to me. At first, he stayed right behind me, stepping on my heels and breathing in exaggerated puffs and grunts.

Several times he stopped. "Hey, gringo! It's this way," he said, and pointed away.

"No, Daniel, stop!" he called. "Hey! I have something to show you. Hey, Daniel. Stop!"

He slapped the flat of the machete blade against his leg. "I have something to tell you!" he called.

I did not stop or turn around.

Hector's trail was easy to find. It had been trampled by the American professors, and I could see where Hector had led

them through the thickest undergrowth and made them clamber
up the waterfalls and rocks when there was a pathway a few
yards to one side.

The Americans had left behind them a wake of possessions.
The first thing I came across was a fisherman's crusher cap,
caught in a branch six feet off the ground. Then there was a
canteen, then a handkerchief, and then a camera case, tangled
in a bramble of vines. Then I saw where the Americans started
lightening their packs. They began by discarding their books.
The first was a heavy Spanish-English dictionary, then several
paperbacks by Latin-American authors. These had been left in
the jungle only a few days, but already they were swollen by
the humidity and beginning to disintegrate. Up the trail, beneath
a mossy cliff the Americans had been forced to scale, I found
two of their backpacks, left leaning against each other, as if
their owners expected to return for them. I looked back for
Hector, but I could not see him.

After two hours, I reached the site of the plane crash where
Hugo and I had spent the night. I smelled the dead the moment
I got there. It smelled like Los Puentes Caidos.

The odor made me slow to a creep. This place was rotten
with death. The tail of the great aircraft still lifted into the air,
but now its ripped metal, with its encumbrance of vegetation,
looked heavy and was beginning to deform.

I found the bodies huddled together in the cockpit of the
broken aircraft. With their gray skin and their flyblown faces,
they all looked alike, as if they had never been alive at all. The
arms of one man embraced the shoulders of the two others. A
sick, salt taste ran down my throat and I dropped to my knees
and vomited.

When I stood up, Hector was standing nearby, watching me.
He clapped his hands and whistled.

"*Bruto*, gringo," he said. "Low quantity but high quality.
Well done."

Hector had changed clothes again. He now wore other things he had rifled from the dead men's packs. He wore a Panama hat with a white silk band, a white sport coat, and a pair of round-lens, tortoiseshell, trifocal eyeglasses. He wore a button-down shirt and a beige silk necktie, tied loosely like an ascot in an overhand knot. In one hand, he held my machete. In the other, he held an unlit cigarette at the very tips of his fingers. He regarded me with his half-lidded, lizardlike gaze and he shook his head. He pursed his lips and blew, as if he were smoking.

Then he tipped his head back and smiled with his mouth open. The trifocals were too big for his face. The strong lenses made his eyes look smaller. They narrowed the sides of his head.

"We are disappointed in you, Hector," he said in the high Ohio voice of the missionary Lester McGuinness. "You could have been the prophet and savior of your people. We gave you food, clothes, education. And Jesus Christ too. Well . . ."

"What happened here, Hector?"

"Hector, you could have been anything," Hector said, "like a multiple choice. A, B, C, or D." He looked at me through each part of the trifocals. "Big, bigger, biggest. Nearer, farther, farthest. All of the above. None of the above. Which of the answers is most correct? Caudillo of the Republic. King of the country. President of the world."

"What happened here, Hector?"

Hector squinted at the wreckage. "This would appear to be an airplane crash. It would appear there were victims. True? Or false?"

I pointed to the bodies.

"They weren't here before," I said. "I've been here. With Hugo."

"Hugo died, gringo. Or don't you remember?"

"And so did these people."

"And so will you."

"These are the American professors."

"So it appears that they could be."

"You killed them."

Hector began to nod, then shook his head. "No. False. And not all of them. One professor got away. And the others all killed themselves. By poison. You know, in a mass suicide. It was like Jonestown in the jungles of Guyana, with the Reverend Jim Jones from California. Not pretty, you remember, but a powerful scene, and spread by the picture newsmagazines around the world. It shocked us all. It made the world pause."

"You poisoned them."

"It was said they poisoned themselves. Unknowingly at first, perhaps. But who knows, finally? Unwittingly at first, we might say. Or so it was rumored. But once one knows . . ."

"How?"

"The lemons, you idiot."

I thought of Santiago, drinking poisoned beer. Hector raised the machete and shook his head. "Damn your eyes. Don't you move, gringo. It is a very slow poison and lingering, too. A hemlock, I believe, or something other. I would have told the professors all about it, but they never asked me, ever. They never asked a single question that ever counted. But in the end, they stopped complaining."

Hector nodded. "They got into the crashed airplane, all by themselves. As sick as they were, they were very brave, very thoughtful professors, in the end. They told each other it was the least they could do. To stick together. Why is it that when people are dying, they suddenly get so reasonable? Why do they always get reasonable after it's too late?"

Hector viewed me through the three lenses. I got ready to run, but he waved the machete. "No, gringo. Don't you try it. I can throw this right through you."

He smiled like a lizard. "Come over here," he said. "I have something more to show you."

Hector led me a few paces to an abandoned jungle camp. The place was torn up, with nylon cord and plastic plates scattered around. I recognized the camouflage tent of William Bodean. It had been slashed to ribbons by a machete.

Hector held the machete up to his lips. "Shhh," he whispered. "This way."

He led me a few steps more to where a decomposed body hung by one leg from a blue nylon rope. I knew it was Bodean. Ants had turned the corpse's head into a dripping nest of matted leaves.

"The survivalist himself," Hector said. "*El sobreviviente*. Very well camouflaged now, don't you think? He fits in well with his surroundings."

Hector looked at me. "I did not kill him either, although I did watch him die. When everyone worried, I came back to look for him, and here I found him like this. Caught in his own trap, it appears. Snared! Hah! Imagine his surprise. Imagine my surprise when I found him. I talked with him. But I could not cut him down. I could not trust him. What might he do to me? I did not know him. You knew him. You spoke with him often. Maybe you would cut him down. But he was trained in killing and he was abusive to the end. In the end, he begged me to finish him, angrily, unreasonably, and I would not. By then I was too much insulted. I am still insulted. I gave him a lemon, but he would not eat it, although I tried to explain. With him, it was pain all the way.

"With you, we'll have more time to talk. Like with Finalina, the modern way out. And believe me, gringo, I will never forget your very last words."

Then Hector caught his breath and held up a finger. There was a moment when the jungle went silent. It stank.

"Now!" Hector whispered. "Now!"

The earth jerked sideways. Litter rained down from the trees.

Hector watched me and smiled. I felt cold and I shivered. I realized I was afraid.

"I can smell you, too, gringo, and you smell like you are going to die."

Hector pulled a lemon from his sport coat pocket. "So let's eat our lemon," he said. "Come on now and die. Come on and tell me about it. Santiago ate his."

Hector tossed me the lemon.

"Go ahead and eat it and don't worry," he said. "Don't worry, it tastes like a lemon. Sour but refreshing. Death has no after-taste. No after-nothing. Once you eat it, it's over. Pfft! Over! Well, it's over, but it's not. It is not quite over yet. It is just too late, and that is better because you still have time to think about it. Hours sometimes. Sometimes half a day. But that doesn't matter because it all goes so slowly. They say time itself slows. It's like a second lifetime, a second-class chance at some reconsideration. Now that is exceptional, don't you think? Such slow . . . Such lazy . . . Santiago will love it, when he figures it out. When he figures out that he can still ask his questions right up to the end."

I felt sudden hate for Hector Tanbueno. "You . . ."

"Shhh! Don't worry, gringo. Don't worry about me. Don't worry about Santiago. These lemons take time. So eat yours. Now."

I dropped the lemon.

Hector stamped his foot.

"I will kill you," I said to him.

Hector blinked behind the thick trifocals, and cocked his head back to get another view. "I was going to say that to you," he said.

"You are going to die."

"Let us not be abusive, gringo. Who do we think we are? We are not Bodean. The survivalist was abusive to the end."

"I'll kill you," I said.

Hector set his feet farther apart. "Eat the lemon, gringo. Don't be difficult. Believe me, this will hurt more." He raised the machete in his right hand.

I began to circle him. I moved left so he would have trouble swinging. From behind the thick glasses, Hector could not see me well. When I leaned left or crouched, he cocked his head back to keep me in view. I circled left, getting ready to spring, but the undergrowth caught my heels and I fell. Hector laughed and he reached up to take off the glasses. I scrambled to my feet and rushed him.

I grabbed his machete hand and slammed my shoulder into his chest, but he stood solid and I fell back. He swung now and caught my ear with the flat of the blade. My skull rang, but I grabbed Hector's ankle and pulled. He fell backward and I clambered on top of him. I thrust my knee into his chest and I grabbed the blade of the machete with both my hands and I forced it down against his throat. Hector gagged. I had him, I thought; the back of the blade had cut off his air. His face darkened and his temple veins swelled into purple snakes, writhing and pulsing beneath his skin.

Now Hector reached up and took my throat in his powerful grip and he began to choke me. My vision dimmed and my ears pounded. I rolled forward against the machete blade. Its sharp edge cut into the heels of my hands as its back edge broke Hector's larynx. I heard cartilage popping. The whites of his eyes shot red with veins and his hands squeezed my neck harder. My head filled with pressure. I pressed down on the blade until it sliced into his throat. Blood gushed hot over my hands and a rasp of hot, stinking breath rattled across my face. Hector's face paled and went blank. He released me and died.

I ran back down the mountain to Los Puentes Caidos.

17

I had been gone a few hours, but the village had changed again. Now the Army was there. The place swarmed with soldiers and military vehicles, and a big blue and gray Chevy Suburban with the seal of the United States Embassy stood parked beside the burned bus. I ran past officers in uniforms and civilians in suit coats and I bounded up the steps of the cantina. Inside, a reporter, or a tourist, was taking pictures.

Santiago lay on the table in the center of the cantina. His head rested on a big blue pillow. Napoleon was there, and Consuelo. Angelina stood beside Santiago, holding his hand.

"Santiago!" I said. "It's me!" I grabbed his other hand, but Santiago did not move. I leaned over the table to put my face in front of his. "Santiago. I am back."

Santiago's gaze traveled my face and it took several seconds before it found my eyes. "Ah? Daniel!" he whispered. He sounded surprised, but he said, "Well then, all right. This makes sense."

He looked for Angelina. "Daughter," he said, "you can take away the pillow now. My head has gotten softer."

Angelina started crying, and then she laughed, the first time I had heard her laugh in a year. Her laughter was free and light, and almost happy. It made me laugh too, and cry, and I wished Hector were there so I could kill him again, could kill him for Santiago. Angelina kissed the pillow and set it aside.

Consuelo picked up the pillow and buried her face in it. She was beginning to cry. "It hurts!" she said. "It hurts to cry!"

Santiago smiled at her. "It's supposed to, Consuelo. You are getting well."

Angelina took her father's hand and kissed it.

"But don't pull the shroud over my face until you are sure I have stopped talking," he said. "My lips are growing numb now. I may be dead and still talking and you not know it. And just as it's making sense."

He looked for me. "And what if I am dead?" he asked. "Can you hear me, Daniel? Can you see me?"

"Yes!" I said. "Yes."

Santiago's eyes gave me another look of surprise. He moved his head slowly from side to side. "It's slowing down now, Daniel. It's slowing down. Like a story at the end."

I looked up at Angelina and then at Napoleon. He shook his great head.

"It's slowing down," Santiago said, "and it's getting better."

Consuelo began to cry harder now, with the pain of grief. "It hurts!" she cried.

It hurt worse than anything.

Soon it was over. Santiago died. Just when, I could not tell.

Angelina left.

"And I love you," she said, and she left.

She moved to the capital, and then to the U.S. I stayed in the country, and Consuelo and I moved up the mountain to a ridge above the highway, by a high waterfall, where we have a broad view of the jungle and a sweet evening breeze. The earthquakes shake oranges out of our trees. Our two daughters hunt butterflies and they send them to Angelina to sell in Miami. I love Angelina. And Consuelo. But I never see Angelina.

Los Puentes Caidos is abandoned, for now. The sickness that destroyed it was diagnosed as a viral encephalitis called St. Vitus's Waltz, a brain fever affecting balance and emotion. It worries the doctors because they don't know how it is passed. Consuelo once said that it felt like being in love.

"Only sicker," she said.